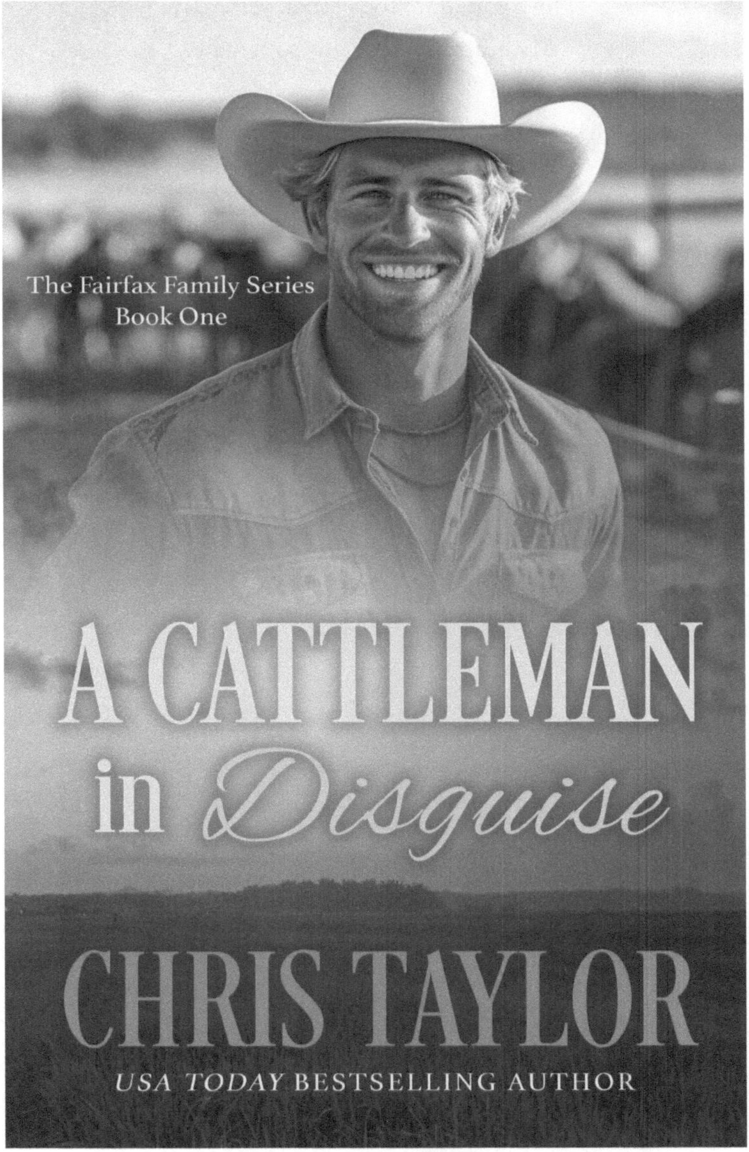

The Fairfax Family Series
Book One

A CATTLEMAN
in Disguise

CHRIS TAYLOR

USA TODAY BESTSELLING AUTHOR

This book is dedicated to my husband, Linden Taylor.
I love you more today than yesterday.
My heart, my rock, my soul mate.
I love you.

Also By Chris Taylor

The Munro Family Series (in order)
The Profiler
The Investigator
The Predator
The Betrayal
The Deception
The Negotiator
The Christmas Vigil (A novella)
The Ransom
The Defendant
The Shooting
The Maker

The Sydney Harbour Hospital Series (in order)
The Perfect Husband
The Body Thief
The Baby Snatchers

CHRIS TAYLOR

The Final Bullet
The Debt Collector
The Lab Test
The Stolen Identity
The Cliff-top Killer
The Likeable Fraudster

The Sydney Legal Series (in order)
An Accidental Murderer
At the Hand of her Father
A Woman Scorned
Lies and Deception
Ordinary Evil
The Ties That Bind
The Perfect Crime
A Toxic Inheritance
Malicious Love

The Craigdon Family Series (in order)
Callum
Joel
Isabella
Nicholas
Sophia
Flynn
Noah
Logan
Elizabeth

The Barrington Family Series (in order)
Broken Lives
Broken Promises
Broken Bonds
Broken Spirits
Broken Minds
Broken Vows
Broken Hearts
Broken Dreams
Broken Homes

The Fairfax Family Series (in order)
A Cattleman in Disguise
A Cattleman's Quest
A Cattleman's Daughter
A Cattleman's Secret Baby
To Catch a Cattleman
The Doctor and the Cattleman
To Rescue a Cattleman
A Cattleman's Heart
For the Love of a Cattleman

Bachelor and Brides Series (in order)
Matilda
Austin
Farrah
Benjamin
Verity
Denver

Ebony

Tyrone

Willow

Books by Chris Taylor writing as Bella Christian

This is Where it Ends series (in order)

Jessie's Story

Ryan's Story

Holly's Story

Sarah's Story

Veronica's Story

Chapter One

♥

With the back of his hand, Brock Fairfax swiped at the sweat on his brow. It was early May in downtown Brisbane. The temperature outside was a pleasant twenty-six degrees Celsius. The air conditioner in the boardroom of Fairfax Investments had been set a few degrees lower. Brock had no excuse to perspire. Except he and his brother were waiting for a manager from the New World bank. The fate of Marlowe Downs, their family cattle station, rested in her hands.

No reason to be nervous...much.

He grimaced and glanced at Raine seated across the wide red cedar boardroom table where many a deal had been struck over the years. Though there was no sheen of perspiration on his brother's forehead, there were other indicators that Raine was just as nervous as he was about the upcoming meeting. A tug of his Italian silk tie. A finger that tapped an irritating rhythm on the polished wood, while the other hand scrubbed through his thick auburn hair. The same auburn hair he'd inherited from their father.

They both jumped at the sound of Raine's phone.

"Shit. I thought I'd switched it to silent," Raine muttered. He pulled the phone out of his suit jacket and checked the screen. The annoyance that had marred his features only seconds earlier disappeared. "It's Isabella."

Brock rolled his eyes. His brother had been married for more than a year. He ought not to be so gaga over his wife at this point. They were still so lovey-dovey, it was embarrassing. Raine pushed away from the table and stood. Turning his back to Brock, he hurried toward the exit before answering the call.

Brock pushed down a wave of irritation. He and Raine had once been tight. They'd never had any secrets between them, had even gone into business together. They trusted each other implicitly. But lately, his brother had taken to lowering his voice to almost inaudible murmurings whenever his wife called in Brock's presence, or leaving the room altogether, like he'd done now.

It had taken some adjusting to no longer being Raine's wingman. Brock understood that as Raine's wife, Isabella had the right to usurp Brock's position, but that didn't make it any easier to accept. The brothers were only twelve months apart in age. From the time they'd become adults, they'd known they wanted to work together, go into business together, conquer the investment world side by s ide.

And they'd done that. Fairfax Investments was one of the most successful companies in the country, along with an enviable reputation abroad. They had an instinctive nose for good business deals and had invested well and wisely over the years. It was ironic that though the company was flourishing, they weren't in a position to hand over five million dollars to help the family cattle business out of a difficult situation. Hence, the need for the loan.

Brock blew out a breath and glanced at his watch. The woman was late. One thing that irritated him no end was tardiness. It was rude, an implicit statement that their time was more important than his. If they didn't need the money so badly, he'd be tempted to call the bank and cancel the appointment.

Raine returned to the boardroom. His cheeks were slightly flushed. His glance landed on Brock and then skittered away.

Brock frowned. "What is it?"

Raine scrubbed at his hair and stared at something over Brock's shoulder. "Um, I hate to do this to you, but I have to leave."

Brock's frown deepened. "What? The manager from the bank's due any minute. She specifically asked to meet with both of us. You're not going anywhere."

The color in Raine's cheeks intensified. He still wouldn't meet Brock's gaze. "Something's come up. I have to go."

Anger licked at Brock's insides. He sat up straighter. "Hey, I don't think you appreciate how badly we need this money. We've already been to all the other banks. No one wants to lend us the money. If we don't get that loan, Marlowe Downs goes under." His gaze narrowed on his brother. "You know what that means."

"Of course, I know what that means." Raine's tone was lined with frustration. "I want this money as much as you do. I want to be at this meeting. It's just that..." His voice petered off.

Brock sat forward. His gaze bore into his brother's. "What the hell's going on? What's more important than saving the station?"

Raine broke eye contact and softly cursed. "I swore to Isabella I wouldn't say anything."

Brock shook his head. "About what?"

Raine blew out his breath, his hands on his hips. He stared down at Brock. "About...the baby."

"What baby?"

"Our baby. Mine and Isabella's."

Brock blinked in surprise. "She's pregnant?"

Raine ducked his head and grinned. "Yeah."

"Wow. Congratulations. That's great news."

Raine's smile widened. "Yeah. Yeah, it is. We've been trying for a while. It's finally happened."

"I'm pleased for you, bro. But what's that got to do with this meeting?"

Raine grimaced. "That's the problem. Isabella has her ultrasound appointment today. It was scheduled for this afternoon, but the clinic just called and asked if she could reschedule. They want her to come in right away."

Brock nodded. "I see."

Raine looked contrite. He held out his hands. "I'm sorry, Brock. I need to be there. It's our first ultrasound. The first time we get to see our baby."

A pang went through Brock at the wonder and awe that colored his brother's voice. Brock loved the thought of being a father. He hoped he'd be in that same position one day.

"Of course, you have to go," he said. "No father-to-be should miss such a momentous event."

Relief flooded Raine's features. "Thanks for understanding, bro."

Brock waved off the thanks. "Go, go. Be with your wife. I'll give your apologies to the bank manager."

"I can't wait to see it. Our baby." He paused and then added, "Do you mind keeping this to yourself? We haven't told anyone yet.

Isabella wants to get past the first trimester before giving anyone the news. The first twelve weeks are the most dangerous time as far as miscarriages go."

Some of Raine's excitement dimmed. Brock saw it and forced a smile. "Hey, everything's going to be all right. I'm sure the ultrasound will confirm that. Go and share this moment with your wife and enjoy every minute. Don't worry about the bank manager. I'm sure I can sweet talk her into giving us the money."

Concern flashed through Raine's eyes. "Are you sure? I wish I didn't have to run out on you like this, but..." He shrugged helplessly.

"Go. If this loan falls through, we'll think of something else. The most important thing right now is your wife and baby."

"You're right. Thanks again for understanding," Raine said.

He hurried toward the exit and pulled the door closed quietly behind him. Brock released a sigh and mentally prepared to make their case to the bank manager alone, if she ever turned up.

Kelsey Garland's three-inch stilettos clicked on the polished marble floor as she crossed the foyer and stepped inside the impressive high-rise that housed the offices of Fairfax Investments. She was running late and that was something she hated, but she'd been caught up in unexpectedly heavy traffic after an accident and there had been nothing she could do. She'd tried to phone ahead to explain, but the line had been engaged. In the end, she'd resigned herself to offering her apologies once she arrived.

She'd used the enforced extended time in her car to reread her notes on the Fairfax brothers. Brock and Raine Fairfax, who'd started Fairfax Investments, were twenty-nine and thirty respectively. From all accounts, theirs had been a meteoric rise. Call it good judgment, good management, good luck, or a combination of all three, they'd turned a startup investment company into one of the major players in the world of business.

But one investment had run afoul. Four years earlier, they'd invested a sizable sum into the family business. A cattle ranch—or station, as they called it in Australia—in Central Queensland. Three years of drought, followed by a flood, and the family business was now hemorrhaging money. Kelsey had checked their finances. Though Fairfax Investments was worth millions on paper, most of their money was tied up. There was no ready cash on hand. Certainly not the kind of cash needed to bail out an operation like Marlowe Downs.

She'd looked over the figures. Had dug deep to find a solution. But she'd come there bearing bad news. That was one of the reasons she'd opted to come in person. She wanted to make a personal connection with the two men who'd already proven themselves to be movers and shakers in the business world. She might not be able to help them out this time, but there was always the next time. They weren't the only ones filled with ambition.

There was another reason she'd chosen to come in person. Thanks to her mean-spirited grandmother, there was a million dollars riding on her being married before she turned thirty. That was six months away. With that in mind, she'd stalked the Fairfax brothers on the Internet.

Her research had revealed two formidable business operators who were also seriously good-looking. According to the social pages, the older one—Raine—had gotten married a year earlier, but Brock appeared to be single. That was good news for a woman on the hunt for a husband.

The sound of her phone ringing cut into her thoughts. She hunted around in her briefcase and pulled out the device. Checking the screen, she smiled and answered the call.

"Hi, Mama. How're you doing?"

"Not too bad, honey. All things considered."

The sound of her mother's weak voice on the other end of the line filled Kelsey with concern. Three months earlier, her mother had been diagnosed with a rare blood cancer. Though she'd undergone conventional treatments, so far nothing had worked. A few weeks ago, her doctor had mentioned an experimental treatment that had so far produced promising results. Though there was no guarantee of a cure, the doctors were hopeful the treatment might slow the cancer's progression. The problem was, the treatment wasn't covered by Medicare or her mother's insurance. The cost was way beyond what either of them could afford.

"Have you seen your doctor this week?"

"Yes, honey."

"Did you get your blood results?"

"Yes. They weren't good."

Kelsey's heart sank. "Oh, Mama. I'm so sorry."

"Hey, don't be sorry. It's not your fault."

A wave of helplessness washed over her. "I wish there was something I could do. I've looked into every which way I can come up with the money for your treatment and I've fallen short every time.

I'm a bank manager! If anyone should have access to money, it's me. And yet, it's beyond me." Her voice hitched. "I've failed you."

"Don't be silly, honey. This isn't on you. And we're talking thousands of dollars. Probably more. I wouldn't expect you to pay that kind of money, even if you could."

"Oh, Mama! I'd pay it in an instant if that meant saving your life! If only I had it…" She blew out her breath on a heavy sigh. "That settles it. I need to find a husband."

"Your grandmother should never have made that offer," her mother scolded. "Imagine dangling a million dollars in front of your granddaughter provided she marries by a certain time. Utterly disgraceful. She's richer than King Midas. She could simply give you the money with no strings attached. But no, she has to always be in control, even dictating when you should marry."

"It's so mean. Especially when she's aware of your situation. It's too bad granddad passed away. He might have had some chance of convincing her. I don't understand why she's not willing to pay for your treatment herself."

Her mother sighed. "There's a lot of history between us, none of it good. She never wanted your father to marry me."

Kelsey made a sound of impatience in the back of her throat. "I know. But you were together for twenty-seven years. And you were happy. Surely, that had to count?"

Her mother didn't respond, but Kelsey understood. There were no words to explain why her grandmother continued to hold a grudge. It was Kelsey's turn to sigh. "We could really use that money right now," she murmured. "I need to try harder to find a husband."

"I'd never want you to marry for the sake of it, Kelsey. Marriage is a lifelong commitment. At least, I hope that's how you feel about it."

Kelsey sighed again. "You know I do, Mama. I had the best role models, after all. You and Daddy were still in love, right up until the day he died."

"Twenty-seven years with a wonderful man," her mother said softly. "My only regret was that we didn't get to grow old together. I miss him so much."

"I miss him too." Kelsey choked past the lump in her throat.

"I want you to have what we had. Please, promise me you won't settle for anything less."

Kelsey remained silent. She wished she could give her mother that promise, but the truth was, she'd do anything to save her. If that meant marrying a stranger in time to collect the million-dollar prize, she wasn't going to rule that out.

"Kelsey?"

"I'm sorry. I'm running late for a meeting. I have to go."

"Okay, honey. But remember what I said. Don't go rushing into marriage for my sake. Knowing you were married to someone you didn't love would be worse for me than dying of cancer."

Kelsey briefly closed her eyes against a surge of emotion and cleared her throat. "Take care, Mama. It was great to talk to you. I love you."

"Love you too."

Dropping her phone back into her handbag, Kelsey reached the bank of elevators and pressed the Up button. She flicked her long blonde hair over her shoulders and then smoothed it into place. She'd taken the time to freshen her lipstick and pump mint-flavored mouth freshener onto her tongue. No doubt she'd gone a little overboard, but the pressure was on to make a good impression. It wasn't every day she got up close and personal with two gorgeous men, at least one of whom was an eligible bachelor.

Since her arrival from Florida six months earlier, she'd joined numerous online dating sites. Even before her mother's diagnosis, she'd been keen to try her hand at landing the million-dollar windfall. All she had to do was find the man of her dreams before she turned thirty. No big deal.

She'd been immediately bombarded with requests for dates. Even now, her phone vibrated with notifications. It was too bad she didn't have time to deal with them. It was also disheartening that so far, she'd had as much luck with the Aussie men as she'd had with their American counterparts. Dozens of dates later, she was no closer to finding her soul mate.

She swallowed another sigh. She still had six months to find Mr Right. And she was moments away from meeting Mr Potential, Brock Fairfax. From what she'd learned about him on the Internet, he appeared to tick a lot of her boxes: smart, ambitious, fun. On top of that, he was gorgeous. Though she'd come there bearing bad news, the phone call from her mother now gave her pause. Time was running out. If her mother didn't start treatment, even an experimental one, there was a good chance she'd lose her fight. Kelsey couldn't bear the thought of that.

Perhaps I've been too hasty in turning down the Fairfax loan? Maybe I should run the numbers again, see if I can get it over the line?

If she could somehow get it approved, she'd get to spend more time with the brothers. More time to make a good impression, get to know Brock, maybe get him interested in her... He'd definitely feel kindlier toward her if she approved his application. It could be a win for both of them.

No, it wouldn't be fair to let him think there was still a chance she might approve the loan. Best to be honest. That was always her preferred course of action. Then again, her mother's life had never been on the line before. She sighed. When had things become so complicated?

The elevator dinged, announcing its arrival, and the stainless-steel doors slid open. Raine Fairfax stood before her. Kelsey blinked, struck by his sudden appearance. As he stepped out of the elevator, she automatically stepped forward and stuck out her hand.

"Raine Fairfax?"

His gaze sharpened. "Yes?"

"Kelsey Garland. I'm from the New World Bank."

He flushed and shook her hand distractedly. "Oh, Ms Garland. I'm sorry. I've been called away to an urgent appointment. Please accept my apologies. My brother, Brock, is upstairs waiting for you. He can answer any questions."

She started in surprise. "I was meant to meet with both of you."

His flush deepened. "Yes, I'm sorry. Something unavoidable has come up. I'm sorry. I have to go."

Kelsey watched as Raine hurried across the foyer's wide expanse and disappeared through the revolving glass door.

Well, at least it's the married one doing a runner...

Momentarily distracted by her bemusement, she quickly pulled herself together. Determined to make the most of what was left of her opportunity, she straightened her shoulders and summoned the elevator again.

The door to the boardroom opened on a brisk knock. Brock's aging secretary, Yvonne, appeared.

"Kelsey Garland from the New World Bank is here," she announced brusquely and then turned on her heel and left.

Brock's stomach clenched. He stood and tugged at his suit jacket and straightened his tie. A moment later, the bank manager appeared and Brock's heart skipped a beat.

The woman was not at all what he'd expected. For a start, she was young, probably around his age. She was also stunning. He'd been around his fair share of attractive women, but this one glowed. White-blonde hair flowed around the shoulders of her suit jacket. Long, silk-covered legs were enhanced by an elegant pencil skirt, and a pair of sexy black stilettos. His gaze tracked their length and then looked up to see bright blue eyes watching him with a mixture of challenge and amusement—like she was completely aware of his visceral reaction to her beauty and took that as her due. He flushed.

No doubt she's used to men gawking at her...

Giving himself a mental shake, he did his best to recover. Holding out his hand, he strode toward her.

"Ms Garland. I'm Brock Fairfax. It's nice to meet you."

They shook hands. Her skin was soft, her fingers long and slender. Like her legs. The black-and-white-checked skirt reached halfway to her thighs and there was a lot of shapely leg on show. He was tall. Six foot three. She stood eye to eye with him in her heels.

"Please, call me Kelsey."

Her voice was low and husky and intimate. He imagined her naked, stretched out on a rug by a fire, sipping whiskey. Blood rushed to his groin. He deliberately shifted his thoughts to something safer and cleared his throat.

"Kelsey. It's nice to meet you. I'm afraid my brother Raine had to duck out. He—"

"That's fine. He's already apologized."

Noticing his frown of confusion, Kelsey added, "I ran into him downstairs."

Brock flushed again. "I'm sorry. Raine really wanted to be here. Securing this finance means as much to him as it does to me. We're trying to save our family home and livelihood."

"And yet, he had somewhere else to be," she chided.

Brock compressed his lips. "He had good reason." He paused and then blurted, "His wife's ultrasound appointment was brought forward unexpectedly. It clashed with our meeting time. I'm sorry, but it's their first baby. He had to be there."

Kelsey's eyes widened in surprise, and then she smiled. "I see. Well, I guess I can understand that. An ultrasound is the kind of important event that can't be repeated. He's forgiven for standing me up. By the way, I also apologize for running late. There was an accident on the freeway. Traffic was backed up."

Brock nodded. "I understand. Thank you. I hope I'll be able to fill the gap. If you have any questions, please ask away. I'll be happy to answer them. Shall we?"

He indicated the boardroom table behind him, large enough to hold sixteen ergonomically sound and environmentally responsible chairs.

"Thank you," she murmured and took a seat at the head of the table.

It was a position of power, but he wasn't about to argue. They needed her—or her bank—more than she needed them, and they both knew it. In silence, Brock pulled out the chair to her right and sat.

"Do I detect an American accent?" he asked in an effort to fill the awkward silence.

She smiled easily. "Yes. I'm from Florida."

"How long have you been in Australia?"

"Six months. I'm halfway through a secondment from the New World bank head office in Tampa."

Brock's eyebrows rose. "They brought you all the way out here on secondment. You must be good at your job."

She inclined her head and replied in a no-nonsense tone, "I'm exceptional at my job."

"What exactly have you been brought in to do?"

"Our Australian branches haven't been performing so well. I've been sent out to investigate and to look to turn things around."

Brock's stomach sank. If the bank was in financial difficulty, it would be unlikely to lend. "And what have you found?" he forced himself to ask.

She grimaced. "That's confidential. But I will say, our loan officers in Australia appear to have been a little too willing to approve loans. Far more willing than I would have been."

Brock's stomach sank further. Her news didn't bode well for their application. This was going to take all his persuasion skills. Despite his rising disappointment, he shot her a disarming smile. "How are you liking Australia?"

She laughed briefly. "I love Australia! Everyone's so laid back and friendly. G'day, mate! Did I say that right?"

Her blush was charming. He chuckled. "You did indeed." His gaze drifted to her ring finger, and he was pleased to discover it was bare. Then he gave himself a silent reprimand.

Quit thinking like that. You're done with relationships. Remember Cecelia? Besides, this is business. At least until the loan's approved...

As if aware of his thoughts, she cleared her throat, her manner once again businesslike. She opened her briefcase and pulled out a sheaf of papers and started leafing through them.

"So, Mr Fairfax. I've been over your figures."

"Please, call me Brock."

"Yes, well. Brock. As I said, I've checked your figures." She glanced up at him. "They don't look good."

Shit. Time to focus on the job at hand.

It was as he'd feared. Still, he wasn't prepared to give up so easily. "I understand. But we've had three years of drought, followed by a flood. Our herd was almost wiped out. But we can restock, breed up our numbers. Become viable again. All we need is time...and money."

"I understand too, but the bank can only go on what you've provided to us right now. Future projections are all well and good, but building up your herd again won't happen overnight. It could be years before you're back to where you were before those natural disasters. Who's to say there's not another drought around the corner? Or another flood?" She smiled faintly. "This is a land of extremes, is it not?"

He compressed his lips and tried to stem his panic.

Hell. She's going to turn us down, just like all the rest of them... Then what will we do?

"Please, Ms...Kelsey. Marlowe Downs has been in our family for generations. We can trace our history all the way back to the very first cattle barons. We've faced natural disasters before. We'll come back from this. We have investments, but we need cash. Without it, we're screwed, along with all the people who rely on the station for their living. If Marlowe Downs goes under, then so do they."

His voice had grown louder, along with his passion. When he stopped speaking, his cheeks felt flushed.

While her expression remained sympathetic, her lips had tightened, and she slowly shook her head.

"I'm sorry, Brock. I wish I had better news. My job is to make decisions that are in the best interests of the bank, and I'm afraid approving your loan application just isn't. Please, be assured, this isn't personal. Since the rise of inflation and interest rates across the world, including here in Australia, the bank's tightened its lending guidelines, particularly in Australia. A lot of people are struggling. We can't save them all. And certainly not at the risk of losing money." She stacked the papers into a neat pile and looked at him again. "I'm afraid as things stand, I have no choice but to recommend that your loan application be denied."

Desperation clawed at Brock's insides, but he was determined to remain in control. "I'm disappointed to hear that. What can we do for the bank to reconsider?"

She continued to regard him with sympathy. "I'm sorry, Brock. I can't see any other way that the bank can help you based on the figures provided."

"But you don't know anything about us, about our operation. What's there on paper can't give you a proper idea about how Marlowe Downs works and its potential to deliver on investment. What if you came out and visited the station? Got a firsthand look at who we are and what we're trying to do? Let me do my best to convince you that Marlowe Downs and the Fairfax brothers are worth the risk."

The surprise on her face reflected his own. The invitation had come from nowhere, a desperate act founded on nothing but instinct and a genuine certainty that the station would struggle to remain viable if they weren't able to secure sufficient finance. He was also just as certain that once back on track with an injection of cash, the station would become lucrative again.

As a variety of expressions flitted across Kelsey's face, he crossed his fingers beneath the table and prayed she'd take him up on his offer.

Her bank was their final play.

Chapter Two

♥

Kelsey's chest tightened at the panic in Brock's startling green eyes. She'd always hated this part of her job. Disappointing applicants. Destroying dreams.

Brock's online pictures hadn't done him justice. His thick, straight hair was a deep caramel color and had a habit of falling into his eyes. Or maybe he was just overdue for a haircut. He spoke with a slow drawl that sent shivers of awareness down her spine. His tanned skin, hollowed cheeks, and chiseled jaw, shadowed with the beginnings of a beard, reminded her of a leading man in an old Western movie, despite the fact he wore business attire. She could clearly picture him astride a horse, complete with cowboy hat and c haps.

She smiled inwardly at the image. She didn't even know if he rode. He looked at ease in the boardroom. The custom-tailored suit fit him perfectly. The gray-and-black-striped tie was silk, probably Italian. The expensive shiny black leather boots. They all complemented the luxurious surroundings. The generously proportioned boardroom was all polished timber, high-quality floor coverings, shiny chrome and acres of glass. Perhaps all his ranching work was done from the comfort of his office? Then again, he'd invited her to Marlowe Downs to see for herself. Did he intend to accompany her?

The possibility gave her pause. This was exactly what she needed. More time with him to build a connection, see if there was a spark between them, something more than physical attraction. She'd seen the flare of heated attraction in his eyes earlier upon meeting. The possibilities of where a visit might lead were suddenly tantalizing. And there was always the slim chance that seeing the ranch in person would change her mind.

A part of her was filled with curiosity about the place. He'd appeared genuinely alarmed upon hearing that she was unable to recommend the loan application. That attitude was endearing. Besides, a day or two with a sexy cowboy in the iconic Australian outback sounded romantic to a Florida girl. What better way to further their acquaintance than to spend more time together? Who knew where that might lead...

Her research had shown that the Fairfax name was well-known in Australia. Their family ties went all the way back to Sir Sidney Kidman, who was considered Australia's most successful cattle producer. Kidman founded his pastoral company in 1899 and became known as Australia's "cattle king." Though he'd died in 1935, the Kidman family business continued to thrive today with cattle properties across Queensland and the Northern Territory.

When the loan application had come across her desk, Kelsey's interest had been immediately piqued. She wasn't the only one in the office who was interested. Her senior loans officer had practically begged to be given the account. The moment Rochelle Williams discovered the Fairfax family was seeking a loan, she'd hounded Kelsey constantly about it.

As the boss, Kelsey had the final decision about the allocation of work. Most of the time, she divvied up the work based on the level of experience required and who had extra capacity, but a little imp inside her had urged her to keep the Fairfax account for herself.

At the time, she didn't know how their financials would stack up, but she knew enough about the Fairfax family to know it might be fun to be involved. Then, of course, there was the little matter of finding a husband. With her mother's health deteriorating, there was an added urgency to that quest. It might seem cold and calculating to go about finding a mate so clinically, but she no longer had the liberty of taking her time and letting things develop in their own time. If her mother didn't get that treatment, she would die.

The Fairfaxes were a well-known family with four daughters and six sons. Raine was now permanently off the marriage market, and some of the younger brothers were only in their early twenties. Probably a bit young for her. But that still left Brock.

Now having met him, she wasn't disappointed. He was every bit as sexy in real life. His obvious love for his family made her want to help them. If spending a few days on his ranch helped her to revise her initial decision, then that would be a good thing for all of them. Apart from that, having the chance to tour outback Australia was vastly appealing. She'd grown up around Tampa, minutes from the ocean. She knew nothing about the heat and dust and flies of outback Queensland, but she'd always been the adventurous type. She'd left her family and friends and familiar life in Florida and had taken a job on the other side of the world, hadn't she?

"I'll have to check my schedule. It's normally completely full. Still... I might be able to rearrange a few appointments. I'll see what I can do."

Brock's expression turned earnest. "There's no better way to get a feel for what we're all about than to visit the station and see for yourself. I'll have Yvonne clear my schedule. We can leave whenever it suits you."

"Thank you, but just so you know, there's only a slim chance I'm going to change my mind about the loan. I'm sure your ranch is beautiful, but you need more than that to secure the money you're after. I don't want to give you false hope."

Brock nodded. "I understand. But you haven't seen Marlowe Downs. It's the most amazing place on earth. Once you see it, you'll understand and then hopefully, you'll feel the same way I do and pull out all the stops to approve our application."

His face was alight with emotion. For a moment, she got lost in the golden specks in his deep green eyes. Then she collected herself and nodded.

"Okay. I accept your invitation. I'll call you and let you know when I have a few days free."

His answering smile was blinding. Kelsey's pulse took off at a gallop before she had a chance to rein it in. She hoped for his sake that the trip to Marlowe Downs would change her decision, but even if it didn't, she was definitely up for a few days in the outback with a hot guy. In fact, she couldn't think of a better way to spend her time and maybe, just maybe, she might snag a husband and save her mother in the meantime.

After seeing Kelsey out and obtaining a promise from her to call him within the next few days with her available dates, Brock returned to his office. He immediately called Yvonne in and asked her to flag anything in his calendar that wasn't absolutely urgent.

"Any reason?" she asked.

"Yes. I need to go to Marlowe Downs for a few days."

"When are you going?"

"I'm not sure yet. Hopefully next week."

She nodded and left on the promise that she'd do what he'd asked. Brock swung around in his chair and stacked his hands behind his head. Oblivious to the spectacular view of the Brisbane River outside his floor-to-ceiling plate glass window, his mind centered on the woman who had him in such a spin.

If she was serious about her decision to deny them finance, they'd be in a terrible mess. Things were dire. Though the recent floods meant they now had plenty of water and fodder, they needed money to increase the size of their herd, and though they were rich in assets, cash flow had become tight. They needed Kelsey Garland to come through for them, and if that meant spending time with her on the farm to convince her, then that was a sacrifice he was willing to make.

Liar. She's a beautiful woman. It's not going to be difficult spending a few days with her...

Okay, he conceded that. Just like he grudgingly admitted to being instantly attracted to her. Not that his response meant anything. That was nothing more than a man's natural response to a beautiful woman. A spontaneous physical reaction. He was still recovering from the damage Cecelia had inflicted to genuinely be seeking female companionship again. Still, Kelsey sure had a way about her that drew him. Perhaps it was the American accent? He'd always been a sucker for accents, and hers was a sexy Southern drawl.

But his first priority was Marlowe Downs and securing the finance they needed to continue their grazing operation and keep their staff employed. He was determined to do all he could to impress the bank manager and convince her to change her mind. If they didn't get the money, the family business would be facing grim times indeed. He hated to think how that might affect his parents.

"How did the meeting go?"

Brock dropped his arms and swung around to face the doorway. Raine filled the opening.

Brock grimaced and shook his head. "Not so good. She turned us down."

Panic flared in Raine's eyes as he moved farther into the room. "What? She turned us down? Without that money, we're screwed. What are we going to do? We can't lose the farm. It would kill Mum and Dad. Shit."

Brock held up his hand. "Hang on a minute. All's not lost yet."

Raine stopped pacing and frowned. "What are you talking about?"

"I've managed to convince Kelsey to visit Marlowe Downs for a hands-on look around the operation. I'm hoping I might be able to get her to change her mind."

Raine's gaze filled with curiosity. "Kelsey? You're on a first-name basis? How did that happen so quickly?"

Brock merely shrugged. "My natural charm, I guess."

Raine chuckled. "Easy to be charming around such an attractive woman."

Brock widened his eyes with mock innocence. "Really? I didn't notice."

Raine grinned. "Bullshit."

"Hey!" Brock protested. "You're married."

"That doesn't mean I'm blind. And you're not fooling me. Any man with a heartbeat and a modicum of eyesight would have noticed. No wonder you poured on the charm."

Brock waved a hand in surrender. "Okay, so she's hot. So what? Surely I don't need to remind you about what happened with Cecelia. I'm done with relationships for now."

"Who said anything about a relationship?" Raine wiggled his eyebrows. "There's a lot to be said for a hot and heavy affair. If it gets us that loan approval, then why not?"

"Raine! I'm offended you'd think I'd stoop to something like that."

"Hey, I'm not suggesting you deliberately try to seduce her for only that purpose, but as you say, she's hot. What's the harm in a little fling?"

"Um, Cecelia?"

"Oh, Cecelia." Raine waved his hand dismissively. "Forget about her."

"That's easy for you to say. You weren't the one who got their heart broken when the woman you were madly in love with turned out to be the biggest liar on the planet. Have you forgotten the lengths she went to? She lied about everything, and all to impress me. She knew I was from a wealthy family, an eligible bachelor. She made sure our paths crossed. Then she lied about being a doctor, a neurosurgeon, no less. She took me to that flash waterfront apartment in her late-model Audi and pretended both of them were hers."

Raine grinned. "Didn't she have a white lab coat on the back seat?"

"Yes! She even wore a pager and had her friends page her to pretend she was needed at the hospital. All of it to deceive me into thinking she was someone she wasn't. I'd fallen in love with her! To discover none of it was real gutted me! I'm not sure I could ever fully trust a woman again. Could you?"

Raine walked over to Brock's desk and propped a hip against it. He waved away Brock's question.

"You have to get over that. Not every girl's like Cecelia. You need to open yourself up to the possibility of love again." Raine frowned. "Don't you want to get married? Have kids?"

"Of course, I do," Brock said impatiently.

Raine shrugged. "Well, you can't do either of those things alone. That means trusting again and risking another broken heart. The greater the risk, the greater the reward, right? Look at me and Isabella. When we first met, I thought she was an escort."

"She *was* an escort," Brock said dryly.

Raine flushed. "Yes, well, she was also a brilliant doctor and a woman with the kindest heart. Smart, sexy, funny... What more could a guy want? My point is, you need to forget about Cecelia and get back on the horse, so to speak. There are plenty more fish in the sea. The sexy bank manager might just be the woman to help you get over your heartbreak."

Brock sighed. Images of the gorgeous Kelsey flooded his mind. No doubt Raine's outlook on love was clouded by the fact he was deliriously besotted with his wife, but getting back into the dating scene was definitely something for him to think about, and what better way to do that than to spend time with Kelsey on Marlowe Downs? The station was in the middle of nowhere. Unless she took up with one of the station hands—or one of his brothers—Brock would be her only source of entertainment and companionship.

The reminder that four of his single younger brothers would also be on the station made him frown, but then he pushed the thought away. He had an advantage over them. He'd already met Kelsey. Better still, she was there at his invitation. That gave him an automatic call on her time, and if he hadn't been mistaken, he was almost certain he'd seen something that looked very much like interest in her bright blue eyes.

Anticipation warred with panic. He wasn't sure if he was ready to risk his heart again. Then again, Raine was right. If he wanted to find someone to settle down with, he needed to get over his trust issues. Maybe this was just the opportunity he needed?

Belatedly, he realized he hadn't asked Raine about his appointment. "How did the ultrasound go?"

Raine's face lit up like a Christmas tree. His eyes sparkled with excitement. "It was amazing. The most amazing thing I've ever seen. The detail! The pictures were incredible. And everything was perfect. It's so hard to believe Isabella and I have created that tiny being and that in about six months, we'll get to meet him."

Brock raised an eyebrow. "Him?"

"Or her." Raine shrugged. "It's too early to find out the sex. We probably won't, anyway. It doesn't matter to us what it is, and we'd rather wait for the surprise."

Brock stood and moved around his desk to thump his brother on the back. "Congratulations, bro. I can't wait to meet my little nephew or niece. The first Fairfax grandchild. Mum and Dad are going to be thrilled."

"Yeah. But remember what I said? Don't tell anyone yet. We want to wait until we're past the first trimester."

Brock thought fleetingly of Kelsey and was filled with guilt.

Perhaps I should tell her to keep the pregnancy thing quiet?

Something in his expression must have given him away. Raine's eyes narrowed. "Shit. You've told someone already, haven't you?"

Brock grimaced and nodded. "Kelsey."

"Kelsey? Why the hell would you tell *her*?"

Brock flushed. "I'm sorry. She seemed a bit put out that you hadn't stayed for the meeting. I told her where you'd gone so that she realized you had a good excuse. Lucky for you, she agreed."

Raine blew out his breath. "I guess there's nothing you can do about that now. Let's hope she doesn't say anything while she's out at Marlowe Downs."

Brock shrugged. "Why would she? Besides, she's going to be there, like, five minutes. She's hardly going to get into personal conversations with the family."

"I guess. Still..."

"If you'd rather I call and ask her to keep it to herself, I will."

"Thanks, I'd appreciate that. I mean, in a couple of weeks, we'll be telling everyone the good news ourselves, but for now, let's just keep it under wraps."

"It'll be here before you know it."

"Yes. So, when are you going to the station?"

"I'm waiting to hear back from Kelsey. She had to check her calendar. I hope to leave in the next few days. As soon as I hear from her, I'll be booking the flights."

"Sounds good," Raine said, nodding with approval. "Let's hope you manage to convince her to change her mind and we get the loan so we can move forward."

Brock winked. "I promise to lay on the famous Fairfax charm."

Kelsey squeezed the last pair of jeans into her suitcase and then used all her weight to zip it closed. She'd packed way too much for a three-day trip, but she'd never been to a cattle ranch before, and she wasn't sure what to take.

No, not a ranch. They call them stations out here... I'm in Australia. I need to use the lingo.

She'd done some research on cattle stations in outback Queensland and had been interested to discover Queensland grew more head of beef cattle than any other state in Australia. In fact, notwithstanding the drought, Queensland had twice as many head as the next largest state. Brock had booked her a flight to Roma. Apparently, that was the closest airport to the station. The flight was expected to take about seventy-five minutes. Then there was an hour's drive through the outback to Marlowe Downs.

When she'd half-jokingly expressed concern that she might get lost trying to find the place, Brock had assured her he'd meet her at the airport and drive her to his family home.

At the thought of seeing the handsome cowboy again, her heart skipped a beat and her stomach flooded with nerves. It had taken longer to clear her schedule than she'd anticipated, and it had been nearly two weeks since she'd seen him. Though the timing had been out of her control, she'd chafed at the delay. Not only because of her mother's deteriorating condition, but because her instant attraction to him hadn't waned. If anything, it now burned hotter. He'd consumed her waking thoughts, distracted her from her work. She couldn't wait to see him again.

Of course, unless there was something he hadn't included in the loan application that would enhance their financial position, no matter how much she liked him or his family, or how much she enjoyed her experience at Marlowe Downs, she likely as not wouldn't change her mind about declining the loan. If it came to that, she hoped Brock would accept her decision was nothing personal.

With a final tug, she got the zipper closed. The sound of a horn from below her apartment window alerted her to the taxi's arrival. Lugging the suitcase off her bed, she slung her handbag over her shoulder and then set her brand new Akubra hat on her head.

She winked at her reflection in the mirror and smiled. Teamed with jeans and boots, she made a fine-looking cowgirl.

Let's just hope Brock feels the same way...

She might not score a new client, but a new boyfriend who could be potential husband material? That was worth the effort. There was a million dollars up for grabs that could be used to potentially save her mother's life, and the sexy, single Brock Fairfax was fair game.

Chapter Three

With the air conditioner cranked up, Brock sat in the driver's seat of his single-cab Toyota Land Cruiser utility tapping a nervous rhythm on the steering wheel with his index finger. The plane from Brisbane was late, and the longer he sat in the airport car park waiting for Kelsey, the more tied up in knots his gut became. It was ridiculous how nervous he was about seeing her again. It wasn't like he hadn't dated beautiful women before. But those beautiful women hadn't held the future of his family's treasured Marlowe Downs in their hands.

He was still a bit bemused by his immediate reaction to her. The way his gut had clenched, how butterflies had swarmed in his belly, how he'd been almost tongue-tied in her presence. He was just glad Raine hadn't been there to witness his awkwardness. He'd never have heard the end of it.

The whole sordid episode with Cecelia had seriously dented Brock's confidence and trust in women and relationships and, more importantly, in his ability to discern the truth. They'd been dating for months before he'd discovered her deception. His normally reliable bullshit detector had completely failed him. What if it failed him again?

He had to remember that not every woman was a Cecelia in disguise. Not every woman deliberately set out to lie and deceive. Besides, Kelsey was out here on a business trip. Securing that finance was the only priority he had. She'd been upfront with him about their prospects, had even warned him there was still a good chance that even after her visit to the station, she wouldn't change her mind. And he was okay with that. He appreciated her honesty, but he was also prepared to rise to the challenge. He had confidence that the financial potential of Marlowe Downs would speak for itself and of course, there was also his ability to woo and charm.

The sound of the plane coming in to land snagged his attention. His stomach clenched on a fresh wave of nerves. They hadn't seen each other for nearly two weeks. He wondered if his reaction to her would be just as visceral, just as immediate, as it had been the first time. With anticipation, he climbed out of the ute, closed the door behind him, and locked it with the remote. Taking a Mument to adjust his Akubra over his eyes, he strode toward the small arrivals lounge.

He watched her as she entered the building. With her long legs encased in blue jeans and a cream-colored Akubra perched on top of her head, she stood head and shoulders above most of the incoming passengers. He lifted his hand slightly to get her attention and was rewarded with a wide grin. His gut tightened with desire.

Shit. It's worse than I expected. She's even more beautiful than before... Shit. I'm in trouble...

"Hi," she said. Her smile was all perfectly straight white teeth and full lips covered in shiny red lipstick. Lips that looked so kissable...

"H-hi," he stammered and then ducked his head to cover the blush.

"It's good to see you again," she said.

"You too," he managed. "Love the hat."

She touched the brim a little self-consciously. "Thank you. You don't think it's too much?"

"Not at all." He touched his own. "A hat with a good brim is essential out here. It might not be the middle of summer, but even the autumn sun can have a bite to it. Besides," he added, his confidence restored, "it suits you."

It was her turn to blush. "Thanks."

"Let's go get your bags," he said and turned toward the baggage collection area.

She walked in silence beside him. The arrivals lounge was filled with people greeting friends, family members, work colleagues. Akubra-covered heads were everywhere. Some battered and worn. Others pristine, like Kelsey's. The condition of his was somewhere in between. He only wore it when he was at the station. It felt out of place in the city. He usually left it on a hook on the back veranda of the Marlowe Downs homestead, where he'd retrieved it that morning.

"You're right," Kelsey murmured. "Everyone's wearing a hat. I feel like I've arrived in Texas."

He shot her a look of mock outrage. "Surely you can't be comparing the Aussie Akubra to a Stetson? They look nothing alike!"

"Hey! They're both cowboy hats, aren't they? And they both keep the sun off, right?" She grinned. "They have more in common than you think."

He chuckled. "Just so you know, we don't have cowboys out here. We call them station hands. Or jackaroos."

She looked bemused. "Jackaroos? Like, kangaroos?"

He rolled his eyes. "No, not like kangaroos. A jackaroo is a bloke, a man who works on the station. He's usually young and inexperienced. One day, he might obtain enough practical skills to become a ringer."

She scrunched up her face. "A ringer? What's a ringer?"

"An older, more experienced station hand or stockman."

"You sure have some strange titles to describe cowboys. What about the women? Do women work on your ranch?"

Brock laughed. "First of all, we don't use the word 'ranch.' It's a farm, or a station. Depending on size and use."

She blushed again. "That's right. I read that," she muttered.

Brock grinned. "Second, yes, there are women who work on the stations. The young, inexperienced hands are called jillaroos."

Her blue eyes sparkled with laughter. "Jillaroos? Really?" And then her eyes widened with sudden comprehension. "Oh, now I get it! Jack and Jill! Jackaroos and jillaroos! How cute!"

They'd arrived at the baggage carousel. A few minutes later, Kelsey spied her suitcase. She pointed it out to Brock, who stepped forward and pulled it off the carousel. He gave an exaggerated groan at the weight of it.

"What do you have in here, woman? This thing weighs a ton!"

She shot him an innocent look. "Do you know, one pair of jeans weighs two pounds on their own."

"Hell, you're only here for three days. How many pairs of jeans do you need?" he grumbled good-naturedly.

She flicked her long hair over her shoulder and merely grinned. He caught a whiff of her sweet-smelling shampoo. His body reacted instinctively. He cursed silently and, ignoring the blood pumping through his veins, he wheeled the suitcase in the direction of the exit.

Kelsey matched his long stride. She wore tall black boots that cupped her slender calves. The high heels gave her the extra few inches she needed to equal his height. He wasn't sure how practical the boots would be on the station, but they sure looked good on her.

His gaze ran up the length of her long, jean-clad leg. She'd looked sexy in her business attire, but he liked her even more in the casual wear. Her pink-and-white-checked shirt was tucked into the waistband of her jeans. A black leather belt sporting a shiny silver buckle was fastened around her narrow waist. The first few buttons of her blouse were undone and revealed a stretchy white top underneath that drew his eyes to her impressive cleavage. All in all, she was a very tidy package, and he looked forward to spending the next few days with her.

Images of Cecelia crowded his mind, and some of his enthusiasm dimmed. Despite what Raine had said, rushing headlong into another relationship—even a fling—was the last thing he needed. Besides, this was a business trip. They needed that loan. It was important to do everything he could to get her to change her mind. Seducing her probably wasn't the best way to go about that. If anything, it might jeopardize their chances, especially if things ended on a sour note between them.

The safest thing to do would be to keep his hands off her. Treat her with the same courtesy and respect he'd offer any guest. Show her around Marlowe Downs. Show her how important it was to him and his family and how many people relied on them for work. If the station went bankrupt, it wouldn't just be his family affected. The station employed five full-time workers and dozens more casual workers who came and went, depending on the seasons. They'd all be looking for new jobs if the station went under. He wanted Kelsey to appreciate that, and he was quietly confident she would. She'd agreed to come out for a look, hadn't she? That was a positive first step.

No one had forced her to do that. She could have simply thanked him for his invitation and reiterated her decision to decline the loan. Instead, she'd taken him up on his offer, and here she was. Had even made an effort to look the part. New boots, new Akubra. The thought filled him with satisfaction and gave him hope. He'd managed to get her here. Now it was up to him not to screw things up.

As they reached his truck, he hefted the suitcase into the tray back and unlocked the doors. Kelsey climbed into the passenger seat and pulled on her seat belt. Excitement shone in her bright eyes.

He climbed in beside her and gave her a wink. "You ready?"

She laughed and flicked her hair, sending a whiff of her shampoo his way again. "You bet."

As Brock's truck ate up the miles between Roma and the cattle station, Kelsey took in the scenery. The asphalt highway stretched in front of them, a single dark line that cut through the bush surrounding them. Undulating hills were covered in dull, olive-green scrubby trees that were as unfamiliar to Kelsey as most of the Australian countryside.

She'd been in Brisbane for six months already, but she hadn't ventured farther outside the city than the Gold Coast, which was about fifty miles southeast of Brisbane and the Sunshine Coast, which was only a little bit farther, but in the opposite direction. While both locations had plenty to offer in the way of unspoiled beaches, golden sand, high-quality restaurants, and great shopping—along with plenty of buff surfer dudes—they weren't all that different from where she'd grown up in Florida.

The landscape they now traveled through was like passing through a foreign land. So hot, so dry. The place had been flooded only a few months ago, but the water had long since drained away or evaporated, leaving in its wake a thick carpet of vegetation and trees that had been given a new lease on life.

"Those are gum trees, right?" she asked, pointing out toward the passing landscape.

"Yes."

"I read that there are hundreds of species. What kind are they?"

"Mostly coolabah and red gum. Those smaller, scrubbier trees are tea tree and native wattle. The wattle are the ones with the yellow flowers. Smells great. The bees love it."

"I'll have to take your word for that. I've never smelled wattle."

He grinned. "No wattle in Florida?"

She laughed. "No. Our climate's hot and humid, not dry like this."

"I'd take dry heat over humidity any day," he quipped.

"It gets pretty humid in Brisbane."

He nodded. "You're right. They're the days when I have to remind myself, I choose to live in Brisbane. I could be living on the station away from the humidity, with the rest of my family."

"Tell me about them."

"There are ten of us altogether. A neat dozen, counting Mum and Dad."

"*Ten?* Your parents have *ten* children?" she exclaimed, feigning surprise. It wouldn't do for him to know she'd done extensive research on him.

"Yep. Six boys and four girls. A fair handful, to be sure."

She laughed. "I'll say. Do they *all* live at Marlowe Downs?"

"Most of them. Not Raine, of course. He and his wife have a place in Brisbane, where he spends most of his time with our investment business. But the rest of my siblings still call the place home. Two of the younger ones are studying at university and working in Brisbane, but they all have cattle blood in their veins. My sister Emma is with the RFDS, so she's all over the place, but she's single and has no fixed abode and still loves coming home whenever she can."

Kelsey frowned. "The RFDS?"

"The Royal Flying Doctor Service," Brock explained. "They provide twenty-four-hour aeromedical emergency services to people living in the outback. They service an area of nearly five million square miles."

Kelsey's eyes widened in surprise. She could hardly fathom such a large area for a flying medical service. Sure, there were large, open, and dramatic landscapes in the US, and long distances, but there were more people, which didn't make it feel as vast as the world passing by her window seemed to be.

She turned to look out the window again. She slid the tinted glass down. This time, she noticed the scrubby bushes with their dots of yellow flowers. A fly flew through the open window and landed on her cheek. She laughed and brushed it away.

The truck continued forward in a straight and unrelenting line. There were miles and miles of bush for as far as the eye could see. It was unbroken by anything that resembled civilization. The last town they'd passed through had been little more than a small collection of houses, a post office, and a bar. She'd seen no signs of life. That had been half an hour earlier, and there was no evidence of the next township on the horizon.

"We're traveling on the Carnarvon Highway," Brock said, as if reading her mind. "It stretches for about four hundred and thirty-three miles from Rolleston in central west Queensland, all the way down to Moree in New South Wales. There are only a handful of small towns scattered in between."

"How far is Marlowe Downs from Roma?" she asked.

"About sixty miles."

"Wow. And how many towns in between?"

Brock shot her a quick grin. "Six. And you've already passed through three of them."

"You're kidding! They could hardly be called towns. If I'd blinked, I would have missed them."

He chuckled. "Yep."

"What about the other three? Are they worthy of the name 'town'?"

"I guess that depends on how you define a town. All of them are home to the people who live there, but none of them have a population exceeding two hundred."

She gaped. "Where do they go to shop?"

"Roma, mostly."

She turned to him in disbelief. "They drive more than an hour just to go shopping?"

He shrugged. "Some people drive even farther. Marlowe Downs is about an hour from Roma. That's where we mostly go to shop, see doctors, do business. But the town only has a population of around seven thousand. Not exactly huge. The Internet has improved access in that regard. Now we're able to do some of that stuff online."

Kelsey shook her head and once again pondered the vastness outside her window. She couldn't imagine living in such isolation. And yet, people chose to do it. She wanted to know what kept them there. A surge of anticipation went through her. This was one of the reasons she'd taken a job on the other side of the world. She wanted new experiences. She wanted adventure. And the fact that she would get to do those things with a hot-looking cowboy by her side, was icing on the cake.

No, not a cowboy. Not a rancher. A station hand. A cattle farmer. Or in this case, a station owner. Well, at least his family was.

Those terms didn't quite have the same ring to them, but what did that matter? He was charming and sexy and made her heart flutter.

"So, I guess you have family in the States? How do they feel about you being so far from home?" Brock asked, interrupting her thoughts.

"Yes, I have family, but it's just my Mum and my grandmother and me. I'm an only child. I lost my dad a couple of years ago in a car accident."

Brock grimaced. "I'm sorry."

"Yes. So am I. He was a good man. I still miss him."

"What prompted you to take a job on the other side of the world?"

She shrugged. "Several reasons. I love new challenges, new experiences. When the job offer came up, it appealed to my sense of adventure."

"I'm surprised your mum was willing to let you take a job so far away."

She smiled. "My mother's amazing. She's always encouraged me to live the life I want. It's probably not the best time to be so far away from her right now—"

Kelsey broke off, becoming aware of what she'd been about to reveal. They barely knew each other. There was no point in getting bogged down in personal details. Besides, if he knew about her mother's cancer and the complications that came with her treatment, that might lead to other questions. Best to keep all that under wraps for now. She didn't want to scare him off.

But Brock proved far too perceptive. "Why not?" he asked.

Kelsey forced a nonchalant smile. "Is there ever a good time for an only child to be so far away from home?"

She could see the questions in Brock's eyes and hurriedly changed the subject. "How about we listen to some music? Do you mind if I Bluetooth my phone to your truck? I have some great playlists to choose from. What do you like?"

The questions came out in a rush, but she didn't give him a chance to answer. Instead, she pulled out her phone and in no time at all had connected to his car's audio system. Scrolling through her playlists, she chose a mix of her favorite female singers.

When the first song started playing, Brock groaned in mock horror. "Who's this?"

She smiled sweetly. "Beyoncé, of course. We also have Taylor Swift, Katy Perry, Pink, and a bit of Spice Girls. What's not to like about that lineup?"

He groaned again. "How about some good old country music? Luke Combs? Morgan Wallen? Cody Johnson? Hell, I'd even be happy to listen to Garth Brooks."

Now it was Kelsey's turn to look horrified. "Country music? You like country music? Oh, dear. Stop the car. I can't travel any farther with a man who's a country music fan."

She softened her words with a giggle, and Brock laughed. She sent him a cheeky wink and then settled back against the seat.

The first indication Kelsey had that they were nearing Marlowe Downs was when Brock began to slow the vehicle and then told her to put up her window. She did as he instructed and watched curiously as they took a left turn off the highway and onto a red dirt road. Clouds of red dust immediately billowed behind them.

"Wow. Now I understand why you told me to put up my window." She chuckled.

Brock glanced at her and grinned. "Welcome to Marlowe Downs."

Through a break in the dust, she glimpsed a dusty white rail fence that spanned either side of a wide driveway blocked by double iron gates. The words "Marlowe Downs" were set in tall black steel letters above the gates, making the entryway even more impressive.

"I can't believe we're finally here," she said.

He smiled. "Well, almost. We're on Fairfax land at least. The homestead's another six miles farther down this track."

"Six *miles*?"

Brock laughed and climbed out to open the gate. Kelsey could barely fathom driving six miles across a single farm, and that was only to the homestead. She recalled from the figures Brock had supplied on the loan application that the station comprised two hundred thousand acres of prime grazing land, with verdant valleys, well-improved country, and an abundance of water in normal seasons. Now that she was there, with wide-open red and brown land for as far as the eye could see, the vastness before her boggled the mind.

"How many cattle do you run?" she asked when he slid back behind the wheel.

"In a good season, up to twenty thousand head. At the moment, our pasture's been ravaged by the drought. That's why we had to sell so much stock. We're down to five hundred head of our prime breeding stock right now. The recent floods have helped restore some of the ground cover and replenished the dams, but we still have a long way to go before we'll be back to where we were before the drought."

Hence, the need for the loan from my bank...

The thought went unspoken, but she could tell it was on Brock's mind. He climbed back out of the vehicle and secured the gate behind them. Dread stirred in her stomach. The figures supplied by Brock and his brother hadn't convinced her they were a good enough risk. She wasn't sure there was anything he could show her on the ranch that would change her mind. Still, she was here, and she'd do her best to keep an open mind.

He climbed back into the truck, and they kept going. Kelsey looked around at the passing countryside.

"Who looks after the cattle in a good season? Twenty thousand head sounds like a lot."

"My father and brothers, mostly, along with the station hands, jackaroos, jillaroos, and stockmen. This station employs nearly a dozen people, including family. Believe me, when the going's good, this place is a thriving metropolis."

He gave her another quick grin. She smiled back. It was hard to imagine. Never in her wildest dreams would she describe the wide-open land spread before them, dotted with scrubby wattle bushes and gum trees with zero evidence of habitation—let alone a shopping center—as a metropolis, but she appreciated the joke.

Surreptitiously, her gaze slid over him. Dressed in faded blue jeans that hugged his ass and a long-sleeved emerald-green plaid shirt that brought out the color in his eyes, he'd replaced the sophisticated veneer of the boardroom with the raw earthiness of a cowboy. Teamed with the chocolate-brown Akubra and with his sleeves rolled up to his elbows, he could have been any one of the cowboys she'd seen on TV. She'd never seen an American cowboy in real life, but she imagined they'd look something like Brock. Even his speech sounded different. Slower, lazier. His vowels less rounded. His speech less clipped. And then she realized what it was: He was more relaxed.

No doubt that had something to do with the fact their first meeting had taken place in his boardroom, and he'd been anxious about the outcome of the loan application. Now, it was almost as if he'd forgotten the reason behind his impromptu invitation. It felt more like she was there as his guest, rather than this being a business trip.

Without warning, a kangaroo bounded across the road in front of them, and Brock slammed on the brakes. She gasped. The animal hopped safely out of the way. Before Kelsey could utter a word, three more followed in quick succession. Brock came to a halt and let them pass.

"I can't believe I just saw real live kangaroos!" she said, her heart thumping.

Brock grinned. "You'll see plenty of them out here. Along with a lot of other wildlife. Emus, wallabies, bandicoots. Echidnas, possums, even the odd koala, although they're rarer because they only eat one particular type of gum leaf. Then there's all the birdlife. During a good season, when there's plenty of water, we're blessed with hundreds of different species of birds. Seeing the sky filled with them is something to behold. That's one good thing about a flood. It brings the birdlife back."

They continued forward. Ignoring the dust, she lowered her window and stared at the passing landscape. At first glance, she'd dismissed it as nothing more than red dirt and scrubby trees. But now she saw it through Brock's eyes. The different shades of brown and green and red on the trees. The tufts of straw-like grass. Bursts of color in the wildflowers—red and white and yellow—dotted along the ground.

It suddenly reminded her of a painting she'd seen in a Brisbane art gallery by a well-known Aboriginal artist. Though the painting had been abstract, she recognized the same patterns and colors that were reflected in the landscape around her. A harsh land, to be sure, and not for everyone, but there was a wild kind of beauty about it, something free and unrestrained. She could see the appeal of living out here, so far removed from the hustle and bustle of the city.

And then she gave herself a mental shake. She was on a business trip. A few days to look around the place, spend some time with Brock, and see where things led. If her efforts came to nothing, she'd head back to Brisbane and get on with her life.

As several farm buildings came into view, her heart gave a kick of excitement. Brock steered the vehicle toward a large weatherboard homestead, with screened-in verandas and wide stone steps leading to the front door. There were well-established trees in the tidy front yard. Several other trucks of the same make and model as Brock's were parked outside the fence.

Brock turned to her with a grin. "So, we're here and it's right on lunchtime. Are you ready to meet the family?"

Chapter Four

♥

It was a little before one. Stepping out of the truck, she looked around quickly before following Brock through a garden gate and a short walk along a path and then up a few steps to a weathered timber veranda. They crossed over it and made their way through an open door, down a wide entry hall, and into a large and airy country-style kitchen, where they found the family sitting down to lunch.

No one seemed surprised to see her, which meant Brock had already brought his family up to speed. But whether he'd told them that she'd more or less decided to reject their application remained to be seen. She found herself bracing for signs of anger and suspicion.

Brock glanced at her and made the introductions. "Mum, Dad. This is Kelsey Garland."

An attractive older woman with short, dark brown hair liberally streaked with gray nodded a greeting from where she was seated at the long table.

"Hello, Kelsey. I'm Ellen."

Taking into account the age lines around her blue eyes, Kelsey guessed her to be in her mid-fifties. The man beside her, with his gray-flecked auburn hair and brilliant green eyes, stood and offered his hand. There was no guessing from whom Brock had inherited his eyes.

"Bob Fairfax. It's nice to meet you, Kelsey. Welcome to Marlowe Downs."

His hand was rough from years of farmwork. Kelsey smiled in response, her nerves easing. "Thanks for having me."

She sat beside Brock in the chair he held out for her and then noticed three other good-looking men seated across from her. She caught the eye of the one closest to her, and he held out his hand.

"I'm Cayd. I'm Brock's younger, much better looking brother."

Brock snorted. "Younger in age and, unfortunately, in maturity."

Ignoring the gibe, Kelsey shook the proffered hand and smiled. "It's nice to meet you, Cayd."

His hair was darker, longer, and with a reddish tinge, and his eyes were blue. He gazed at her with a mixture of curiosity and laughter.

"I'm Lachlan," the man seated beside Cayd said.

Kelsey turned in his direction and smiled again. Lachlan was a younger version of Brock, though he didn't exhibit quite the same degree of confidence. She murmured a greeting.

"I'm Justin."

Kelsey smiled a greeting toward the man seated opposite Cayd. He was younger than the other two and had thick dark hair and twinkling blue eyes he'd obviously inherited from his mother. He gave her a cheeky wink.

"Last, but certainly not least, I'm Aiden."

Kelsey turned her attention to the youngest man at the table. Long, unruly blond hair hung messily around his face. Sparkling green eyes that reminded her of Brock's smiled back at her.

She smiled back. "Hi, Aiden. It's lovely to meet you."

Brock tensed beside her and leveled a warning glare on his brothers. Kelsey was amused. She wasn't sure if he was warning them off, or merely silently ordering them to behave. Not that Brock's brothers made her heart race like he did. They might be every bit as good-looking as he was, but there was something about Brock that had drawn her from the start. Still drew her.

Quit thinking like that. He invited me here to assess the farm from the bank's point of view. Nothing more.

Though she'd seen signs of Brock's attraction to her, she had no idea if he'd follow up on it. She'd been blessed with more than her fair share of good looks. She was used to men doing a double take when they passed by. Her popularity on dating sites was further testament to her physical attractiveness.

But no matter the endless dates she'd endured, she still hadn't found "the one." That was partly her fault. She intimidated a lot of men. More than one of her ex-boyfriends had complained about that. She wasn't sure if it was because of her high position in the bank or just the way she conducted herself with confidence and authority. Still, she wasn't about to change her ways or lower her standards, although her pressing circumstances meant that she might have to find a compromise.

She liked Brock's confidence. Even when he'd been a little awkward upon meeting her in the boardroom and at the airport, he'd recovered quickly and taken charge. He was obviously a successful businessman who commanded authority and respect, His commitment to and protectiveness toward his family's heritage intrigued her. His determination to save it despite the odds and the cost was impressive.

Could Brock be the man I've been searching for? Only closer acquaintance will tell.

Brock was acutely aware of Kelsey throughout lunch. As serving platters piled high with food were handed around and conversation about the farm flowed between his father and brothers, he found it difficult to focus on anything but her. How close she was seated beside him. The brush of her arm as she reached for a plate. The smell of her perfume. Then there was the occasional whiff of her shampoo whenever she flicked back her hair, which she did so often it was slowly driving him crazy.

Focus. I need to focus. This is a business trip. She's here in a professional capacity. We need that loan. Don't do anything to jeopardize that. Picture Cecelia. That should do the trick.

At the reminder of his last disastrous relationship, all thought of igniting some romance with Kelsey disappeared. Letting the conversation flow around him, he busied himself with his food. Prime beef steak, cooked to perfection, accompanied by fresh garden salad and fluffy mashed potato. Delicious, wholesome food that left everyone feeling satisfied.

Kelsey cut into her steak and took a bite. "This is so good!" she enthused.

Brock winked. "The best of Fairfax beef."

Her eyes widened. "This is your meat?"

"Absolutely," he replied and then indicated the other food on her plate. "Everything on your plate has been grown here on Marlowe Downs."

"Wow. I'm impressed," she replied. "Who tends to the garden?"

"Mum," they all chorused.

Ellen Fairfax smiled, looking pleased. "The garden's always been my domain. I enjoy growing things. Bob and the boys take care of the paddock. I take care of the plate."

Kelsey smiled. "Well, everything tastes terrific. So much better than store-bought. It's quite a treat."

Ellen nodded. "We're glad to have you here. I hope you have enough time to take a look around the station."

"I managed to get away for three days. Hopefully that's enough." Kelsey looked at Brock's mother. "Thank you for having me. This place, so far from everywhere... It's like nothing I've ever experienced."

"Where are you from?" Bob asked from his position at the head of the table.

Kelsey filled them in on her background, including her spontaneous decision to take up a position with her company in Brisbane, despite not having traveled much outside of Florida.

"How did your parents feel about your decision?" Ellen asked.

"Dad passed away a couple of years ago. It's only my mother now."

There were murmured apologies for her loss.

"Your poor mum, all on her own and having her baby living on the other side of the world. I bet she had plenty to say about that," Ellen said.

Kelsey shrugged and answered honestly. "I'm twenty-nine. She's okay with me wanting to stretch my wings. Besides, these days, with Zoom and social media, it's easy to stay in touch." Even when her mother had been diagnosed with cancer and Kelsey had offered to throw in her job and come home immediately, her mother had urged her to stay.

"Do you think she'll come and visit while you're in Australia?" Bob asked.

Kelsey bit her lip. There was no way her mother's current health would allow for that. In response to Bob's question, she merely shrugged and said, "We'll see."

"How long are you here for?" Ellen asked.

Beside her, Brock stilled. There was a general hush around the table, as if everyone was interested in her response.

"Another six months. I'm halfway through my secondment."

"What will you do then? Return to the US?" Ellen asked.

Kelsey looked down at the table. Everything hinged on her being able to secure the money for her mother's treatment, but she didn't want to tell them that. "I'm not sure. There's still so much of Australia I haven't seen. I'd like to do some more traveling. Sydney. Melbourne. The Northern Territory."

"It's a big country," Bob agreed and sliced off another piece of steak. "There's plenty to see."

Kelsey nodded. "Yes. A bit like the US. People think they can travel across all fifty states in a week or two. They're surprised to discover the distance between everything. It's like that here."

"So, where have you been in Australia?" Brock asked.

Kelsey shifted slightly in her seat to face him. "Not many places, I'm afraid. I've been to the Gold Coast and the Sunshine Coast. Checked out the beaches and the shops. But other than that, I've been too busy working."

"But you live in Brisbane. You must have seen some of the city's sights," Brock insisted.

Kelsey shook her head. "Not really. A few of the bars. Shopping malls. Jogging tracks. That's about it."

Brock's eyes widened in mock amazement. "You mean you haven't watched a game at the 'Gabba? Been on a riverboat ride? Had a day trip to Stradbroke Island?"

Kelsey smiled. "No, afraid not. None of those things."

"Well, you've been to the Sunshine Coast. I assume you visited Australia Zoo?"

"That's the one set up by the late Steve Irwin, right?"

"Right," Brock replied.

Kelsey shook her head. "Sorry, no."

Once again, Brock's expression was one of mock disbelief. "You haven't been to visit Steve Irwin's sanctuary! What's wrong with you, woman!"

"All right, Brock. Give the lady a break," Bob chided.

Kelsey shot him a reassuring look. "It's okay, Bob. Brock's right to be horrified. I've been here six months and barely seen or done anything. That's my fault. I've been working too hard. I need to learn to take some time off. At least a weekend every now and then. You wouldn't believe how hard it was for me to arrange the time to come out here."

"Well, we're pleased you did. It will be a pleasure having another woman around, even if it's only for a few days," Ellen said.

After the meal, Kelsey helped the boys to gather up the plates and bring them over to the sink. Ellen was already stacking the dishwasher.

"One good thing about the flood," Ellen said, "it means our rainwater tanks are full." She gave Kelsey a wink. "That means we can use the dishwasher again."

"What happens when it's dry?" Kelsey asked.

Ellen chuckled. "The boys get to do the dishes by hand."

"Cayd's chief dishwasher," Justin said. "Aiden scrapes the plates. Lachie and I wipe up. Mum puts everything away."

"What about Brock? What does he do?" Kelsey asked.

"Brock lives in Brisbane most of the time," Cayd said. "I'm pretty sure he stays away on purpose so he doesn't have to do dishes."

Brock rolled his eyes and handed his mother a stack of dried plates. Kelsey laughed, enjoying the friendly ribbing. It was nice to be around a big family, feel the love, the camaraderie. The noise. Growing up an only child, that was something she'd never had.

"I've put you in the guest cottage," Ellen said, wiping her hands on a tea towel. "I hope that's okay?"

"Of course. I'm excited to be here, away from the city chaos."

"I know what you mean," Ellen said. "I was a city girl once. A lifetime ago."

Kelsey started in surprise. "Wow! You seem so much at home out here."

"I am. Bob and I have been married thirty-three years this year. I arrived here as a blushing bride. I had no idea what I was in for, but we made it work. Now, I wouldn't want to live anywhere else."

Kelsey pondered Ellen's words as she wiped over the table and straightened the chairs. Brock met her on her way back to the kitchen and removed the cloth from her fingers. He tossed it in the direction of the sink and took her by the hand. Her heart skipped a beat at the casual contact.

"Let me show you to your cottage. We'll drop your suitcase off and then go exploring. What do you say?"

She grinned on a surge of excitement, her fingers tingling from the contact with his skin. "Sounds good to me."

"Great."

As they walked down the hallway toward the front door, Kelsey paused beside an antique dresser that was covered with framed photographs. Curious, she picked one up. She scanned the faces of all ten Fairfax children who were crowded around their parents. The homestead could be seen in the background.

"Which one am I?" Brock asked with a grin.

Kelsey regarded the photo closely, slowly scanning from one child to another. She already knew Brock was one of the older ones. That certainly helped to narrow things down. Every one of the ten offspring looked similar enough to make guessing difficult. The oldest child looked to be around thirteen. The youngest, a brown-haired, blue-eyed toddler, about three.

At last, Kelsey stabbed a finger at a boy who stood tall and proud with his hands on his hips. He wore jeans, a T-shirt, and a dark-colored cowboy hat that was pushed back on his head. He stared confidently at the camera, a challenging grin on his face.

"That one."

He laughed. "Wow. I'm impressed. It's usually only the people who know me well who guess right the first time."

"It was the smile that gave you away."

Their eyes locked on a sudden surge of awareness. Kelsey's breath caught in her throat. Her chest went tight, making it difficult to breathe. With an effort, she dragged her gaze from his and looked back down at the photograph she still held in her hands.

"What are their names?"

It was the first thing that came into her head. Brock cleared his throat and replied, "Oldest to youngest: Raine, me, Cayd, Maggie, Lachlan, Justin, Emma, Aiden, Marnie, and Skyla."

Feeling more in control, Kelsey smiled. "Wow. Just...wow."

"I can't imagine what it must be like not to have any siblings."

She chuckled. "Nowhere near as noisy as your house, I bet."

Brock smiled again. "Yep, noisy is just one of the ways to describe it."

"You must have had some fun times growing up together. You all look close in age."

"Yep. A bit over ten years between the first and last. Mum sure had her hands full."

Kelsey shook her head, bemused. "Unbelievable. Did she have any help?"

"Yes. We always had a cook, and a couple of Aboriginal women from the camp would come in for a few hours each day and help, but Mum did the heavy lifting."

"She's a remarkable woman," Kelsey mused.

"You bet. Dad did his bit too, of course. He'd work outside all day and then come in at night and help with baths and feeding time."

Kelsey grinned. "Sounds like a zoo."

Brock chuckled. "Believe me, some days, I think that's exactly what it was like."

"But you loved it, didn't you? You loved growing up out here, surrounded by your family."

He nodded and reached out to pick up another picture. This one showed some of the children on horseback, while the younger ones clowned around beside them. All ten children were grinning madly at the camera. It was such a happy scene.

A sentimental smile lit up Brock's face. Kelsey smiled too. It was obvious how deeply he cared for his siblings and for the farm. The family had been there for generations. So many memories. So many good times. It was a shame to think it might all be taken away.

Unfortunately for Brock, sentimentality had no place in a bank's business decisions. Cold, hard figures were all they went on, and the figures she'd seen indicated Marlowe Downs was already on life support.

Chapter Five

♥

Brock retrieved Kelsey's suitcase from the back of his ute and hefted it toward the guest cottage. She strode quietly along beside him in her high-heeled boots, apparently content for him to do the heavy lifting. He didn't mind. In fact, he wouldn't have it any other way. He was pleased Kelsey hadn't made a big deal about it, insisting she could do it on her own. While he was all for women being treated as equals—hell, he had four sisters—no one could argue with science. In general, men were stronger than women. That was an undeniable fact, no matter the modern-day narrative that surrounded gender these days. He refused to buy into that.

He was, however, grateful the cottage wasn't too far away from the main house. They still had twenty yards to go, and his muscles screamed for a break. If it were possible, he'd have wheeled the suitcase there, but the grass growing between the homestead and the cottage put paid to that idea. During the drought, the ground had been as bare as a granite tabletop, with not a blade of grass to be found anywhere. That wasn't the case now. The thick cushion of buffalo grass was soft underfoot and would have made dragging a suitcase across it impossible, particularly a heavy one.

On the other hand, he was pleased his mother hadn't set Kelsey up in one of the unoccupied bedrooms in the homestead. She could have stayed in Skyla's room. His sister wasn't due home until the end of the school term, another four weeks away. But that would have meant Kelsey would have been right next door to him. He could do without the mental torture of knowing she was so close. Running into her in the bathroom in the middle of the night in her pajamas... That's if she wore pajamas... Maybe she slept naked, like he did.

The possibility sent an immediate rush of blood to his groin. He was glad he was a few steps ahead of her so that she didn't notice how uncomfortably tight the front of his jeans had suddenly become. He might not be keen to rush headlong into another relationship, but he still had all the physical wants and needs of any man, and it had been far too long since he'd been with a woman. Swallowing a groan of annoyance, he forced the alluring images away.

Setting the suitcase down on the cottage's front veranda, he opened the screen door. It squeaked on its hinges in protest.

"Sorry. That sounds like it needs a bit of attention. Since the flood, there have been so many other maintenance issues to see to. We lost miles and miles of fencing, and the cattle yards were completely washed away. I guess no one's gotten around to looking at the cottage."

Seemingly unfazed, Kelsey merely smiled. "Don't worry about it. That squeak only adds to the ambience."

She looked up at the clear blue sky. Brock watched as her gaze drifted around the yard, with its shady silky oak trees, towering gums, and well-tended flower beds. She didn't bother to hide her appreciative gaze.

"The place doesn't always look as inviting as this. Aside from filling the tanks, the recent rains have done wonders for Mum's garden."

Kelsey breathed deeply. "It's so beautiful out here. The air is so fresh and clean. It's nice to be out of the city and experiencing some of the Australian bush."

Brock tried not to notice how attractive she was with the sun shining on her face. Her blue eyes were bright and sparkled with good humor. Her flawless skin glowed. Reining in his heart rate, he merely inclined his head. "As Mum said, it's nice to have you here."

Kelsey brushed past Brock as she entered the cottage and did her best to ignore the brief frisson from the contact. She'd been acutely aware of him from the moment he'd met her at the airport, and that awareness hadn't diminished over the ensuing hours they'd spent together. She'd noticed his every movement, every tilt of his head when he listened, the way he held his knife. Every breath he drew as he ate. It was ridiculous.

She was behaving like a giddy teenager, dizzy with the prospect of falling in love for the first time. She might be picky about her lovers, but she'd done her fair share of dating over the years—even more so lately. Once or twice, when she was younger, she'd even fancied herself in love. But none of her former boyfriends had set her pulse racing over every little thing like Brock did.

As she stepped past him, a whiff of his cologne followed her—something fresh and woodsy that perfectly suited their surroundings. Steadfastly ignoring her body's reaction to his closeness, she stepped into a small, open-plan kitchen and living room and smiled in surprise.

"This is gorgeous!"

The walls were painted a rich cream color that emphasized the red brick of the fireplace at the far end of the room. Large, framed black-and-white portraits of people she guessed were Fairfax ancestors lined the walls. The furniture consisted of a floral-patterned settee with matching armchair and an antique, cherrywood coffee table in between. Drawn back from the front window were heavy, pale blue damask drapes. Little knickknacks lined the mantel, along with a vase of fresh flowers, giving the place a welcoming, homey feel.

"Your mother's gone to a lot of trouble," she said.

Brock hauled her suitcase further into the room and waved her comment away. "Mum doesn't get a lot of visitors out here. At least not visitors that aren't family. She likes it when guests come to stay. It breaks up the monotony of her day and gives her something else to focus on. As you can imagine, the days often all roll into one on an outback station."

"Doesn't she find it isolating?" Kelsey murmured.

Brock shrugged. "I guess she does now that most of us aren't home that often. But Roma's only an hour away for her to catch up with friends. And as you know, there's a direct flight to Brisbane if she needs a change of scene. Of course, the roads become unusable in the wet, which means she can't go anywhere. But she loves Dad, and she loves the station. She's made it work over the years."

Kelsey pondered his words as she wandered into a cozy kitchen. An old-fashioned woodstove stood against one wall. Next to it was an electric hot plate, and on the shelf above that was a microwave.

An open-shelved cupboard containing crockery and glassware and three drawers that no doubt held cutlery, cooking implements, and the like. There was no dishwasher.

"Don't worry about the woodstove. No one uses that anymore. The hot plate's as fancy as it gets. Not that you'll have to cook. Mum's got that covered," Brock said.

"Oh, that's okay. I don't expect her to cater for me," Kelsey said.

"It's all good. She'll be insulted if you don't turn up for her meals. Besides, you're a long way from the nearest corner store. I'm not sure where you're intending to stock up on supplies."

Kelsey flushed. "You're right. I spoke without thinking. I've never stayed anywhere that wasn't located near all the modern conveniences. Thank you. This is more than I expected."

"Good old country hospitality." Brock grinned. "We Fairfaxes wouldn't have it any other way."

"I feel like I'm on holidays, not here on a work trip."

"Maybe it can be a bit of both?" Brock suggested. "All work and no play makes Kelsey a dull girl." He gave her a sexy wink.

Her stomach somersaulted with nerves and increased awareness. He was far too good-looking for her peace of mind. Though she'd been looking forward to meeting the handsome, single Fairfax brother, she'd never expected to be so wildly attracted to him. It certainly was encouraging. Her search for a husband might very well have come to an end.

Cut it out… I hardly know him… And I don't yet know how he feels… Interested, yes. Attracted, yes. But who knows whether that might develop into something more…

She had three days in which to find out. With a bit of luck, he'd prove just as attractive on the inside as he was on the outside and maybe, just maybe, he might feel the same way. She felt giddy at the prospect. Her mother's potentially lifesaving treatment might be closer than she imagined.

She smiled, feeling happy at the thought.

"What's so funny?" Brock asked.

Kelsey blinked. A surge of guilt sobered her. She averted her gaze. Though she hoped she'd never get desperate enough to marry for the sake of the money, her mother's deteriorating health had most definitely incentivized her to speed up the process. Not that she'd tell Brock, at least not yet. She needed to play it cool and not scare him off. Besides, she was genuinely attracted to him and interested to see where things might lead and that had nothing to do with the money.

With Brock's expectant gaze still upon her, she scrambled for something to say. "Um, nothing. I... I was just thinking how lucky I am to be out of the city and staying somewhere so gloriously peaceful and lovely. It's so quiet, I'm pretty sure I can hear my own heartbeat."

She gave a half laugh and was relieved when Brock smiled back. "I wasn't sure whether the silence would drive you crazy. Not every city slicker takes to the solitude of the country."

She regarded him steadily. "I wasn't sure either, but...so far, I like it. It's nice to get away from the constant rush and noise and just...chill."

He chuckled, and her heart skipped a beat at the way his eyes crinkled when he smiled. He was sophisticated and sexy in a suit and tie. Relaxed in casual attire, he was devastating. She wasn't sure which Brock she liked the best, but she looked forward to finding out over the next couple of days.

Brock's heart rate accelerated at the frank interest in Kelsey's blue-eyed gaze. Despite his efforts to play things cool, his body continued to hum with awareness. If he hadn't been burned by Cecelia, he might have already propositioned her, or at least asked her out on a date. But he'd learned the hard way about the need to exercise caution—especially when it came to matters of the heart.

Anyway, it was a moot point. Kelsey was here on business. The farm needed that money. Convincing her of the merits of backing Marlowe Downs so she approved their loan was his first and only priority. Forget anything else.

In an effort to put some distance between them, he hefted her suitcase off the floor and carried it into the only bedroom. Leaving it by the door, he returned to the living room and found Kelsey looking at the wall of framed family photographs.

"They are some of my ancestors, the first generations of Fairfaxes to farm here."

"It's great to be part of so much history," she said.

"Yes." He paused and then added, "I'll give you some time to rest and freshen up, then we can take a tour around the place."

She half turned to him, and the impact of her high-wattage grin hit him in the gut.

"That would be great. Do I need to change?"

His gaze swept over her blouse and jean-clad legs. "Maybe the boots. They're not exactly practical for out here, even though they look great."

A frisson of awareness arced between them. Brock took a step backward. A faint blush stained Kelsey's cheeks and her gaze darted away. It was obvious she'd felt it too.

This isn't good... Damn it that she's so attractive... I need to get out of here.

Jamming his hat back on his head, he mumbled a goodbye and made his escape. He'd barely made it halfway across the back veranda of the main house when he was intercepted by Cayd. Brock was taken aback by the thundercloud that darkened his brother's face.

"What the hell's the matter with you, Cayd?"

Cayd glared at him in response. "Don't be getting any ideas, Brock. If you fuck up our chances over a piece of skirt, I'll never forgive you."

Brock pulled up short. The anger in Cayd's voice was palpable, along with the fury that burned in his eyes.

"Whoa! Back up there, brother. What the hell are you talking about?"

"I saw the way you looked at her. Like she's a tasty morsel just waiting for you to gobble her up. We need that money, Brock. More than you need to get laid."

Brock clenched his teeth against a burst of irritation. He hated that his interest in Kelsey had been so obvious. He also hated that Cayd was right. Without the loan, the station would go under. It was as dire as that.

Drawing in a deep breath, Brock blew it out noisily between his lips, easing his tension. He understood Cayd's anger. His brother was well aware of their tenuous situation. Cayd spent most of his waking hours hard at work on the station. If the farm went under, Cayd's future as a cattleman would be dealt a heavy blow. No doubt he'd secure work at one of the adjoining stations, but that wasn't the same as continuing the family legacy that had been established for generations.

"You're right," Brock said. "I'm sorry."

Cayd shrugged. "Hell, I can see why you might be distracted. She's smoking hot. But she's also here to determine the outcome of our loan application and I don't need to tell you how much is riding on a positive response."

Brock nodded. "I'm surprised I've even noticed how hot she is. After the number Cecelia did on me, I didn't think I'd ever want to get close to a woman again."

"You don't mean that," Cayd muttered.

Brock grimaced. He thought about Raine and Isabella and how happy they were. Now they were expecting a baby. Despite the blow to his heart, he wanted what they had. He wanted a wife and a family, someone to call his own.

Is that someone Kelsey?

Frowning, he pushed the thought away and stared hard at his brother. "Marlowe Downs means more to me than anything. There's nothing I won't do to save her. You have my word I'll ignore whatever interest I might or might not have in the bank manager and do everything in my power to secure those funds. But you know there are no guarantees the bank will come to the party, right?"

Cayd accepted his words with a nod and relaxed. "Thanks, Brock. I appreciate that." He paused and then added in a more reasonable tone, "I'm thinking about taking part in a new TV show. You ever heard of *Outback Bride*?"

Brock shook his head. "Nup. What's it about?"

"I don't know a whole lot about it either. Apparently, a handful of single farmers from the middle of nowhere go in search of wives, and they film it all for TV."

Brock chuckled. "Could be fun."

Cayd shrugged. "Maybe. I'm not too sure about it, but it could be good publicity for us. Highlight the station. It might lead to other things."

"What kind of other things?"

Cayd scratched at the five o'clock shadow on his cheeks. "These past few years have been tough. A devastating drought, followed by a destructive flood. All our hard work gone..." He snapped his fingers. "Just like that. And there's nothing we could do about it."

Brock nodded somberly. "It's one hell of a tough life. You'll get no argument from me about that."

Cayd blew his breath out on a sigh. "That's life on the land. You never know what nature's going to throw at you." He looked away for a moment. "I've been thinking about setting this place up as a farm stay. A bed and breakfast. We could renovate the old shearer's quarters. An experience-a-cattle-station-in-the-outback opportunity. It could be another source of income for when the weather's not cooperating. The publicity from the TV show could help kick it off the ground."

Brock blinked in surprise. "Gee, you've really put some thought into this."

Cayd nodded. "Yeah, I have. Being at the whim of the weather's been doing my head in. I need more security than that. This could be the way to achieve that."

"Yeah, maybe," Brock agreed. "It can't hurt to add another stream of income and take the pressure off the farm. That's if you're up for being pawed over by a handful of desperate women all angling for a proposal. Isn't that the point of the show? That they catch a farmer husband?"

Cayd blushed and ducked his head. "Hey, I'm twenty-seven years old. Gotta get married sometime, right? Besides, there's no obligation to make a commitment to any of them. It's all a bit of a lark for the cameras. Spending a couple of weeks with gorgeous, willing women dogging my heels and hanging off my every word kind of sounds like fun."

"Good luck with that, bro. I look forward to watching you wrangle them. Let's hope you wrangle women better than you wrangle steers."

Cayd mock-punched his brother. Brock neatly sidestepped the swipe and laughed.

"You just mind yourself around that bank manager," Cayd growled. "Whether I pull this farm stay thing off or not, we're not going to see any income in the short term. We need that loan. Don't mess this up."

Brock gave Cayd a wry salute. "Aye, aye, brother. I hear you, loud and clear. And don't you worry. I want that money as badly as you do."

Chapter Six

♥

Kelsey hauled her suitcase up onto the bed and zipped it open. Pulling out several blouses and a couple of dresses, she hung them in the antique wardrobe that stood opposite the bed. A matching dresser built of the same carved, dark wood stood against another wall. She half filled it with jeans, T-shirts, and underwear. She really had packed way too much for such a short stay.

A large window that filled the room with natural light took up most of the other wall. It looked out onto swathes of lush green lawn that was dotted with mature fruit trees. Ripening oranges and mandarins hung from the branches.

After setting her toiletries out on the vanity in the adjoining bathroom, she closed the suitcase and put it out of the way. Then, with a sigh, she flopped down on the bed. Its thick, high mattress was firm, but soft and luxurious at the same time. She didn't know what she'd expected from guest quarters on a cattle ranch in the middle of nowhere, but this level of comfort and luxury wasn't it.

Not only was the cottage comfortable and tastefully furnished, it was also homey in the way a hotel room never could be. Reverse-cycle air-conditioning units in both the bedroom and the living areas meant the temperature would be comfortable all year round. She'd read that out here, the temperature could range from the midthirties Celsius at the height of summer to below zero in the middle of winter. A far cry from the milder temperatures of her hometown. It rarely got anywhere near freezing in Tampa.

She was still getting used to the seasons on the other side of the world. This time of year in Tampa, she would have already been feeling the heat of the oncoming summer. Here, there was a distinct chill in the air as winter approached. It was weird to think she'd be bundled up and sitting in front of a fire in July. Probably just as weird for Australians thinking about snow in December.

Still, she didn't regret her decision to come—not to Australia, nor to the ranch. *Station*, she silently corrected. Though the time she spent away from her mother was time she'd never get back, she hadn't lied when she'd told the Fairfaxes that she'd taken the job in Brisbane with her mother's blessing. Maria Garland knew her daughter well.

Long before she'd fallen ill, her mother had been aware of how restless Kelsey had been. She'd worked her way up to a position of authority in the bank, but somehow, it wasn't enough. She'd felt constrained by the monotony of her job and her life in Tampa. She'd been born and bred in the city. Had spent all her life there. And though she had good friends and an active social life, there had been nothing to excite her about any of it. Least of all the eligible men.

Even before her grandmother had come to her with her proposal, Kelsey had lost patience over ever finding Mr Right. She'd been toying with a change of scenery, perhaps moving interstate. When the job opportunity in Australia had come up, it hadn't taken her long to decide to accept it. The new adventure halfway across the world had been going well until her mother had fallen ill.

News of the rare cancer had shaken Kelsey to the core. If it weren't for her mother's quiet urgings to stay, she'd have packed up immediately and returned home. But as her mother had said, there was nothing Kelsey could do. Better to stay where she was and enjoy her time in Australia than sit around in Tampa, despairing over the harsh hand her mother had been dealt.

Then the doctor had offered hope with talk of an experimental treatment. As quickly as their hopes had been raised, they were dashed again when they realized that neither of them could afford the cost. The fact that her paternal grandmother could easily foot the bill but refused to do so was unfathomable to Kelsey and cut her deep.

Alice Garland had never approved of her only son's choice of a wife. Kelsey had never discovered exactly why her grandmother hadn't liked her daughter-in-law, but over the years, Kelsey had suspected from pithy comments her grandmother had made that it had something to do with the fact that the Garlands were from old Southern money and Maria Andrecchio was not. She was the daughter of Italian immigrants who'd made their money through sheer hard work.

Prejudice was nothing new in the South. Kelsey was just sad that her grandmother couldn't get past it to see the kind and loving daughter-in-law she had. Their relationship had only deteriorated with the unexpected death of her father, and while Kelsey had long ago accepted that her mother and grandmother would never be close, her grandmother's refusal to pay for potentially lifesaving medical treatment for her granddaughter's mother—money she could easily spare—incensed Kelsey.

She could still recall every word of the heated argument she'd had with her grandmother about paying for the treatment, but her grandmother had refused to budge. Then she'd reminded her of the million dollars on offer. It was a cruel move, but effective. Her grandmother knew she'd never be able to resist an opportunity to save her mother's life, no matter how slim the chances.

Of course, she'd taken up the challenge, and she'd done so with renewed vigor.

And here I am... On an outback cattle station, with a single, sexy businessman who sometimes masquerades as a cowboy... Maybe fate is smiling upon me?

She flushed at the thought of Brock and his potential, but reined in her fanciful thoughts. She was getting way ahead of herself. She needed to play her hand carefully. Let things develop at a natural pace. She sensed a wariness in Brock that meant he wouldn't be rushed, and that was okay with her for now. She wouldn't turn thirty for another six months. Plenty of time to make the deadline. She crossed her fingers and sent up a silent prayer that her mother's health would hold out.

A knock on the cottage door startled her. Deep in thought, she'd missed hearing the footsteps on the veranda. Climbing off the bed, she crossed the living room and opened the door. Brock stood on the other side, smiling. Her heart leaped.

"You ready for that tour?" He winked.

Her stomach somersaulted. She managed to smile back at him. "Sure. I can't wait. Just give me a few minutes to change my boots and I'm all yours."

Kelsey's loose hair was mussed and the makeup around her eyes was slightly smudged. Brock liked that she hadn't felt the need to redo either. It suggested she was comfortable in her own skin. Enough that she didn't feel the need to look perfect all the time. He liked that too. In fact, he liked a lot of what he saw.

Though she held a position of authority in the bank , she didn't seem to have the staid and serious attitude one might expect in such a role. In fact, she was as easy-going and friendly as he could have hoped. She appeared to be as comfortable in the outback as she'd been in his boardroom. Her self-confidence was hugely attractive. In fact, everything about her was attractive, and that was a problem. At least until they had the loan sorted.

He couldn't believe he was already looking forward to the time when that didn't stand between them. That he was actively thinking about when they might shift from having an impersonal business relationship to something more.

Am I mad? Have I already forgotten the lessons delivered by Cecelia? Am I really contemplating trusting a woman with my heart again?

No. He was getting way ahead of himself. He barely knew Kelsey, and while the next couple of days would throw them together on the station, he needed to keep his eyes on the end goal. He'd do whatever he could to convince her to approve that loan. The future of current and future Fairfaxes rode on him.

He led her toward a quad bike he'd pulled out of the shed. Two helmets hung from the handlebars. If he'd been riding on his own, he wouldn't have bothered with one, but she was here on official business. Best to play by the rules.

"Ever been on a quad before?" he asked as he handed her one of the helmets.

She shook her head. "No. Does that matter?"

He chuckled. "Not at all. I'll do the driving. All you have to do is hang on. Let's go."

He swung his leg over the bike and settled himself on the seat. Kelsey followed suit.

"Don't forget to hold on," he said, as he pressed the automatic ignition.

She hesitated as the bike roared to life, then snaked her arms around his waist. He sucked in his breath at the contact.

Shit. Am I a masochist? Why didn't we just go in the ute? And why doesn't she just hold on to the seat bars? How am I going to concentrate on anything with her pressed up against me like this?

But it was too late for second thoughts, and he didn't want to draw attention to his discomfort. Doing his best to ignore her closeness, he let out the clutch and gunned the throttle. The bike leaped forward. Kelsey shrieked and tightened her hold on him. Brock cursed under his breath. She was now plastered against him, the shape and softness of her generous breasts burned into his skin. Once again, he was bombarded with an image of her naked. His groan was thankfully swallowed up by the noise of the engine.

He'd intended to take her on a leisurely tour of the best parts of the farm. The spring-fed billabong that was now full of sweet, clear water. The west paddock where the cattle were. The range of hills that marked their northern border and the amazing lookout his grandfather had built there.

But the thought of spending so much time up close and personal suddenly filled him with dread. He didn't want to rush headlong into another relationship, and definitely not while a five-million-dollar loan was on the line. Best to leave those points of interest for tomorrow, when he'd opt for a different mode of transport. One that didn't put them in such close quarters where he was aware of her every breath, her every gasp of delight and alarm.

Decision made, he turned away from the cattle and headed in the opposite direction. He'd point out the many improvements they'd made—the clearing they'd done to improve access to pasture, the water storages they'd constructed, the bores they'd sunk. Their access to water was one of the reasons they'd been able to keep at least some of their stock during the drought.

He squinted up at the blue sky above them. The afternoon sun was pleasant on his face. Kelsey's arms had loosened around him as she relaxed into the rhythm of the bike. Contrarily, he was both relieved and disappointed. As they drew close to one of several artesian bores, he brought the bike to a stop and pulled off his helmet. Kelsey did the same.

"What's that smell?" she asked, crinkling up her nose.

He laughed. "That's the sulfur in the artesian water. The smell's not as strong as some of them can be."

The pool was one of the smaller ponds on the station, measuring only a few yards across and about as many yards wide, but at its deepest, it was enough for most people to submerge themselves up to their necks.

She gazed at the dam and frowned. "That looks like steam coming off the water."

He chuckled. "That *is* steam coming off the water. The water temperature's about thirty-five degrees Celsius. Haven't you been to an artesian pool before?"

"No. We have artesian wells in Florida, but I've never seen one, and I always assumed the water was underground."

"Well, it certainly starts underground," Brock said. He climbed off the bike and then held it steady while Kelsey climbed off.

"The natural pressure between the rocks underground—usually sandstone around here—forces the water to the surface," he continued as he joined Kelsey near the pool. "Marlowe Downs is situated in what's known as the Great Artesian Basin. It's the largest and deepest artesian basin in the world and provides the only source of fresh water through much of inland Australia."

Her eyes went wide. "Wow. That's kind of a big deal."

He grinned. "Given that no living thing can survive without water, it certainly is."

She bent low and dragged her fingers through the water. "Wow, it's really warm."

He winked. "Like I said, about thirty-five degrees. I think that's about ninety-five in Fahrenheit, isn't it?"

She smiled. "That's right." She stepped back from the pool and wiped her hand against her jeans. "What do you use the pool for?"

He laughed. "What does anyone use a pool for? We swim in it, of course."

She looked surprised. "You swim in it?"

"For sure. The water's full of minerals that are good for you. Apart from that, there's nothing like a relaxing hot bath at the end of a busy day." He paused and then shot her a cheeky look. "Wanna try it?"

A flush crept up her neck and spread across her face, but there was a twinkle of excitement in her eyes. "Why not?"

His heart leaped and then his pulse began to pound. He couldn't believe she'd taken up his challenge.

"What about a bathing suit?" she asked.

Emboldened by her adventurous spirit, he stared her down. "Who needs bathing suits?"

She gasped a little, and the color in her cheeks heightened, but to her credit, she didn't back down. Instead, she turned her back to him and started pulling off her boots. Next came her shirt and jeans. Within moments, she stood before him wearing nothing but brief black lace panties and a matching bra.

Blood rushed to his groin, and it was all he could do not to groan. Fully dressed, she'd sported a neat figure. Almost naked, she was stunning. Long, slim legs, tanned a golden color. Toned arms that spoke of hours in the gym. Bountiful breasts that spilled over her bra. A taut, flat stomach. His belly clenched with desire.

Her lips quirked upward. "You coming?" she asked.

Brock's lips pulled back in a strained grin. At her question, he'd almost groaned his thoughts.

Yes, almost. I'm a fucking idiot.

Without waiting for his response, he watched as she padded cautiously into the heated pool. When the water reached her hips, she sank into it up to her neck and sighed. "Oh, Brock! This is glorious!"

He couldn't help his answering smile at her obvious delight. Shrugging away his earlier thoughts, he pulled off his boots and socks, shucked off his jeans, and made short work of the buttons on his shirt. In no time at all, he was down to his boxers. His hard cock still strained against the soft cotton, but there wasn't much he could do about that. He held his hand casually in front of his groin in an effort to shield his erection from her gaze and joined her in the pool. She was right. The water was fabulous.

No doubt it wasn't appropriate to indulge in something that was only just short of skinny dipping with his bank manager. Cayd's warning not to fuck this up resonated in his mind—but he'd worry about that later. He still had time to convince her of the benefits of taking a risk on the station. In the meantime, his attraction to the beautiful woman in front of him was hard to resist. He could have no more stood by and watched her enjoy the pool alone, than he could have held back the floodwater that had so recently ravaged the farm.

He flicked at the water with his fingers and sent a spray into her face. She gasped and laughed and then sent a torrent back his way. The water hit him full in the face. He shook his head and laughed, excited by her sense of fun. She wasn't afraid to enjoy herself.

Her blonde hair floated around her. Water beaded on her thick lashes, the droplets glinting in the sun. They indulged in another round of splashing which had him move in close and when he grabbed her waist and dunked her under the water, she came up spluttering with a look of fake outrage on her face.

"You don't play fair!" she protested, swiping at the water on her face and pushing back her hair.

He grinned. "No one said I had to play fair."

She poked her tongue out and then giggled. In response, he sent another wave of water her way. He liked that she could have fun. Cayd's warning again played in his mind, reminding him that her being here wasn't about him or the way he felt. This was about the station and securing the finance they needed to get the farm back in the black. He couldn't let having fun with Kelsey, no matter how innocuous, jeopardize that. With his mood sobering, he climbed out of the pool and started to get dressed.

Kelsey stared after Brock, confused. One moment they were fooling around and having fun and the next, his expression had turned stony, and he'd abruptly left the water.

What the hell just happened? What changed his mood?

Unwilling to let him get away without an explanation, she waded out of the pool and wrung the water from her hair. Brock kept his face averted and continued to dress.

"What happened just then? What's wrong?" she asked.

She glimpsed a tightening of his lips. Instead of replying, he sat down on a thick patch of grass and began to pull on his socks and boots.

Stubbornness had her hold her ground. With her hands on her hips, she gave him a hard stare. "Please don't pretend you don't know what I'm talking about. Something happened back there to dampen the mood. What was it?"

Finally, Brock met her gaze. Guilt flashed in his eyes.

So, I was right. There is something…

She folded her arms across her chest and glared at him. They weren't children. She wasn't going to play games.

"Brock?"

He glanced at her again and then his shoulders slumped on a sigh. "It's nothing," he mumbled.

Irritation narrowed her eyes. "Don't give me that nonsense. Tell me what happened."

Once again, he took a moment to respond. She was relieved when he finally did.

"For a while there, I forgot who you were and why you're here. Playing around with you in the water, it was fun. But you're not here to have fun. You're here to make a decision about something that will affect this farm and everyone who relies on it for their livelihood for a long time into the future. In fact, your decision will mean the difference between this station remaining viable or not. I'm not trying to put pressure on you, just stating a fact. When I remembered the gravity of our situation, I guess the fun went out of it. Sorry."

She bit her lip against a rush of guilt and then was immediately irritated with herself. She was there to do a job, just like he'd said, and she had no cause to feel guilty about that. What she did feel guilty about was his misconception that she'd change her mind about the loan. She'd accepted his invitation under false pretenses, no matter what she told herself.

She'd known before leaving Brisbane that there was little to no chance that no matter what he showed her or how much she enjoyed her time on the farm, her recommendation to the bank would remain the same. Okay, so she'd been honest with him about that possibility, but still. It had been obvious that he'd given himself a decent chance of being able to change her mind.

Rather than responding, she went about collecting her clothes and putting them back on. Brock's expression was closed. In silence, he strode back to the bike and climbed on. When she was done dressing, she climbed on behind him. Instead of holding him close like she had on their way out there, she noticed the bars along the side of the seat and grabbed them tightly. They returned to the homestead in silence.

Chapter Seven

♥

Brock dropped Kelsey off at the cottage and then spent what was left of the afternoon with his younger brother, Justin, helping him out with the chores. After graduating from a private school in Brisbane, Justin had returned to the farm. He'd always loved living and working on the station. He was now twenty-three and gave no indication that he'd rather be anywhere else. Brock admired his brother's commitment to the rural lifestyle and to making the station a success. It underscored his need to ensure he secured the finance required to keep the place going.

In companionable silence, they fed and watered the dogs, collected the eggs, and threw out feed for the chickens. They mucked out the stables and then forked out fresh hay for the horses. While his business in Brisbane kept Brock occupied for most of the year, he enjoyed his visits home and was always prepared to lend a hand when needed. Normally, physical activity kept him too busy to think, but on this occasion, his thoughts kept returning to Kelsey.

He'd blown it with her, for sure. She hadn't said a word to him on the trip home, and he couldn't blame her. He hadn't spoken either. The awkwardness between them had rendered him mute. One moment, he'd been flirty and having fun, and the next, he'd flipped and frozen her out. It wasn't her fault he'd momentarily lost sight of her purpose for being there and the weight of his responsibility, not to mention the echo of Cayd's warning not to mess up.

He ought to be grateful things had cooled between them before they'd had a chance to really get going. He wasn't ready to jump into another relationship, and hot sex, which he had no doubt would be mind-blowing, wasn't worth jeopardizing the end goal.

"That's probably enough. You're going to start another flood."

Justin's dry drawl cut through Brock's feverish thoughts. He blinked and shook his head and then stared at the hose in his hand. He'd been topping up the water troughs for the horses, and now water ran over the top and down the sides and had begun pooling at his feet.

"Shit. Sorry."

He pulled the hose out of the way and directed the stream onto the grass while he hurriedly turned off the tap.

"Looks like something's got you distracted. Or should I say, *someone*," Justin said, raising an eyebrow.

Brock blushed and then cursed under his breath for being so transparent. Was his interest in Kelsey so obvious? Of course, it was. Cayd had seen it. No doubt others had too.

Justin merely chuckled. "Hell, bro. You ought to see your face! Personally, I think it's good you're so worked up about a woman. After the number your last girlfriend did on you, I wasn't sure you'd ever be interested in dating again."

Brock grimaced. Though he'd made no secret about the fact that he'd been upset over Cecelia's treatment, he wasn't aware the whole family were so well informed. He shouldn't have been surprised. No doubt he had Raine to thank for that. Not that it bothered him, really. They were a close family. They tended to band together in support when one of them was going through something difficult. That's just the way the family rolled.

"She's here on business. We need that money. I can't afford to let anything else interfere with that," he said sternly, as much as a reminder to himself as to Justin.

Justin nodded. "Yeah, I understand that. Still, she's hot and she seems nice. And at lunch she looked fairly interested in you too."

Brock was beset with a giddy rush of emotion. "You think?"

Justin nodded. "For sure. She couldn't take her eyes off you."

Brock nudged his brother with his shoulder. "Looks like I've still got it." But his grin suddenly collapsed at the thought of how he and Kelsey had parted, not exactly on friendly terms. He needed to repair the damage, get things back on track. If not for himself, then for the future of the station.

She was here for a couple more days. He could use the time to convince her to approve the loan and maybe, just maybe, after their business was out of the way, they could concentrate on the attraction between them for however long it lasted.

As soon as Brock had brought the quad bike to a halt outside the homestead, Kelsey had climbed off and, with a muttered goodbye, escaped to the cottage. The seat of her jeans was damp from her wet panties and her blouse was also wet in patches. She needed to change out of her clothes, and she also needed to get away from Brock Fairfax. The more time she spent with him, the more she liked him, and that was dangerous, particularly if he was going to blow hot and cold.

One moment, he was warm and friendly, flirty even. The next, he was withdrawn. At least he'd had the decency to tell her why his demeanor had changed so abruptly. She should have known it was over her reasons for being there. She wasn't a guest passing through. She held in her hands the power to destroy his dreams of restoring the station to its former glory. That wasn't something she took lightly, and she did feel bad about it, but she didn't make the bank's policies.

It was obvious he was attracted to her. She'd seen his awkward attempt to conceal his erection tenting his boxers. It had been sweet. But she didn't kid herself that his feelings would go deeper than physical chemistry, no matter how sad that made her feel. They barely knew each other.

There was a good chance he'd be angry and disappointed when she turned down his loan application for a second time, if that's how things played out. She was the instrument of his family's demise. Okay, so she was only doing her job, but somehow, she didn't think he'd quite see it like that. All the more reason to bring a halt to her own fantasies of a possible future with him, no matter how giddy he made her feel.

With a sigh, she peeled off her damp clothing and padded into the bathroom. She walked past a large, inviting bathtub and started the shower. Stepping under the steamy water, she lathered her hair with shampoo. After rinsing and toweling dry, she applied moisturizer to her freshly shaved legs. She told herself unconvincingly she was doing it for herself and not on the off chance she might get up close and personal with Brock.

The truth was, she *wanted* to get up close and personal with him. She wanted to press herself against his hard body again. She wanted to kiss his full lips. Being so wildly attracted to a man she barely knew was completely foreign to her, but she couldn't deny the strong pull of chemistry. Still, given that their time together might very well be fleeting and that things might end on a sour note, she needed to proceed with caution. Getting hurt wasn't part of the plan. It was one thing to engage in a casual fling. It was quite another to have her heart broken in the process, and given her strong attraction and fanciful daydreams, Brock Fairfax could very well break it if she let him.

Wrapping herself in a thick robe she'd pulled from a hook on the back of the bathroom door, she walked across the living room to her handbag and dug through it, looking for her phone. There were several notifications from the dating apps she'd joined. She sighed and ignored all of them, clearing them from her screen. She'd been dating men for months now, and none of them had come anywhere close to making her feel the way Brock did.

The truth was, she dreaded the moment when she'd have to tell him she was there under false pretenses. That so far, she hadn't seen anything that would change her mind about approving their loan. Despite the fact she'd warned him about this, her very presence there would have given him some hope.

She sighed. *When did life get so complicated?*

She had another hour before dinner. Enough time to call her mother. She usually felt better after talking to her. Though it was early morning in Tampa, her mother was always awake well before dawn. It had been two days since they'd spoken, which was longer than they normally went between calls. Kelsey had promised to phone and tell her about her trip to the outback.

The phone dialed out. After four rings, it was answered.

"Kelsey, darling! How are you?"

Her mother sounded weak and very far away. Kelsey was struck with a wave of homesickness, made worse by the knowledge her mother was so unwell.

What if she doesn't make it? What if she dies before I get home? My hunt for a husband will have been for nothing...

No. She refused to think like that. She'd taken the job in Australia with her mother's blessing, and that hadn't changed after the diagnosis.

"How are you, Mama? How have you been?"

"Oh, you know how it is, honey. I have good days and not so good days. But let's not talk about me. How are you doing? Have you arrived at the cattle ranch?"

"Yes, but they call it a cattle station down here, remember? And cowboys are jackaroos. And there are ringers. That's a more experienced cowboy. It's hot and dry and dusty. I can't believe they were flooded not so long ago. At least there's plenty of grass. That's helping to keep what little livestock they still have alive.

"I'm staying in this cute guest cottage. It looks like someone's home, full of family photographs and odds and ends that someone might collect over time. Very comfortable. And the Fairfax family are just great. They've been so warm and welcoming."

Kelsey's mind snagged on an image of Brock. Broad, naked chest. Well-defined pectorals. Wet hair that glinted in the sun. He'd been very warm and welcoming—at least for a time—and even then, she understood the reason why his attitude had cooled.

Her mother's laugh suddenly cut through. "It sounds like you're having a wonderful time. You've hardly drawn a breath."

Kelsey flushed. She hadn't realized she'd been babbling on with so much enthusiasm. That had everything to do with Brock, and she'd been there less than a day.

"Do I take it you're enjoying your time in the outback?" her mother asked.

"You could say that. This place is nothing like I could imagine. It's so different from Tampa, from anywhere I've ever been. So vast and isolated, but so beautiful."

"And what about the Fairfax sons? Didn't you say the other day there were six of them?"

Kelsey's face warmed again. She was glad her mother couldn't see her. "Yes," she managed. "Six sons. I've now met all of them. One of them is married. As far as I know, the rest are single."

"I see."

The speculation in her mother's voice made Kelsey grin. "Yes, Mama. They're all of marriageable age. One in particular has caught my eye. His name's Brock."

"Brock. That's a nice name. Tell me about him."

Kelsey grinned. She settled herself onto the couch and tucked the phone against her ear. "Well, he's twenty-nine, like me, and sinfully good-looking. Blond hair, green eyes, tanned and toned and tall."

"He sounds dreamy."

Kelsey laughed. "You're right. He *is* dreamy."

"How does he feel about you?"

"I'm not sure. There's definitely a mutual attraction. Whether that can develop into anything more, I guess we'll have to wait and see. It's early days."

"What about the loan? Do you think you'll change your mind?"

Kelsey sighed. "I'm not sure. Probably not."

"How do you think Brock will take that?"

"Not well. He's desperate to help his family, and they certainly need the money."

"Well, don't go feeling guilty about it. However this works out, you're only doing your job. Surely he'll understand that?"

Kelsey compressed her lips. "I hope so. I really like this guy. He's really special, and the added incentive of collecting all that money can't be denied."

"We've already spoken about this. Please don't rush into anything. I don't want you to give your grandmother's crazy proposal another thought. Getting the money for my treatment shouldn't factor into your decision to make a lifelong commitment, no matter what. Do you understand?"

"Yes, Mama. I promise not to rush into anything."

She bit her tongue on the small fib she'd made to ease her mother's concerns. Whatever arrangement she needed to make to secure the money for her mother's treatment, she'd make it. But she'd ensure the arrangement had an exit clause.

Her mother sighed quietly. "We'll find the money from somewhere. In the meantime, I'll continue the way I am. God willing, I still have plenty of years in me yet."

Tears sprang to Kelsey's eyes. She swallowed against a lump in her throat. She hated that she couldn't wave a magic wand and make her mother well again, and she hated that she didn't yet have the means to foot the bill. She also hated that her wealthy grandmother had put them in such a cruel predicament. She was just grateful she'd had her mother in her life for as long as she had.

That didn't mean she was ready to give up on the money. There was every chance she could fall in love with Brock. If they managed to spend a bit more time together, he might even begin to feel the same way. She could marry for love and collect the money. It would be a win for everyone.

If only I could find some way of approving that loan...

For a brief moment, she wished she could set aside her principles and approve the loan anyway, no matter that the numbers didn't stack up. Then she remembered the reason she'd been sent to Australia in the first place. Too many of their loan officers had approved applications they shouldn't have. She'd been sent out to clean up that mess, not add to it.

Her shoulders slumped on a heavy sigh.

Seated on the opposite side of the dining table, Brock eyed his brothers balefully as his gaze came to rest on Kelsey. With Cayd on one side and Justin on the other and Lachlan and Aiden seated across from them, from the frequent way she tipped back her head in laughter, they were obviously keeping her entertained.

Jealousy ate at him, souring his appetite. His mother had dished up a feast of tender roast lamb, crisp baked vegetables, thick gravy, and freshly baked rolls in honor of their guest and yet he could have been eating cardboard. He couldn't concentrate on anything other than Kelsey.

She'd greeted him politely enough as she'd stepped into the homestead for dinner, but then she'd proceeded to seat herself as far away from him as possible. Short of raising his voice above the din emanating from the far end of the table, he had to be satisfied with quiet conversation with his parents.

"Did you take a look at any of those fences on the western side of the house paddock while you were out with Kelsey?" his father asked.

Brock blinked. His father regarded him expectantly. With a concerted effort, he cleared his thoughts of the woman in question and managed to respond.

"Um, no. We spent most of the time at the bore well."

His father's eyes narrowed momentarily. "I bet the water was nice."

Brock flushed. "It was."

Bob Fairfax's expression turned speculative. "We still have a lot of flood damage to the fence lines. We've been doing what we can in the way of repairs, but there's a long way to go. More time and money's what we need. And help. How long are you here for?"

Brock's cheeks warmed again under the force of his father's direct gaze. While neither of his parents had pressured any of their children to remain on the station, they were obviously pleased when some of them had elected to stay and work there. It took a lot of effort to keep an operation the size of theirs viable. Brock was glad too.

But station life had never been for him. The bright lights of the city and the cutthroat world of business had proven to be too much of an allure. It had been the same for Raine. They'd established an investment company and had worked long hours and made wise, if not risky, investments to get it to where they were now. The business was flourishing, and it would continue to go from strength to strength with him and Raine at the wheel. But unfortunately, they were just not at the stage of being able to inject the needed cash into the family cattle station. Short of liquidating assets, the five million they needed to get the farm back on its feet was beyond them.

"Sorry, only a few days," he replied. "I came out to show Kelsey around, then I'll have to return to the city. We're snowed under at work at the moment, and now that Raine and Isabella are—"

He broke off suddenly and hoped his parents didn't notice. He should have known better.

"Raine and Isabella are what?" his mother asked, her eyes gleaming with curiosity.

Brock stuffed his mouth full of food and started chewing. His mother's gaze remained fixed on him. When he couldn't draw it out a minute longer, he swallowed and reluctantly answered.

"Nothing. I just meant they're busy with stuff of their own. Isabella's been on call at the hospital all month, and Raine and I have been tied up with back-to-back meetings. It looks like we might have caught the eye of some wealthy Japanese investors who are keen to get a toehold in the resources sector."

"Didn't you and Raine make a play for one of those companies not long ago?" his father asked.

Brock breathed out a surreptitious sigh of relief and nodded toward his father. "Yes. And it's going really well, but that also means our cash will be tied up for some time to come. I wish we could afford to loan you the money, but we just haven't got access to that kind of cash at the moment."

His mother reached over and patted his hand. "We've already been over this. It's not up to you and Raine to bail us out. This is a family business. We all have to do our bit. Going to bat for us with the banks has been invaluable. Let's hope between you and Kelsey, we get a positive result. And if we don't, well, we'll find another way to survive. We always do. We're Fairfaxes, aren't we? We never give up."

He managed a tight smile, but his gut tightened with dread. The thought of letting his parents down was almost more than he could bear. Which was stupid. They'd love him no matter what, and everyone knew he wouldn't be responsible for the bank's decision, no matter which way it went. All he could do was to try his best to convince Kelsey they were worth the risk. The fact that she'd agreed to accompany him there gave him a degree of hope that all wasn't lost.

As if aware of the direction of his thoughts, Kelsey looked over at him. Their gazes locked. Her tongue stole out and licked at a spot of gravy caught on the side of her mouth. His heart skipped a beat and then proceeded to tap out a frantic rhythm against his chest. He might have been burned by a woman in the past, but every time he looked at Kelsey, he could barely remember that.

He wanted her with a fierceness that took him by surprise, but he also wanted to get to know her, spend time with her, laugh and mess around. She'd shown him she was fun, and given time, he probably wouldn't be averse to exploring something more than a casual fling.

The thought of exploring a future should have scared the hell out of him, but instead, he was filled with anticipation. Their chemistry was off the charts. He was sure she felt it too. If only there wasn't a loan application standing between them. Still, that would be resolved one way or the other, and soon. After that, they'd be free to explore their feelings and see where they might lead.

His gaze drifted to Cayd, who stared at him with a narrowed gaze that flared with anger. Brock tamped down rising embarrassment at being caught out. He'd made his brother a promise, and he was determined to keep it. No messing around with the hot bank manager until that money was in the station's account.

Chapter Eight

♥

The next morning, straight after a hearty breakfast of bacon, eggs, fried tomato, buttery toast, and sausage, Brock surprised Kelsey with an invitation to accompany him on another tour of some part of the station.

"We got distracted by the bore bath yesterday. You barely saw anything of the place," he said with a smile.

Her mind flashed instantly to the sight of Brock half-naked and wet, his erection straining against his boxer shorts. Her nipples tightened involuntarily in response.

Don't you worry... I saw plenty.

She forced the tantalizing thought aside and managed to nod.

"Thank you, that would be great. The more I can see of the station, the better."

She bit her lip on her impulsive response and was flooded with guilt at the hope that flared in Brock's green eyes. No matter how impressive the station was, the figures told a grim story. But she wanted to spend more time with him. She was far from done with getting to know him, exploring the chemistry between them, and seeing where they might lead. She couldn't do that from her office.

His eyes crinkled as he smiled. "Great. Let's go, then."

She followed him out of the homestead and across the yard. Instead of heading toward the shed that housed the quad bike, he deviated toward the stables. A sleek black horse was tied up to the slip rail next to a smaller chestnut one. They were both saddled. When Brock came to a halt beside them, her stomach nosedived. Panic gripped her insides.

"We're going horseback riding?" she asked tentatively, hoping she was wrong.

He grinned. "We are. And by the way, we just call it horse riding. After all, there's only one way to ride a horse, right?"

A tiny smile fought its way through her fear and briefly widened her lips. "Touché. I don't know why we call it horseback riding. That's just what we say."

"A bit like when you say 'tuna fish.' We just call it tuna. We all know tuna's a fish, right?" He winked.

She grinned reluctantly. Some of her fear receded, but even so, she kept a wide berth of the horses. Up close, they seemed huge, especially the black one.

Brock shot her a curious look. "I take it you've never been on a horse?"

"You'd be right about that. I was born and bred in the city. Not a horse in sight. The closest I've been to one is when my family took a drive out into the country when I was about nine. There were a few grazing in a paddock near the road. We stopped to take a look."

"Then you're in for a treat. Come and meet Shiloh. She was born and raised on Marlowe Downs. This place is the only home she's ever known, and there isn't a trail or valley she doesn't know."

"Okay, I guess that's a good thing," Kelsey replied, slightly reassured. "What about if she bolts?"

"She won't bolt. She's as sweet and gentle as can be. Come here and I'll help you up."

With that, he reached out and took her hand and drew her closer to the horse. She tried not to think about how nice it was to have her hand in his. And then he released his hold on her and reached for the stirrup.

"Okay, so you put your left foot in here and hold on to the saddle here. Then swing your leg over the other side. Just like you did with the quad bike. Okay?"

She stared at the stirrup dubiously, misgivings stirring inside. But she'd always been adventurous, and she wasn't about to chicken out now. If Brock wanted to go horseback—um, wrong, horse riding, then horse riding she would go.

"Come closer. She won't bite," he urged with another devastating smile.

Kelsey took another step and then another, until she was within reach of the beast. She seemed so big.

"Put your hands up here, and once you have your foot in the stirrup, use your hands to pull yourself up into the saddle," he instructed again.

Kelsey did as he said. As she took the weight on her foot in the stirrup and prepared to hoist herself up, Brock's large palm pressed against her ass. In one smooth motion, he helped her up onto the horse. Her face flamed with embarrassment. At the same time, her ass burned from his touch.

He passed her the reins. "Take these and hold her steady while I mount Calypso."

Keeping her gaze fixed firmly on Shiloh, Kelsey once again did as he said. The horse danced around a little, sensing Kelsey's nervousness and sending her wildly beating heart into her throat, but a quiet word from Brock and the mare settled. Kelsey watched while Brock swung himself up into the saddle of the black devil he'd called Calypso. The smooth and practiced way he settled himself on the back of the horse told her he'd done so many times

Of course, he would have. He's been born and bred on the station.

No doubt he'd spent all his growing-up years there before leaving for the city. Horses and ranches were in his blood.

"Is Calypso a boy or a girl?" she asked, curious.

Brock chuckled. "Can't you tell?"

She blushed. "I'm a city girl, remember? I've never been around horses."

"Well, Calypso is a boy. A stallion. He's a thoroughbred. We use him to breed with the mares."

The look he sent her way had her blushing again. Studiously, she ignored it and asked him another question. "Do you round up the cattle on horseback?"

He nodded. "Yep. That and on the bikes. By the way, we call it mustering in Australia."

"I read somewhere that they round up—sorry, muster in the outback with helicopters. Is that right?"

"Yes. That's right. That's how they do it on the bigger stations."

"There are bigger stations than this?"

"Hell, yes. We're only a modest family operation. Some of those big corporate holdings can run to over a million acres."

Her eyes widened with disbelief. "A *million* acres?"

He chuckled. "Yep. Now *that's* a lot of ground to cover with a horse."

She shook her head. "I had no idea one ranch could be so big. No wonder they need to muster with helicopters."

He flashed her a wide grin. "Stations, not ranches."

She blushed and ducked her head to hide her reaction to his teasing. Her pulse beat faster but this time, desire was in the mix. Her stomach clenched with butterflies every time he drew near, and right now, he was only a foot away, albeit on horseback.

As the stallion drew closer, her mare snorted, flicked her tail, and lifted her head. It was as though Shiloh was as aware of Calypso as Kelsey was of Brock. As he pulled on his reins and steered his horse toward the nearest paddock, she took a moment to admire the way he sat his horse.

Tall and upright in the saddle, he pushed his Akubra back on his head. Another plaid shirt—this one red—stretched across broad shoulders that tapered into a narrow waist. She now knew firsthand how muscular and toned his chest was. His long legs were covered in denim that ended in feet that were hidden inside well-worn leather boots. He was an alluring package and altogether too sexy for her equilibrium. Dressed for business in the boardroom, he was devastatingly attractive. Out here in the middle of nowhere, astride a horse and looking every bit the true-blue cowboy, he was incredibly dangerous to her heart.

"Give her a kick and tell her to walk on," Brock instructed over his shoulder.

Cautiously, Kelsey did as he said. Shiloh took a step forward and stopped. Kelsey grimaced.

"Grip her flanks with your thighs and dig your heels into her side a bit harder. You need to let her know you're in charge. And talk to her. Tell her what you want her to do."

"Come on, Shiloh. Let's go, girl."

Kelsey kicked the horse a little harder. "Come on, girl. Let's walk."

To her relief, Shiloh began walking slowly. Brock waited until she'd caught up with him and then urged his stallion forward. This time, Shiloh moved without prompting, keeping up with Calypso, who pranced alongside her, clearly unhappy to be reined in tight.

When they reached a gate, Brock slid off his horse and deftly undid the latch. He led Calypso through the opening and then stood to one side and waited while Kelsey walked Shiloh through. Regaining his seat, he turned his horse in a westerly direction.

"Dad asked me to check out some of the fence lines along here. We suffered a lot of damage from the floods. The water was more than six feet deep in places. There are still lots of fences that haven't been repaired."

She smiled. "So, we're doing some reconnoitering, are we?"

He chuckled. "That's exactly what we're doing."

"And I take it the money you're after will be put toward these repairs."

"Among other things, yes. Our first priority is to rebuild our herd. That won't happen overnight, and the sooner we get started, the better."

Kelsey refrained from responding. She hated that her very presence there was giving Brock hope, but it was too late to think like that now. She was determined not to let bank business interfere with her enjoyment of the day. She'd been gifted a few hours alone with a sexy, single cowboy. She intended to make the most of it.

As Kelsey bounced up and down on the back of her horse, it was all Brock could do not to groan. From the moment she'd appeared at the breakfast table dressed in another blouse and tight jeans, he'd been battling a hard-on. That hadn't eased since they'd started out. If anything, the brief contact his hand had made with the perfect curve of her ass had only increased the blood that continued to pump to his groin. It made riding very uncomfortable.

The sky blue of her blouse enhanced the color of her eyes, deepening them to cobalt. Her lips were coated with a shiny pink gloss that kept drawing his gaze. He wondered what it would feel like to kiss her. She was obviously uneasy being on the back of a horse, and yet she'd found the courage to give it a go. There had been no whining or complaining. Simply a quiet acceptance and determination that filled him with admiration and respect.

And thoughts like that were bad for so many reasons. He needed to curb them, get control over his physical reaction to her presence. Okay, so she was sexy, smart, and brave, but he barely knew her, and it wasn't that long ago that he'd sworn off women forever... Or something to that effect.

Then there was the loan business. He was almost certain she was professional enough that her decision wouldn't be influenced by anything that might or might not happen between them, but it was an added complication that needed to be resolved. And if she did follow through on rejecting their application, how would he feel toward her? He'd like to think he'd accept her decision gracefully, but he didn't know.

She'd make a final call on their loan either at the end of her stay in two days' time, or shortly thereafter. He was hopeful he might be able to persuade her to their side, especially after seeing firsthand how the farm operated. So he'd best get on with the tour as time was ticking and wishful thinking wasn't going to get them across the line.

Up ahead, he spied Cayd repairing part of a damaged fence. Working alongside him were three teenage Aboriginal girls. The four chatted companionably together as Cayd showed the girls what to do. They didn't notice the approaching horses until Brock and Kelsey were almost upon them.

"Brock. Kelsey. What brings you out here?" Cayd asked, pushing his hat back farther on his head.

"I'm giving Kelsey a tour. Thought she might like to see a bit more of the station. How's the fencing going?"

One of the Aboriginal girls gave Brock a white-toothed grin. "It's going great. We'll be experts in no time!"

Everyone laughed. Brock swung down off his horse and helped Kelsey down from hers. She shot him a grateful look and murmured her thanks. No doubt she'd be sore later. He'd have to remember that.

Taking the reins of both horses and giving Kelsey a chance to stretch her limbs, he shifted closer to Cayd. "Dad said there's a fair bit of damage along the western side of the house paddock. Have you been by that way yet?"

Cayd shook his head. "No. We've been working on this stretch all week. Thought we'd do one section at a time. We don't have enough fencing materials to fix everything. At least, not until we find the money to order more."

Brock's gaze went instinctively to Kelsey. She stood a short distance away. From her somber expression, it was clear she understood the significance of Cayd's comments.

"How much do you need to repair all the fencing?" she asked quietly.

"A hundred thousand," Cayd replied.

Kelsey started in surprise. "One hundred thousand just for fencing?"

Cayd's expression remained hard. "Yep."

"What happens if you can't afford to repair them all?" she asked.

"It means we're restricted to the number of paddocks where we can run the cattle, which also affects the number of stock we can hold," Brock explained. "We need to be able to contain them. Broken fences don't do that very well."

She nodded. "Of course."

Her expression grew thoughtful. Brock hoped the reality of what the bank's money could do for them and how much they needed it had started to set in for her. She continued to look thoughtful when they bid Cayd and the girls farewell and climbed back on their horses. They continued on their way.

"Are the girls jillaroos?" Kelsey asked a little while later.

Brock chuckled. "No. They're taking part in a government program involving local station owners to provide opportunities for young Aboriginal people to learn new skills that will ultimately increase their employment prospects. They come for three days at a time several times a year and learn about working on a station."

"What kind of work do they do?"

"All sorts of things. Horse riding and grooming, cattle welfare and safety, feeding the horses, cattle, pigs, and chickens, and general cattle management, including mustering, branding, dehorning and vaccinating." He glanced over his shoulder. "Cayd's got them fencing today."

"They seemed to be enjoying it," Kelsey commented.

"Yes. Most of them are very enthusiastic about coming out here and being given the opportunity to learn new skills. Some of them will stay on as employees. Others will find work on other stations and nearby farms. It's a win for everyone. Being so remote, it isn't easy finding staff. This program helps the station owners find employees, and it gives the young people a job."

Kelsey's face was full of admiration. "I love how everyone involved gets something out of it. Learning new skills, feeling useful...that's good for self-esteem. And of course, there's the economic benefits for both sides. It's probably not easy to find jobs."

"Yes. The program coordinator tells us how much the young people benefit. There's a lot of interpersonal development. Many of the activities with the livestock are designed to build confidence, increase communication, and build relationships based on trust."

"That sounds incredibly empowering," Kelsey said, her eyes shining.

Brock nodded. He'd witnessed firsthand the change in confidence in many of the program's participants from day one to graduation. It always gave him a warm feeling of satisfaction to know they were making a difference in those young people's lives.

"We've only been participating in the program for a year and we've already had forty-seven young Aboriginal youth graduate. Let's just hope we can continue to take part in it."

"Where does the funding come from?"

"A little bit comes from the government. We're fortunate to have the support of one of the big mining companies. They support the bulk of the program in the form of private grants. Any shortfall is picked up by us."

Kelsey regarded him steadily and then nodded. "It would be sad to see it come to an end."

From her demeanor, Brock could tell Kelsey understood that if Marlowe Downs became unviable, there would be no more participation in a program that had the potential to help so many more people. He hoped she'd think about that when it came time for her to make her decision.

They rode the next stretch of fence line, quietly taking in their surroundings. Occasionally, Kelsey would ask a question about various flora, most of which she'd never seen before, including several species of wattle, majestic eucalyptus, and a paddock carpeted with native wildflowers. Brock pointed out a flock of galahs, their bright pink chest feathers even more brilliant against the clear, blue sky.

A few yards along, he drew his horse to a halt. Kelsey did the same. When she shot him a look filled with curiosity, he pressed a finger against his lips and indicated with his head the large goanna that lumbered its way slowly across their path.

Kelsey gasped, holding a hand to her chest. "Oh my goodness!" she half whispered. "What is that?"

"A goanna."

"A goanna? It looks like some prehistoric animal! Are you sure it's not some long-forgotten dinosaur?"

Brock chuckled. "I'm not sure about that, but it's generally believed they arrived here from the Northern Hemisphere, moving south into Australia and Africa about fifteen million years ago. But we have more species of goanna here than in Africa."

Kelsey stared at the lizard, her eyes wide with excitement. "Wow. It's huge! That must be at least six or seven feet long, and I can't even imagine how much it must weigh. I've never seen such an enormous lizard."

"This one's known as the perentie goanna. It is the largest lizard in Australia and the fourth largest lizard in the world. It can grow more than eight feet long and weigh up to fifteen kilograms. That's about thirty-three pounds."

Kelsey shook her head. "That's amazing. And it looks so pretty! The pale yellow-and-brown pattern on its skin is quite intricate. Do they all look like that?"

"Yes. Some of them are a bit lighter brown than this one, but the markings are all the same."

They both watched in silence as the lizard finally disappeared from view beneath a thick clump of kangaroo grass.

Kelsey turned to Brock, her eyes wide with wonder. "Oh my goodness! That was...the most fabulous experience! I can't believe I just saw that in real life!"

"More fabulous than the kangaroos you saw yesterday?"

She laughed. "Now you've got me. Seeing real live kangaroos in the wild was also a great experience." She sighed happily. "This place... It's amazing. Thank you for inviting me here."

Brock tipped his hat toward her and grinned. "My pleasure."

Their gazes locked. An arc of awareness ran between them. They were so caught up in each other, they didn't even notice the newcomer until he spoke.

"Well, if it isn't the boardroom cowboy home for a little taste of the outback."

Chapter Nine

♥

Kelsey eyed the sinfully good-looking stranger with open curiosity. He'd ridden up on a horse that was every bit as intimidating as Brock's stallion and came to a halt beside them. He looked to be about her age, and with his chiseled jaw, thick black hair, and piercing blue eyes, the newcomer could have been a leading man straight off a Hollywood movie set.

Brock bristled beside her. His expression turned dark. From the snide expression on the stranger's face, it was obvious the two men disliked each other. Kelsey could almost cut the tension in the air with a knife. She glanced from one man to the other, trying to determine the reason behind their obvious acrimony.

The stranger's gaze slid over her with lazy insouciance. He did nothing to hide the avid interest in his eyes. His gaze paused pointedly on her breasts, before continuing lower and finally coming back to rest on her face. Kelsey noticed that Brock's hands tightened on his reins, his jaw clenched, and his lips thinned. She wasn't sure if his reaction was just male testosterone or something more.

"And who do we have here?" the stranger drawled.

"None of your business, Whittaker," Brock almost snarled.

The stranger merely chuckled, clearly unperturbed by Brock's antagonism. Instead, he nudged his horse closer toward Kelsey and stuck out his hand.

"I'm Todd Whittaker. My family own Wyambee Station right next door."

Kelsey shook his proffered hand. "Kelsey Garland. I'm from the New World Bank."

A muscle in Brock's jaw contracted as he clenched it again. Todd's expression turned feral.

"The New World Bank, hey? A bank manager doing the rounds of Marlowe Downs. Fancy that." The chuckle that accompanied his words rang flat.

Kelsey bit her lip. She'd spoken without thinking. She glanced again at Brock. His body was tense. Anger and wariness glinted in his eyes.

"Of course, it comes as no surprise that you're here," the other man continued in a lazy drawl, his gaze still fixed on Kelsey. "It's only a matter of time before the Fairfax family go broke. Everyone knows that." He laughed mirthlessly again and shifted his gaze to Brock. "Seeing as how you have your bank manager here, you might as well tell her my family are willing to buy Marlowe Downs whenever you give the word. We'll pay you a fair price, of course. As fair as you can expect under the circumstances."

Whittaker shot Brock a knowing look and then laughed. A muscle ticked in Brock's jaw.

"I'd rather give this farm away to charity before I sell to the likes of you," he snapped.

Whittaker clucked his tongue. "Temper, temper. Be careful what you wish for, Fairfax. Everyone knows you sold off most of your livestock and you don't have the money to buy more. The once illustrious Fairfax empire is clinging on with its fingernails, and unless you manage to persuade this pretty little woman to hand over some serious cash, you're done for. We both know it's only a matter of time. You can't hold out forever."

Kelsey tensed at the man's insult. Anger heated her face. She opened her mouth to give him a piece of her mind, but he beat her to it.

"You might want to go and check on what little cattle you have left. I've just ridden by that way and saw some of them. They're looking off. When was the last time you checked on them?"

"I only arrived the day before yesterday. I haven't had the chance to investigate. But I'm sure one of my brothers has it in hand."

Whittaker merely nodded. "Yeah, that's what I thought. You're a city boy now. You work behind a desk. You're only out here now pretending to be a cattleman because you're trying to impress a piece of skirt. Oh, sorry, ma'am. A bank manager." He smirked and. tipping his hat in her direction, pulled hard on his reins and kicked his horse into a gallop. Mocking laughter and a cloud of dust followed in his wake.

Kelsey turned to Brock, whose face was as dark as a thundercloud. "What was that all about?"

Brock made an effort to control his anger, but it was difficult. Todd's gibe about being a boardroom cowboy had drawn blood, and the prick knew it. There was nothing Brock could do to deny it. It was true. He spent most of his time in the city. But that didn't mean the station wasn't in his blood or that he no longer cared about what became of it. He still loved it out here, loved to visit whenever he could. Just because he chose a different career path didn't change that.

Still, this wasn't Kelsey's fault. The antagonism between him and Todd had been there a long time. What had made things worse right then was Todd's obvious interest in her. At least it appeared the interest wasn't reciprocated. She'd regarded Todd with nothing more than curiosity, and Brock could tell she'd been annoyed when the asshole had called her a pretty little woman. The fact she hadn't appeared interested in the man filled him with relief, and then he was immediately mad at himself for feeling like that.

He liked her a lot. Could even fall in love with her, if he allowed himself. But that was the problem. Right now, she was off-limits. He'd promised himself. He'd promised Cayd. Every member of his family was counting on him to pull this off or at least do all he could possibly do to make that happen. He needed to get his head back in the game and stop thinking with his cock. In fact, the wisest thing to do would be to stay the hell away from her. Starting now.

"I need to go and check on the cattle and see if there's anything to what Todd has said or whether he's just full of shit," he muttered.

Kelsey regarded him with surprise. "Would he lie about something like that?"

A sudden breeze lifted her hair and brought a waft of her sweet perfume toward him. His gut clenched. Irritation at his response had him frowning. "Who knows?" he snapped.

She leaned back as if he'd slapped her. He cursed under his breath. The best thing for him to do was to put some distance between them, give his body and his head time to cool down. With that, he turned away and dug his heels into Calypso's sides, urging the beast forward into a canter.

Kelsey stared after him, perplexed. She understood he was angry over his encounter with his neighbor, but he had no right to take that out on her. She was merely a bystander.

She blew her breath out on a sigh and clucked at her horse and was grateful when Shiloh began to walk without further prompting. She was also relieved the mare hadn't taken off at a gallop after the retreating pair. She was finding it hard enough to stay in the saddle as it was.

She followed Brock as best she could as he all but disappeared into the distance. Luckily, his path was clearly visible from the cloud of red dust kicked up by his stallion in their wake. By the time she reached them, Brock and Calypso had come to a halt beneath the shadow of a huge gum tree. Brock had dismounted and leaned against the trunk, watching her. She was relieved to discover his anger seemed to have dissipated. Too bad for him, hers was about to blow at his nonchalant expression and rudeness.

"Feeling better?" she asked.

"Nothing like a gallop on the back of a fast horse to blow off some steam. What took you so long?" he drawled.

Her anger simmered just below the surface. "I would have been here sooner if I knew how to ride. Thanks for leaving me to follow in your dust."

His expression filled with remorse. "I'm sorry."

"Look, I'm sorry your neighbor upset you, but you shouldn't have just taken off like that, leaving me in the middle of nowhere on the back of a horse I'm doing all I can to stay on."

Brock grimaced, and his cheeks flushed with guilt. "You're right. I've been an ass. I'm sorry. It had nothing to do with you, and I treated you as if it did. Todd Whittaker and I have been butting heads for years. Our animosity isn't new."

"Why can't you just tell him your farm isn't for sale and put an end to it?"

He snorted humorlessly. "Todd and his father have been after our land forever. As if they don't have plenty of their own. Wyambee Station is more than double the size of our holdings, and still they want more. It's pure greed, that's all this is. Todd takes every opportunity to rub in the fact we're only a modest operation and that it's only a matter of time before we go under. Then he and his father will be waiting, ready to pounce. Scavengers, that's what they are. Without significant financial assistance, they might just get their way." His gaze bore into hers. "We need that money, Kelsey."

She bit her lip. "I wish it were that easy. The bank has strict criteria that need to be met. Things are tough for everyone, including the bank. They're accountable to shareholders."

He waved away her words with a sharp movement of his hand, his expression flooding with frustration. "You don't need to explain it all again to me. I get it, okay? Just promise me you'll keep an open mind while you're out here, that you'll look at what we do here and allow a bit of emotion into your decision. We're good for the money. I promise you."

She shook her head sadly. "I wish I had the liberty of making the decision with my heart and not my head. It would be a no-brainer to approve your loan if that were the case. Unfortunately…" She lifted one arm in a sign of surrender. "The world of banking doesn't work like that."

Brock's lips thinned with disappointment.

She filled the silence. "I hate it when a bully thinks they have the upper hand. And that's what Todd Whittaker is: a bully."

Brock grimaced. "He's just doing what his old man expects. Alistair Whittaker's been at my father for decades, trying to convince him to sell. We were able to stand strong during the good years, but the last few years when things haven't gone so well… It's tough."

Kelsey was flooded with sympathy for this family that was only doing what they could to keep hold of their heritage for future generations, but for all the power she had to make decisions, she had to make them in line with bank policies.

She averted her gaze and followed the landscape up to the endless blue sky. The sun had climbed higher, and a trickle of sweat ran down between her shoulder blades. She swiped at her lower lip and thought longingly of a drink of cool water. She also needed to climb off Shiloh. Her ass and thighs were already a little sore from the unfamiliar position astride the horse.

As if sensing her discomfort, Brock walked the few steps over to her side. "Come on, let's get you down off that horse for a few minutes and rest in the shade. Have some water and stretch those muscles."

Looking down at him, she smiled. "You read my mind."

He took hold of her reins. "Swing your right leg over and put your weight on the left stirrup," he said.

She did as he instructed, although it took a couple of tries to get her thighs to unclench from the horse's flanks, and then slid awkwardly down the side. As her muscles readjusted, she stumbled slightly, and his arms came around her. For an instant, she was pressed against the rock-hard wall of his chest. Awareness arced through her, sending heat rushing to her face and other regions. She caught the sound of Brock's sharp intake of breath before he released her and turned away. He led Shiloh to the tree beside Calypso and secured her reins to a branch.

She watched as he untied a stainless-steel canteen from his saddle and walked back toward her. He handed it to her. Their fingers brushed. She determinedly ignored another frisson of awareness. She glanced cautiously at Brock, but he too appeared determined not to acknowledge the physical attraction between them. That was fine with her. For now.

Unscrewing the lid, she took grateful swallows of the cool water until her thirst was quenched, then she handed the canteen back to him.

"Thank you. That was delicious."

"The cleanest, clearest bore water to be found for miles around. Just another reason the Whittakers want to get their hands on our land. Having clean and reliable water around here is invaluable."

Pleased to be out of the sun for a while, Kelsey folded her arms across her chest and leaned back against the shady tree. "Tell me more about them."

Brock swallowed a few mouthfuls of water before tightening the cap on the canteen and securing it back onto his saddle. He didn't particularly want to spend any more time talking about his neighbors, but if it helped her to better understand what was at stake, then he'd do so. He was also surprised at her continued interest, but in the short time he'd known her, he'd found himself enjoying her company and was keen to extend his time with her so that he could get to know her better.

"What do you want to know?" he asked.

"How did the Whittakers survive the drought and the flood? I assume they were hit as hard as you were."

"Yes. No one out here was spared. But the Whittaker family have plenty of money. Apart from their agricultural holdings in Queensland, Alistair owns a couple of gold mines in Western Australia. I'm pretty sure he also has a share in one of the iron ore companies. The bottom line is, they have other sources of income. Farming cattle is just a hobby to them. Not like us. This is our life. Without the station, my family has nothing. Mum and Dad have invested everything they have into Marlowe Downs. If the farming enterprise fails, they might still have a roof over their heads, but they'd have no source of income. They'd have to move, maybe even start over again. My parents are too old for that.

"Then there are my brothers who live and work out here. They wouldn't cope well in the city. They love it out here. They need the wide-open plains, fresh air, dirt and dust, heat. The whole thing. It's in their blood. They wouldn't be happy anywhere else."

Kelsey regarded him steadily. "Surely, they must get lonely with no one around for miles. What do they do for entertainment? A social life? They're young men in the prime of their life."

Brock shrugged. "They go out sometimes to the local bars."

She shot him a wry look. "An hour's drive away."

Brock waved her comment away. "You might have guessed, distance is of no concern to people who live in the outback. I once drove two hours to play a game of tennis. Besides, we make our own fun out here. Someone's always throwing a barbeque on one of the adjoining farms to celebrate a wedding or a baptism or a birthday, even a funeral. We might be spread out and be sparse in numbers, but you can live in a city of a million people and still be alone."

She nodded. "That's true. I've been in Brisbane six months, and I don't have any close friends. Some acquaintances and friendly work colleagues, that's it. Before that, I lived in Tampa, a city of just under four hundred thousand people. The dating scene is also challenging. I've been dating on and off since I graduated from high school. But no Mr Right or even Mr Maybe anywhere to be found."

She spoke lightly, but he thought he detected a note of urgency. His gaze zeroed in on her. "So, you're single, then?"

She flushed. "Yes."

He ignored the sudden zing of elation and forced a casual note in his tone. "So, what are you looking for? What's the plan for say, the next decade? Marriage? Kids?"

"Yes. All that. What about you?"

Their gazes caught and held. His heart pounded. "I guess. Yes."

The air between them became charged. Time stopped still. He straightened from the tree and leaned closer, his head angling down. His gaze fell to her lips. Her eyes watched him intently from beneath the brim of her hat.

As he stared, her mouth parted on a tiny intake of breath. The sound of it sent a shiver of desire tingling through his veins. He pushed his hat further back on his head. He could almost taste the sweet softness of her lips. He was a breath away from kissing her when he came to his senses.

What the hell am I doing? I can't kiss our bank manager. At least, not until I secure that loan...

With an effort, he pulled back and deliberately stepped away, putting some distance between them. He busied himself with checking on the horses, giving himself time to get his breathing back under control and cool the fire in his veins that centered in his cock. He glanced at Kelsey. Her color was high. Her chest rose and fell in rapid breaths, as if she were also doing her best to calm down.

The realization she was in as much turmoil as he was filled him with satisfaction. It had been awhile since he'd felt the emotional disruption of raw need. Though he was leery of engaging his heart, there was something about this woman that tempted him to give it a shot. Still, he needed to exercise caution. The last time he'd thrown himself head over heels for a woman, things hadn't ended so well. Best to remember that.

Kelsey drew in surreptitious breaths in an effort to slow her heartbeat and stem her disappointment. She'd seen the look in Brock's eyes, the flare of desire, the rapid pulse in the side of his neck, just moments before he went to kiss her. At least, she was pretty sure that's what he'd intended to do. But then, he'd changed his mind, and now an awkward silence had fallen between them.

She didn't care. It was early days. It was enough that he'd once again shown his attraction to her. And while her time on the station would soon come to an end, she was more determined than ever to pursue their connection once they'd returned to Brisbane and dealt with the matter of the loan. She needed to keep things professional between them until then. After that, if he was still speaking to her, everything would be up for grabs, including Brock Fairfax.

The thought put a smile on her face. She ducked her head to conceal her expression, but she wasn't quick enough.

"What are you smiling about?" Brock asked, a tentative grin lifting the sides of his mouth.

Unable to stop herself, she smiled more broadly. "Nothing in particular," she fibbed. "I was just thinking how lucky I am to be out here, experiencing the beautiful Australian outback with a handsome cowboy as my guide."

Brock flushed, but she could tell he was pleased with her comment.

"Not a cowboy," he mumbled.

She laughed. "Oh, right. Sorry. I forgot. You're a cattleman in disguise."

The bellow of a cow caught her attention and she almost laughed at the reminder of why they were there. She lifted her head and stared off toward the sound. Brock followed the direction of her gaze.

His expression became focused. "You ready to go and inspect some livestock?"

She smiled back, and butterflies swarmed in her stomach.

"Let's do it," she said.

He untied her horse and helped her remount. Once again, as his hand palmed her ass, awareness rushed through her, despite the ache of protesting muscles. She was so going to pay for this tomorrow. She watched from beneath her lashes as he mounted Calypso, admiring the authority he commanded from his handsome stallion.

Swallowing a sigh, she took a firm grip on her hormones and tapped her heels against Shiloh's flanks. Thankfully, her obedient little mare started walking. Together, they ambled toward the herd.

Chapter Ten

♥

Brock's stallion stepped out smartly beside Kelsey's mare, his head and tail held high. It was almost as if he were trying to impress the little chestnut. Brock smiled at the image, but quickly suppressed it. He needed to be focusing on the business at hand.

Down, boy. Patience...

They rounded a thick stand of eucalyptus and came upon the herd of cattle.

"Wow, they're huge. What breed of cows are they?" Kelsey asked, pulling on her reins and bringing Shiloh to a halt.

"They're Droughtmasters. It's an Australian breed of beef cattle. They were developed from around 1915. They crossed Zebuine, primarily Brahman cattle from the US, with British origin Beef Shorthorn and came up with the Droughtmaster. They were specially bred for the tough conditions experienced in North and Central Queensland and are resistant to ticks, heat, eye cancer, and, funnily enough, drought."

"And yet you lost so many over the past years," she murmured.

Brock compressed his lips. "Yes. They're drought resistant, but two years of extreme heat and dry without a break... There was no feed; water was scarce. We made the decision to sell all but our top breeders. Then came the flood. What cattle had survived the drought were then forced to swim for their lives. We lost more than I can count when the river broke its banks."

"You've had a tough few years," she said quietly, her face full of sympathy.

Brock shot her a grim look. "You bet. But we won't be beaten. We Fairfaxes are made from stronger stuff than that. We might be down, but we're not out. Not by a long shot."

Kelsey's eyes shone with admiration. Brock hoped that meant she might be softening her stance on their loan. Then again, that was probably wishful thinking. He turned away and scanned the herd, looking for signs that something was awry. Of course, there was every chance Todd Whittaker had been simply pulling Brock's chain. He wouldn't put that past the asshole.

As he rode into the herd, he eyed them closely, but they looked as healthy as they had the last time he'd seen them. He relaxed into the saddle, convinced that Todd had simply been toying with him. His brothers were in regular contact with the cattle. They would have known if something was wrong.

Then he spied a cow standing off to the side on her own. He frowned. A cow on her own was unusual. They preferred to be part of a mob. A cow separated from the herd often indicated sickness. The thought made his gut clench. He glanced across at Kelsey. The last thing he wanted to do was alert her to a possible problem with the herd. Hell, if she got even a whiff that there was something wrong, they'd never get that money.

As casually as he could, he flicked the reins and kept ambling through the cattle. As he'd hoped, Kelsey remained where she was, well clear of the edge of the herd. Continuing forward at the same steady pace, he nudged Calypso in the direction of the solitary cow.

He heard her cough. As he drew closer, he saw a flood of thick snot and mucus hanging out of her nose. His stomach filled with dread.

Shit.

It looked suspiciously like the cow had a cold. The runny nose, the cough... In the back of Brock's mind was the awful possibility that she was suffering from something far more serious: tuberculosis. Though the disease had been eradicated in Queensland since 1997, it was still possible, particularly if it had been spread via a mob of infected deer or some other infected animal that might have come into contact with the herd. The symptoms were often the same as a common cold. The only way to be sure was to test.

Tuberculosis was a notifiable disease. It was highly infectious and could spread from one cow to another very quickly. It could also be transmitted to humans. Cattle owners had a legal obligation to inform Biosecurity Queensland as soon as a case of tuberculosis was suspected. A positive test would result in the cow being put down.

Just when I thought things couldn't get any worse... How much more of this can we take? No, I won't jump to conclusions.

But if it was tuberculosis, the disease could wipe out what was left of their stock. He tamped down on a growing sense of urgency. He needed to get back to the house as soon as possible and have a quiet word with Cayd and his father. He didn't want to alert Kelsey to the potential threat. Biting his lip hard, he drew in a deep breath and eased it out, forcing himself to relax. Plastering a smile on his face, he swung his horse back around and meandered back through the cattle toward her.

"I take it your neighbor was teasing when he expressed concern about your cattle," she called out.

He chuckled. "Yeah, it looks that way. As I said, Todd Whittaker's a prick." He arrived back at Kelsey's side. "Let's forget about him. We've wasted too much time discussing him. I wouldn't care if I never hear his name again."

"Well, at least you know your cows are all good."

He kept his grin firmly in place. "Absolutely. Anyway, we've seen all we need to see here. How about we head back to the homestead? No doubt Mum has lunch ready. Race you?"

"No! Don't leave me! I won't be able to find my way home," Kelsey protested and then stopped when he began to laugh.

"Just kidding. I'm not going to leave you out here all alone. Come on. Let's go."

As fast as he could with Kelsey plodding a few yards behind him, Brock returned to the homestead. Tamping down his impatience, he tied up the horses at the slip rail and helped Kelsey down from Shiloh. With unseemly haste, he suggested she take a few minutes to freshen up in her cottage before lunch and then hurried toward the main house, leaving her to stare after him, nonplussed.

No doubt she was as confused as hell about his abrupt departure, but there was nothing he could do about that. He needed to find Cayd or his dad or one of his other brothers and let them know what he'd discovered, and he had to do that out of Kelsey's hearing.

To his relief, he ran into Cayd just inside the front veranda. He drew in a quick breath and did his best to compose himself.

"Cayd, we need to talk."

Cayd stared at him in surprise. "What's got you so worked up? Or should I say, *who's* got you so worked up?"

Brock waved away his comment with a snort of impatience. "Shut up about that. This has nothing to do with Kelsey. It's about the cattle."

Cayd's expression sharpened. "What about the cattle?"

"I was just out there with Kelsey, showing her around. We ran into Todd. He was an asshole, as usual. He said something about the cattle not looking right. I didn't know if he was telling the truth or just dicking me around, but I went and checked on them anyway." He stared at his brother grimly. "Seems like Whittaker might have been right."

Cayd's eyes flared wide. "What are you talking about?"

Brock filled Cayd in on the lone cow who'd been hanging back from the rest of the herd and the signs she'd exhibited.

"Could just be a cold," Cayd muttered.

"Yeah. Or it could be TB. We need to isolate her and have her tested."

Cayd's lips thinned. Frown lines marked the smooth skin of his forehead. "It can't be tuberculosis. We vaccinate against that now. Besides, it was eradicated in this state decades ago."

Brock nodded. "Right. Except every now and then, a case crops up. Remember that outbreak they had in the Northern Territory? And don't forget how, halfway through the last drought, we made a decision to cut back on costs where we could. We haven't vaccinated against TB for at least eighteen months. Any immunity they might have had would have well and truly worn off."

"Shit. You're right."

Cayd looked as grim as Brock felt.

"How many head looked sick?" Cayd asked.

"I only saw one, but there could have been others. Kelsey was with me. I didn't want to alert her to the possibility that something was wrong. If she thinks the herd's at risk of being slaughtered, she'll never give us that money."

"Shit," Cayd said again.

Brock grimaced. "Yeah."

Cayd's shoulders slumped on a heavy sigh. "We need to notify Biosecurity, get that cow tested as soon as possible."

"Yeah."

"When does Kelsey leave?"

A little disgruntled at Brock's abrupt departure, Kelsey took only a few moments to use the bathroom, splash some water on her face, and run a brush through her tangled hair. She didn't care about the dust that coated her blouse or the horsehair that clung to her jeans. She was in the outback. Other than the family and the station hands, there was no one around for miles. She realized she was enjoying herself more than she could remember or ever expected.

Perhaps I'm a country girl at heart? A country girl born in the city...

The dust and flies and heat didn't bother her. In fact, every moment she'd spent with Brock had been wonderful. She'd never felt more alive. The vastness of the landscape made her feel insignificant and yet, inspired. But maybe that had more to do with Brock than anything else. She couldn't deny the place would likely be far less exciting without him around. He had a vitality that was hard to ignore.

Impatient to be in his company again, she stepped out of the cottage and hurried across the lawn to the homestead. She rounded the side of the house and headed toward the wide stone steps that led up to the front veranda. Male voices snagged her attention. When she heard one of them mention her name, her footsteps slowed.

Eavesdropping is fraught with danger... What if I hear something I wish I hadn't?

But she couldn't have stepped away if she'd tried. With her heart thumping, she flattened herself against the side of the house and strained to hear the conversation.

It was Brock and one of his brothers. She was fairly certain it was Cayd, though she couldn't be sure. The brothers sounded very much alike, and she didn't know them well enough to be able to confidently distinguish their voices. But they were talking about her and the herd of cattle she and Brock had just inspected. The more she listened, the more she realized something was awry. Whatever it was, they didn't want her to know about it. Well, she'd see about that.

Stepping away from the house, she stomped up the stone steps in time to catch the look of surprise followed swiftly by guilt on the faces of Brock and Cayd.

"Thanks for asking. I fly out the day after tomorrow," she said, eyeing Brock.

He flushed and averted his gaze. "Kelsey, I—"

She narrowed her eyes. "What's going on?"

He shifted uncomfortably, glanced at his brother, then back at Kelsey. "It's nothing. I don't know what you mean. I was just—"

"Don't treat me like an idiot, Brock. You've been acting strange ever since we inspected the cattle. Something's up. Are you going to tell me, or will Cayd?"

She turned to Brock's brother and gave him a piercing look, the same look that had caused many a recalcitrant board member to quiver in their boots. It wasn't easy being the one whose job it was to clean up after someone else's mess, but she'd had years of experience and now had it down to a fine art. She'd gone toe to toe with many uncooperative people in the past and had come out on top. Getting information out of the Fairfax men would be child's play.

Cayd held her gaze. Something like admiration hovered around his lips. "I guess you'd better tell her, Brock."

Brock bit his lip and sighed. "We have a sick cow. We don't know whether it's just a cold, or if it's something more serious."

She blinked in surprise. "Cows can get a cold?"

"Yes," Brock said. "Same as us. And with much the same symptoms. Runny nose, cough, temperature. One of the cows is displaying some of those symptoms. It could be nothing. Then again…"

"What else could it be?" she asked.

Brock blew out his breath. "Tuberculosis."

Kelsey had heard of the disease, but only insofar as it affected humans. She didn't realize it could also be caught by cattle.

"How serious is that?"

Brock's lips thinned. "Serious."

"It's a notifiable disease," Cayd replied briskly. "It's mandatory that whenever tuberculosis is suspected, the government's biosecurity department must be made aware of it. Every cow on this farm will need to be tested. Any cow that tests positive for tuberculosis will be destroyed."

It took a moment for that information to sink in. As the full weight of what Cayd had said hit her, she let out a gasp. Her gaze collided with Brock's. The combination of uncertainty and dread in his eyes was difficult to witness. After all this family had been through... Three years of drought followed by a devastating flood. Now they faced the prospect of what little stock they had left being eradicated. Cripes. God had an odd sense of humor at times.

"I'm sorry," she said. "That doesn't seem fair."

Brock's lips twisted in a grimace. "Too right it's not fair. But that's the law. We have no choice but to comply with it."

"I'll go and make the call now," Cayd muttered. "Best get this over with." He turned away and disappeared inside the house.

Kelsey shifted closer to Brock. She could almost feel his pain. He looked so disheartened, almost defeated.

"I wish there was something I could do," she said.

His grunt of laughter was devoid of humor. "Me, too." He paused and then added, "Oh, that's right. There *is* something you can do. You can approve that loan. If this is TB, we'll need that money more than ever."

Her stomach sank. They both knew she couldn't base her decision on anything other than black-and-white facts and figures, no matter how much her heart yearned to help them out. The discovery that their remaining herd could be under threat was a further black mark against their application and if it was TB, that would be the death knell as far as the loan was concerned. She could tell from the look on Brock's face that he was well aware of the implications.

The fact she was developing feelings for him made this even more difficult. She should have known not to let her heart get involved.

She'd always managed to keep her professional life separate from the other, and this time, she'd broken her own rule.

She thought again about whether rejection of the loan application would also be a rejection of her. Brock's easy charm and good looks and their undeniable mutual attraction, along with the unconscious pressure she felt to secure the money that had been dangled so enticingly by her grandmother, had put him squarely in the future she'd begun to envisage. Her grandmother's money would pay for her mother's much-needed treatment and set both of them up for a comfortable life. But it was increasingly hard to ignore the burgeoning panic as the potential future with Brock she'd imagined began to dissipate like smoke.

She hoped that his aborted kiss had simply been about temporary prudence, while they dealt with the loan business, and that in the aftermath of the loan application's failure, he'd still be interested in exploring their chemistry further. Of course, there was no guarantee of that.

The sound of footsteps clacking softly on the wooden floorboards in the hallway alerted her that someone was approaching. She glanced over Brock's shoulder in time to see his mother bearing down on them. She was smiling. Her sons had obviously not yet passed on the bad news.

"There you are!" Ellen exclaimed. "Lunch is ready. Please, come in and sit down before everything gets cold."

Ellen linked her arm with Kelsey's and led her down the hall toward the kitchen. As they entered the room, Kelsey noted that Cayd had slipped in ahead of them and was already seated at the table beside his father, Bob. The two men had their heads together, talking quietly. Aiden, Lachlan, and Justin sat opposite them, their expressions intent on the older men. It appeared they'd already been advised of the potential catastrophe that awaited them.

But when Ellen appeared with Kelsey, all heads turned in their direction. The men's faces lightened and filled with smiles. It was only because Kelsey was watching closely that she noticed the smiles failed to reach their eyes. It was further proof they were keeping the bad news from their mother.

She admired their need to protect Ellen from the harsher realities, at least until they had definite proof. No doubt that's how she'd survived all these years living under such exacting conditions, where their livelihood could be snatched away from them at any time by forces beyond their control.

No wonder they grow them tough out here...

Her gaze wandered over the men seated around the table. Tall, broad-shouldered, strong. Each showed a mental toughness in the set of their jaw, the purpose in their eyes, the never-say-die attitude, she'd witnessed over the past two days. They'd just received news that might have the power to destroy them, and yet, though the mood was subdued, she also sensed a determination to pull together and do what needed to be done.

She was struck with sudden admiration for the family. They were obviously good people who were committed to working hard for each other and their future. A lot of families who worked together ended up being torn apart by egos too big to manage. But not the Fairfaxes. Four of their six sons lived and worked the farm and sat down for meals with their parents every day. There was love, caring, and respect stamped on each of their faces. Kelsey, who had no knowledge of what it was like to be part of a large family, had a growing ache to be a part of it.

Chapter Eleven

♥

Cayd drew Brock aside after lunch to tell him the people from Biosecurity would be out early the next morning. Until then, Cayd would keep the sick cow isolated from the rest of the herd. He'd also check the rest of them over for signs of illness.

"Do you want me to come with you?" Brock asked.

"No. Lachlan's already offered to ride along. We're going to check some more of those fences on our way back. How about you go and keep that hot little bank manager company? After all, she's your guest."

Brock blinked in surprise. "I thought you wanted me to stay the hell away from her? In fact, I think those were your exact words."

Cayd flushed. "Yeah, well. That's before I realized that she seems an okay person. And of course, how much you like her."

It was Brock's turn to flush. Cayd merely chuckled.

"Don't try to deny it, bro. It's written all over your face. And I'm fairly sure she likes you too."

Brock's heart leaped. This was the second brother to make that observation. "Really?"

Cayd grinned. "Really. Now, go and keep her company. You'll be no use to me anyway, daydreaming over her." He managed to dodge Brock's right arm swung at him in mock outrage and laughed. "You'd better get going. I saw her wandering off toward the vegetable garden a few minutes ago. I'd hate for her to get lost."

Brock scowled at his brother, but quickly turned and strode off in the direction of his mother's thriving vegetable patch. His heart raced at the thought of spending more time alone with Kelsey, but he also wanted to smooth over the issue with the cattle—well, as much as he could. It was important for her not to make any decisions until they knew for sure.

He was actually glad she'd overheard him talking to Cayd. He'd never liked keeping secrets, and though this might very well mean the loan money was as good as gone, he felt better that she knew the truth than accuse them later of a cover-up.

After being in a relationship that had been based on nothing but lies, Brock's preferred option was to be honest. Not that he and Kelsey were in a relationship, but he increasingly wanted the opportunity to explore what looked to him like promising signs.

Of course, he was also wary. Things were moving incredibly fast. In truth, they barely knew each other. And then there was the issue that she lived in the States. She was only here on secondment. What had she said? Halfway through a twelve-month stint? That didn't leave a lot of time to get to know each other. And then what?

There was no way he could leave his business and set up shop in the US. He and Raine had worked hard to get where they were. He couldn't walk away from that. Not for a woman. Not for anyone.

Could I?

Shaking his head, he made a sound of disgust in the back of his throat. He was getting way ahead of himself. He and Kelsey weren't even dating, let alone thinking seriously about the future. It was just that he'd never felt so strongly about a woman before. Not even when he'd thought he was in love with Cecelia.

Looking back, he realized his ex-girlfriend's deception had done him a favor. He'd been forced to acknowledge that he'd only seen the person he wanted to see and not the person she was. He'd ignored all the warning signs and niggling questions in his mind. But when he'd discovered her deception, the sense of betrayal had been crippling. More because he'd felt like such a fool. He'd been in love with an image, not Cecelia herself.

So how do I know things will be different with Kelsey?

He just did. He was always levelheaded and focused on the business at hand, no matter how attractive the woman he might be doing business with. With Kelsey, he struggled to maintain his focus on what was the most critical deal of his life thus far. The fact she held the balance of the station's future in her hands, and, from all indications, wouldn't be able to help them out, didn't stop him from wanting her. He was attracted to her personality—her sense of fun, her spirit of adventure, her willingness to give anything a try. And of course, there was his physical reaction. She was drop-dead gorgeous. And she wanted him.

He'd seen the disappointment in her face when he hadn't kissed her. But he was fairly sure she knew the only thing that had been holding him back was the loan application.

Or at least, he hoped she knew. Then again, maybe she didn't? Maybe she thought he didn't like her that way at all, or at least not enough to want to kiss her. The possibility that she might have thought that he'd not been as attracted filled him with panic. He didn't want her thinking that he wasn't interested in her. He was *very* interested.

A flash of color through the greenery of his mother's orchard caught his attention. Kelsey stood among the orange trees, her nose pressed against a piece of fruit. A large, round dish sat at her feet. She had her eyes closed and appeared to be breathing in its scent. A gentle smile tugged at her lips.

"There you are," he said with a grin.

Her eyes flew open, and her mouth formed a cute "oh" of surprise. She stepped back and pressed a hand against her chest.

"You startled me. I didn't hear you coming."

"Sorry. I didn't mean to."

"That's all right. I was just enjoying your mother's garden. After that delicious lunch, I thought I might come and see for myself where all the magic happens."

She turned and began to wander toward the neat rows of lettuce. Their curly, green heads were plump and shiny with health. Brock followed beside her, enjoying being close to her once again. At the same time, his gut churned with nerves and he found himself suddenly tongue-tied.

"So, how was your lunch?" he blurted, desperate for something to say.

She shot him a curious look, and he blushed.

She just told you about her delicious lunch, you idiot...

"I mean, I know you said it was delicious, but... Have you ever eaten vegetables picked straight from a garden?"

Brock cringed as the words fell from his mouth. Could he get any more nonsensical? This was ridiculous! He was a man of nearly thirty and had plenty of experience with women. What was it about this one that made him feel so off-balance? As if the briefest smile of encouragement from her could tilt his world off its axis. It was crazy.

"No, I can't say that I have. Other than last night, of course," Kelsey added. "I live in an apartment. My mother lives in a small duplex with a postage stamp-sized backyard. No room for a vegetable garden. No room for any kind of garden, in fact."

"That's a shame," Brock managed. "I have plenty of fond memories of time spent working and playing in Mum's garden. Me and my brothers and sisters would spend hours playing hide and seek while Mum weeded and pruned and cultivated. Occasionally, she'd ask one of us to fetch her a bucket of water or the wheelbarrow, or a gardening tool from the shed. Sometimes she'd gather us around and tell us stories. Make-believe ones, not real. Of knights and fairies and dragons. Of castles and kings with horses and swords who went to war. We used to love it."

Kelsey smiled. "Wow. What a wonderful childhood you must have had."

"Yeah, it was great. It's times like this that I really miss it out here."

"Would you ever move back? Raise your own family in the outback?"

He shook his head. "No. As much as I love visiting, my life's in the city now. I guess my asshole of a neighbor was right. I'm a boardroom cowboy."

"You say that as if that makes you somehow lesser. As if the work you do in Brisbane is not as important as the life your family leads out here. Do they care that you left the station to work in the city?"

"No. That's the good thing. Mum and Dad were always fully supportive of whatever we chose to do. Raine was the first to leave for the city. When he invited me to go into business with him, I didn't even think about saying no. By then, I'd spent six years in Brisbane at boarding school, and as much as I loved the farm, I loved the city more. It was an easy decision for me to base my life there."

"You're lucky you had your parents' blessing to pursue a life off the farm. Not all families are so supportive or understanding."

"Are you speaking from experience?"

She shook her head. "No, not me personally, but I've come across many family-run enterprises over the course of my job. Not all of them work as well together or are as amiable as yours. In fact, I've seen firsthand how resentment and anger can build when an adult son or daughter is forced to work in the family business when they'd rather be anywhere else."

Brock nodded. "Well, that's another thing in our favor in terms of the loan. There would be no risk of the family breaking up. What you'd get from us is the commitment and drive to make it work."

Ignoring his pitch, Kelsey simply nodded. "If only all families looked upon it that way."

Brock sighed. They'd paused beside a flourishing strawberry patch. The glossy dark-green leaves shaded the ripe plump fruit from the sun. He bent down and plucked a handful of bright red strawberries and dropped them into Kelsey's open palm.

She smiled her thanks and popped one into her mouth. "Yum, that's delicious. I've never tasted a strawberry so sweet."

"They're full of flavor. Mum fertilizes them with manure from the chickens." At the look on Kelsey's face, he hurriedly added, "Don't worry, it's mixed into the soil. It won't be on the fruit."

"I'm sure she also gives them lots of tender love and care," Kelsey added with a smile. "I've heard that makes all the difference." She winked.

Brock's gut clenched with desire and his cock thickened. No matter how many times he cautioned himself to take things slowly, his body had other ideas. The urge to take her in his arms and kiss her was almost overwhelming. His gaze zeroed in on her lush strawberry-stained mouth. It was all he could do not to dive in for a taste.

As if she were aware of the direction of his thoughts, a flush crept up Kelsey's neck and spread across her cheeks. She ducked her head and averted her gaze, staring blindly at the strawberries that remained in her hand. Then she snuck a glance at him from beneath her thick lashes, and he almost gasped at the desire in her eyes.

His resolve to keep his distance crumbled. A single step was all he needed to close the distance between them. His arms came around her shoulders. He drew her toward him, loving the way she fit so well against him. She tilted her head back, and he bent his down. Their lips met in a feather-light touch.

Brock sighed against her mouth. A torrent of emotions flooded through him as his senses registered the soft lushness of her lips, the sweetness of the strawberries, the way her mouth opened under his, inviting him in. His tongue swept boldly into her warmth, and he lost himself in the kiss. Her arms tightened around his neck. She clung to him as if needing support. He held on to her for much the same reason.

The birds chirping in the distance, the warm sun on their faces, the smell of orange blossom, strawberries, and fragrant herbs... All of it faded until there was nothing and no one but her. When he finally came up for air and lifted his head to stare down at the woman in his arms, he felt dazed and a little shocked at the wonder of it. From her bemused expression, she'd been equally affected. That knowledge zinged through him.

"Wow," she breathed and tentatively touched her lips.

He smiled a little self-consciously. "Yeah."

"That was..." Her voice faded off. She looked away, an embarrassed flush staining her cheeks.

"Amazing," he finished.

She nodded, but the glow in her eyes had already begun to dim and was fast being replaced with regret. "We shouldn't have done that."

He forced his disappointment in check. "Because you're my bank manager?"

"Yes. That was unprofessional of me. I admit, I'm attracted to you, and I've been struggling with that because I'm here on business. You're my client."

She flushed again, as if the full import of what she'd done was only now hitting home. Brock hurried to reassure her. "If you don't approve the loan, then that's a mere technicality. My time as a potential client would be so brief as to have been almost nonexistent."

She smiled slightly, but continued to avoid his gaze. Gently, he tilted her chin up with his finger and forced her to look at him.

"Don't be sorry for what we just did. That kiss was mind-blowing. I don't care if we crossed some ethical line. It didn't feel that way to me. And whatever this is between us, I'm mature enough to accept it won't affect your decision. Whatever you decide to do about the loan will be fine with me. We desperately need that money, and I'll be disappointed if we miss out, but if the numbers don't go the way you need them to, then that's the way it is. I'm in business too. I understand that sometimes we have to make the hard decisions. If it doesn't go our way, we'll find another avenue."

She nodded. A reluctant smile tilted up her lips. "Okay." She drew in a deep breath. "Thank you for understanding the difficult position I'm in." She looked around her, focusing on the mountain ranges in the distance. "What you have out here, it's magical. A very special place on earth. And your family loves every inch of it and works hard to look after it. They deserve to be rewarded for their dedication and for wanting to preserve such a beautiful part of this country. In particular, they deserve to be given a helping hand after some extremely challenging years battling the elements.

"But life doesn't always play fair, and you know better than most that it's rarely easy. Your family's not looking for a handout. All they want is a hand up to get back on their feet. I get that. And I admire them for their stoicism. I only hope I can help with this loan, but the figures aren't good. In fact, I've been incredibly doubtful all this time." Her expression grew determined. "But that was before I came here, before I met your family and some of the other people who rely on this station. Before I fell in love with the landscape, the life out here. Rest assured that if it's at all in my power to get that loan application across the line, I'll make it happen. That's the best I can offer."

Brock took her by the shoulders, bent his head, and pressed a quick kiss on her mouth. "And that's all I'll ask of you on this matter."

They continued walking through the garden in silence, inspecting cabbages and broccoli that had just begun to form. The tomato patch stood empty, waiting for the spring before seeds would be sown in the freshly turned soil. The last of the pumpkins had withered on the vine, struck by an unusually early frost.

"You're very protective of your mother, aren't you?" Kelsey murmured.

Brock blinked in surprise. "What makes you say that?"

"No one told her about the possible tuberculosis finding."

Brock nodded. "You're right." He blew out his breath on a sigh. "Life can be very difficult out here. Mum arrived here as a new bride more than thirty years ago. She's been faced with challenges most people never come across. She's tough and strong and resilient, but no one wants her to worry unnecessarily. Until we know for sure that we're dealing with something serious, there's no need to concern her with it."

"Isn't that treating her a little like a child?"

"Not at all. None of us doubt her strength, but these past few years have been especially difficult. Mum's not as young as she used to be. Though she's generally fit and healthy, she's on medication for high blood pressure. Apparently, her mother suffered from that too. Suffice it to say, she doesn't need any added unnecessary stress. If the worst case happens and the cows have TB, then we'll tell her. We're not trying to deceive her, only to save her some worry."

"So, you don't think it's dishonest keeping something like that from her?"

Brock shook his head. "Not at all. We don't even know if it's a thing yet. Once we know for sure there's a problem, then we'll bring her up to speed. Until then, there's no point in concerning her with something that might not even happen."

"That must be hard on the rest of you. What about your father? Is he on board with that?"

"It was his suggestion. It's always been that way. Once we got old enough to understand, he impressed upon us the need to protect Mum as much as we could. We all agreed we only needed to share things when they became real, and not worry her with mere possibilities."

"Does your mother get upset when she discovers you've kept things from her?"

He made a sound of impatience. "We're not keeping things from her! You make it sound like we're deliberately deceiving her by keeping her in the dark. When developments are confirmed, we tell her. There's no point in worrying her with speculation. Believe me. It's done from a place of love. It's not malicious. Hell, I prize honesty above everything else. I'm the last person to be comfortable with deception. I've been there before, in a prior relationship. Let's just say my girlfriend was less than upfront about many aspects of her life. When I discovered the truth, I was gutted. I wasn't sure if I'd ever be able to trust a woman again."

They came to a halt. Kelsey regarded him somberly. "Do you still feel that way?" she asked quietly.

He took a moment to respond. Only a few days earlier, he might have continued to express some reservations as far as women and trusting them went. But that was before Kelsey. Before he'd discovered she was open and honest. She'd answered all his questions about her family, where she'd come from, what had prompted her decision to take a job thousands of miles away. She'd told him from the outset that coming to the farm might not change her decision. In every aspect, she'd been nothing but upfront. She was nothing like Cecelia. But she did have him churned up inside, for good reason. He liked her. A lot. He might even be falling in love with her.

Wow. Now that's a scary thought...

Except, it wasn't. The more he thought about it, the more right it felt. He was glad it appeared Kelsey felt the same way. He couldn't wait to get the loan business over with and focus on the two of them and what the future might hold...

He turned to her and reached for her hands. "No, I don't feel that way anymore. You're nothing like my ex. You're upfront, honest. No subterfuge. What you see is what you get. I like that. I like that a lot. I trust you."

Chapter Twelve

♥

As Brock's head came down for another kiss, Kelsey clamped down hard on her rising panic. Though she very much wanted to kiss him again, his words shook her to the core. While she'd answered all his questions with the truth, she'd omitted the bit about her mother's dire health status, or that her grandmother had dangled in front of her a million-dollar bribe and how that had factored into her decision to actively seek out a husband. In short, she'd set her sights on him, but not entirely for the reasons he was going to think when she told him the truth.

What should I do?

If she told him now, he'd be convinced she'd deliberately kept that information from him, which she had. Though she'd had a good reason, now knowing a little of his previous relationship history, Brock would see it as a betrayal, like she'd had an ulterior motive for wanting to spend time with him that had nothing to do with the farm, the loan, or the attraction between them.

If she told him now, he'd accuse her of being deceitful, the very quality he hated most. His ex-girlfriend's dishonesty had apparently almost destroyed him. Was she prepared to take the risk that he'd understand things from her point of view? That he wouldn't be as upset by her omissions? No, she wasn't.

They were in a good place right now. Things were moving in the right direction. She was fast falling in love with him, and she suspected he was developing strong feelings for her too. It was a heady feeling, thrilling, and overwhelming at the same time.

This is what real love feels like... Now I finally know... I'm so close to having everything I want... But so close to disaster!

As his lips came down on hers and she was once again swept up in the magic of his kiss, she vowed silently to ensure he never found out about her grandmother's deal. After all, there was no guarantee she'd ever receive it, and if she did... Well, it wasn't as if Brock knew anything about her finances. He wouldn't have to know the sudden increase in her bank account had come about because of their marriage... That was, if this led to that. There was no guarantee of that either.

On a sigh, she pushed the tumultuous thoughts aside and surrendered fully to Brock's kiss. His lips were firm and supple. His tongue swept into her mouth. She met his thrust with one of her own and opened her mouth wider to welcome him in. Her arms crept up around his neck and she drew him to her, pressing her breasts against his broad chest, loving the feel of his strength, his masculinity, the hard evidence of his desire against the core of her femininity.

When they finally pulled apart, they were both breathless. Brock's cheeks were flushed. His beautiful emerald eyes glittered with desire. Kelsey knew exactly how he felt. Her nipples were hard. There was an aching in her core that craved to be assuaged. But it would have to wait. At least, until their business dealings were finalized.

She smiled up at him. "Your mother asked me to pick some peas for dinner. She sent me out with a dish to put them in, but I seemed to have misplaced it."

"I think I saw it by the orange grove," he said with a grin.

She cocked an eyebrow. "Would you like to join me?"

"I can't think of anything I'd rather do."

Hand in hand, they walked back to collect the dish and then headed over to pick peas.

Brock was determined to spend as much time as possible with Kelsey during her last day at the station. With the help of his mother, he packed them a picnic lunch and strapped it on the back of his stallion. While he waited for Kelsey, he set about topping up the water troughs.

They'd ended the previous night kissing and messing around on the front veranda of the cottage until Brock had reluctantly called it a night. He wanted their first time together to be special, and he intended to have it all planned out well in advance. He liked to be organized and he wanted to go the extra mile for Kelsey.

He marveled at how quickly she'd become important to him. Not so long ago, the speed with which his feelings had developed would have spooked him, or at least given him pause, but everything felt so good and right with Kelsey, so natural. Like they were meant to be.

It was refreshing to be with someone so open and honest. She'd handled the added complication of the loan application with maturity and professionalism, and he respected her for that. Today, he intended to show her all his favorite places on the station. He hoped she enjoyed them as much as he did.

She'd still been asleep when he'd stopped by the cottage earlier. No doubt she wasn't used to the early rising that happened on the farm. He'd left a note for her on her kitchen table, asking her to meet him at the stables after breakfast.

"Don't tell me you have more horseback riding planned?"

The sound of her voice sent his pulse rate skyrocketing. He spun on his heel and grinned like an idiot. She was dressed in another tight-fitting pair of jeans that cupped her shapely ass and a red-and-white-checked blouse that brought out the color in her cheeks. Her hair was tied back in a loose knot at the base of her neck. Her Akubra was set at a rakish angle on her head.

"I thought we agreed there's only one way to ride a horse?" He chuckled.

She poked out her tongue. "I'm not sure my ass can stand another day in the saddle." She patted her butt cheeks. "They're still sore from yesterday. And don't get me started on my thigh muscles! I'm lucky I can walk at all!"

He laughed. "You'll be fine. In fact, the best way to deal with that is to rinse and repeat. By the end of the day, your muscles will have gotten used to the unfamiliar position. And if not, you can always have a soak in the tub. Mum made sure there was one installed in the cottage for just that purpose. Come on, Shiloh's eager to get started."

He untied the reins and led the chestnut mare over to where Kelsey stood. "Ready?"

She sighed exaggeratedly. "If I must."

"Unfortunately, where we're going today is only accessible by horseback. It'll be worth your while, I promise."

She gave him a mock glare. "It better."

He merely laughed again and helped her to mount. Grumbling good-naturedly under her breath, she turned sideways and fitted her boot into the stirrup. She reached up and grasped the saddle in an effort to pull herself up. The opportunity to cup her ass was far too tempting to resist. He palmed her cheek and hoisted her up. If his hand lingered on her sweet flesh a little longer than necessary, who could blame him?

After Kelsey was settled in the saddle, he handed her the reins.

"Don't look so scared. You've got this. Hey, you were great yesterday. You're almost a pro."

She chuckled. "I thought you said you prized honesty."

He spread his arms wide. "Hey! I *am* being honest. I'm honestly impressed by how well you've taken to this whole riding thing. For someone who's never been on a horse before, you've done a great job."

Color brightened her cheeks. "Thank you, but I didn't get beyond a walk. Hardly a pro," she reminded him, but looked pleased by his compliment.

Brock winked and then untied Calypso. He made short work of climbing onto the horse's back and settling his weight into the saddle. Calypso danced and snorted and shook his head, impatient to be going.

Brock looked over at Kelsey. "You ready?"

She sighed loudly. "Do I have a choice?"

He grinned. "Nope."

"Then I guess I'm ready."

They started off at a brisk walk, which quickly shifted to a trot. Brock glanced at her. "You ready to try a canter?"

A flash of fear appeared in Kelsey's eyes, but it was quickly replaced by a look of determination.

"Sure. Let's do it."

Brock's admiration for her grew. It seemed there was no challenge too daunting. It showed a lot of grit and courage. They were good qualities for anyone to possess. He kicked Calypso into a canter and encouraged Kelsey to do the same with Shiloh. A moment later, they were both cantering down the road. At first, Kelsey bounced all over the place and looked completely terrified, but with Brock's continued gentle instruction and encouragement as he rode by her side, she relaxed into the rocking movement and slowly, her fear and uncertainty eased.

"This is fun." She laughed.

The joyous sound of it, along with the delight on her face, struck a chord deep inside him. The joy on her face seemed to permeate his soul. He couldn't remember feeling so good or so happy to be with someone.

I'm a goner for sure... Who'd have thought I could fall so quickly... Especially after that debacle with Cecelia...

The first place Brock stopped was a natural mountain-fed spring with water breathtakingly clear and sweet. They cupped their hands in it and bent their heads and drank until they were replete. The horses also took their fill.

"It's so sweet and cold!" Kelsey exclaimed. "What makes it that way?"

"The sandstone mainly. The water travels for miles underground before it reaches the surface."

"It's the best water I've ever tasted." She paused and gave Brock a tender look. "Thank you for bringing me here."

He flushed at the warmth in her gaze. "Hey, this is only the start of it. There's plenty more to come yet."

She smiled. "I can't wait."

They climbed back on the horses and started to ascend. The wild scrub and thick brush that covered the ground made progress difficult, but Brock knew this country like the back of his hand, and he continued to lead them upward. There was a lookout at the top of the mountain that Brock and his siblings had discovered when they were kids. Their grandfather had carved out a rough track that was now mostly overgrown, but Brock unerringly found the way forward. Every now and then, he glanced behind him to check on Kelsey and encourage her along.

"How are you doing back there?" he asked when they were about halfway to their destination.

"I'm fine. Are you sure this is okay for Shiloh? It's awfully steep."

"She's used to traversing these mountains. Don't worry. She'll be fine. Just relax your hold on the reins and let her find the easiest path."

When they reached the top, Kelsey marveled at the uninterrupted three-hundred-and-sixty-degree view of the valley and beyond.

"This is amazing," she gasped.

He nodded. "Yes. It is. I always loved coming here when I was a kid. I still love it but it's rare that I have the time to come when I'm home for a visit."

"The view is unbelievable. You can see for miles and miles."

He smiled. "Was it worth all the pain on Shiloh's back?"

Her eyes shone. "You bet."

After securing the horses to a branch of an ancient red gum, he untied the picnic basket and spread out the red-checked tablecloth in an area cleared a long time ago for just that purpose.

"You bought food?" Kelsey exclaimed in delight.

"Absolutely. It's close enough to lunchtime. You hungry?"

"Starving. I skipped breakfast."

"You skipped breakfast?"

"Yes. I found your note when I got up and couldn't wait to see you."

She flushed adorably and looked a little uncertain. He shifted until he was close enough to press a kiss on her lips.

"I love that you were eager to see me again. I couldn't wait to see you again either."

They shared a tender smile. Brock's heart turned over.

"What's that over there?" Kelsey asked, breaking the moment. She pointed toward a nearby mountain range.

"That's the Carnarvon Ranges. They're a plateau section of the Great Dividing Range that runs from Dauan Island, located on the northern edge of the Cape York Peninsula in Queensland, and terminates at the Wimmera plains way down south in Victoria," he explained. "It runs for a total of about two thousand one hundred and seventy-five miles and is the fifth longest land-based mountain chain in the world and the longest mountain range entirely in a single country. The Carnarvon runs for about one hundred miles of it. Of course, our mountain ranges aren't as high as the ones you have in the US. In fact, Australia is the world's flattest continent."

"Well, that hardly matters looking at them from up here," Kelsey responded. "They're spectacular. I love that red color. It looks like it's been set on fire by the sun."

"Yes, it's beautiful, isn't it? It's even more magnificent at sunset."

She looked around them. "I can't believe the cycads. They're enormous. They must be a hundred years old."

Brock chuckled. "There's a reason they're called dinosaur plants."

"We grow them over in Florida too. I've always found them fascinating."

"Prickly, though. You don't want to get too close."

She laughed. "Absolutely."

"Let's eat."

He proceeded to unpack the contents of the picnic basket. He was thrilled to see the wide variety of finger food his mother had thoughtfully supplied. There were mini quiches and sandwiches, home-baked chocolate chip biscuits, and a selection of fresh strawberries, mandarins, and oranges. A carafe of iced tea completed the feast.

"Wow, this looks so wonderful," Kelsey said. "Did you put this together?"

"I had a little help from my Mum," he admitted.

"Thank you, Ellen! She's a treasure."

"That she is."

There was a pause in conversation while they busied themselves sampling the delicious offerings. They even indulged a little in feeding each other strawberries. Brock couldn't remember ever feeling so happy and relaxed. He didn't want the day to end.

"Tell me more about your mother."

Chapter Thirteen

♥

Kelsey froze. When Brock had previously asked about her family, she'd managed to keep the conversation rather vague. It wasn't that she had anything to hide. More a fear that he might misinterpret her actions. It was true she needed the million dollars to help her mother, and to get it, she needed to marry before she turned thirty. But she was hoping not to have to marry for the sake of securing the money. She wanted to marry someone she loved and who loved her.

But with her mother getting sicker by the day, she hoped she wouldn't be put to the test. Because she knew deep down that if she hadn't found someone by the deadline, she'd marry the devil himself, even for a short time, if that meant giving her mother a chance to live. After all, her grandmother hadn't stipulated that she had to *stay* married.

Noticing the expectant look on Brock's face, she cast around for an answer. "What would you like to know?"

He shrugged. "I don't know. Are you close?"

"Yes. I'd say we're very close. I'm an only child. No competition for her time or affection," she quipped.

"I remember you told me she was happy for you to take a job on the other side of the world."

"Yes. She's always been supportive of my career, and it's only for twelve months. Half that time's gone already."

He winced as if the reminder was painful. Kelsey bit her lip, realizing too late that she probably shouldn't have drawn attention to the short time she had left in his country.

"Anyway," she added hurriedly, "we talk on the phone as often as we can. And we Zoom. The time difference makes things a bit tricky, but we manage to make it work most of the time."

"Does she work?"

"No, she's sixty-nine. She used to be a high school teacher, but she retired when she turned sixty."

Brock's eyebrows rose in surprise. "So, she was forty when you were born?"

"Yes. She didn't get married until she was in her mid-thirties. A late starter. Then they had problems getting pregnant. A few miscarriages. Hence the reason why I'm an only child."

She paused and considered telling him about her mother's illness. If they were going to get serious, he needed to know that much at least. He still didn't have to know about the money. Coming to a decision, she took hold of her courage and spoke again.

"Unfortunately, my mother's not in good health. That's the main reason she's not able to travel."

Brock looked genuinely upset. "Oh, I'm sorry to hear that. Is it serious?"

"Unfortunately, yes. She's been diagnosed with a rare form of blood cancer. She's exhausted the conventional treatments, and things aren't looking too good."

Brock's eyes widened in shock. "Wow. That's way more serious than I imagined. How terrible for you both. Are the doctors offering any hope?"

Kelsey nodded. "Some. There's an experimental treatment that's showing promising results. Her doctor's invited her to give a try."

"I guess that's good news. Is she going to do it?"

Kelsey compressed her lips and nodded again. "Yes. Just as soon as we can get the money together. The experimental treatment isn't covered by Medicare or her health insurance. We have to find the money for it ourselves."

Brock shook his head. "Wow. That's tough. I can imagine something like that won't come cheap."

"You're right." She gave him a tight smile.

"So, we're both on the lookout for a windfall," he joked.

She nodded. "I guess so."

He handed her the dish of remaining strawberries, and she popped one in her mouth. He chose an orange and started to peel it. "What are your chances of securing your funding?"

She froze. Here was the moment of truth. The moment when she could come clean about her subterfuge and clear the air between them. Only, things were going so well between them. She was scared to do anything that might disrupt the warm camaraderie they'd established. She wanted to do everything she could to grow those feelings. Coming clean now could jeopardize everything.

Better to wait until she was more secure in the way he felt about her.

Coward.

She grimaced inwardly. It was true. She was a coward. But better a coward than to destroy the fragile connection she and Brock had built.

"I'm hopeful we'll secure the money," she replied.

"Will you return to the States when she undergoes treatment?"

He asked the question in a casual tone, but she saw the sharp interest in his gaze. He cared about her answer. She wanted to hope that meant he cared about her.

"Yes, of course."

His expression shuttered. "I see."

She could tell he was thinking her departure might be imminent. She hurried to reassure him. "It'll probably take another month or so to get the money together. At least. Don't worry. I'm not going anywhere for the moment. You're not going to get rid of me that easily," she quipped in an effort to lighten the mood.

He reached over and ran a finger slowly down her cheek. "Your mother's lucky to have such a loving daughter."

"You're so sweet, but don't make this out to be more than it is. She's my mother and I love her. I'm her only child. If there's anything I can do to help her, I will. End of story."

"I guess that makes me lucky in a way. If anyone in my family ever has a health crisis, there are plenty of us to step up and help out."

"Do you think that's one of the reasons your parents had so many children?" she teased.

"I think that had more to do with the fact that for the first ten years or so living on the farm, they didn't have any electricity."

Kelsey laughed. "It must have been fun having all those brothers and sisters around."

She heard the wistfulness in her tone and ducked her head. Though there had been plenty of lonely times while she'd been growing up, she hadn't realized until now how much she'd longed for a sibling. Her parents had tried, but after several miscarriages and her mother by then nearing forty-two, they'd given up and had focused all their love and attention on her. That had been great, but even one sibling would have been wonderful.

That was another reason why her grandmother was so insistent about her getting married sooner rather than later. Both of Kelsey's parents were only children. If she failed to produce a child, the family line died with her. Like her grandmother, she was also determined for that not to happen. She'd always wanted a family of her own. At least three or four children. She just had to find the man to have them with.

Could that man be Brock?

She stole a look at him from beneath her lashes. The muscles in his strong jaw flexed as he chewed on a piece of orange. His tongue stole out to lick the juice that escaped his lips. Her gaze zeroed in on his mouth. Desire curled in her stomach and heated her core. The same heat that warmed her cheeks.

As if becoming aware of her scrutiny, Brock swallowed what was in his mouth, set the rest of the orange aside, and then scooted close to her side. Their gazes locked. Her breath caught in her throat. As his head descended, her eyes drifted closed, and her lips parted in anticipation of his kiss.

His mouth opened over hers. A delicious warmth and the sweet taste of citrus exploded on her tongue. His lips moved over hers, soft and supple, firm and insistent. His tongue swept inside and met hers, thrust for thrust. Shifting slightly, he clasped the back of her head and buried his fingers in her hair.

His lips continued their sensual onslaught until all her nerve endings were on fire. She leaned into him, desperate to press herself against the solid wall of his chest. Need stirred in her core, flooding her with moist heat. Whimpers of desire escaped from her mouth.

Splaying her hand flat against his chest, she reveled in the taut muscles beneath her fingers. His heart beat a fast tattoo against her palm. She loved that he was as caught up in this craziness as she was, that the same desperate desire raged through his veins.

She couldn't have said how long they kissed and caressed. It was as if time had stopped. When she finally lifted her head to snatch a breath, her chest rose and fell in turmoil and her hands were buried in the front of his shirt.

"We have to stop doing this," she gasped.

"Yes." Brock leaned in for another kiss. "We must."

She giggled. The pure joy of being with him spread through her. She grinned, pushing him back and settling beside him. A neigh from Shiloh caught her attention. Kelsey looked across at the horses and realized the mare's reins had come free.

"Shiloh's on the loose," she said.

Brock got up and secured the horse again. By unspoken agreement, they set about packing up their picnic things. As Kelsey walked toward her horse and prepared for the ride home, she took one last opportunity to take in the awe-inspiring view.

"It's truly magnificent up here. I can see why you love the place so much."

Brock's chest expanded on a deep breath that he eased out. He gazed out over the vista. "Yes. It's always been home to me." Then he turned to her. "I told you it would be worth it, didn't I?"

She laughed. "You certainly did. And when I'm soaking away my sore muscles in a tub tonight, I'll keep thinking about this view." She pulled out her phone and snapped off some pictures, taking care to capture Brock in at least one of the frames. She wanted something to remember this special moment by.

He winked. "While you're at it, don't forget to think about *this*."

With that, he took her in his arms and kissed her thoroughly. They were both breathing hard once again when it was over. Flustered and with her heart pounding, Kelsey climbed back on her horse. All the way down the mountain, she couldn't stop smiling.

It was Kelsey's last night at Marlowe Downs and everyone was in high spirits. Surprising everyone, Raine and Isabella had flown in from Brisbane that afternoon and were now seated together at the table, along with the rest of the family. One of Brock's sisters, Emma, had also managed to get a couple of nights off from her busy job with the Royal Flying Doctors and now sat next to their mother, catching up on the happenings around the farm.

Cayd had quietly filled Brock in on the latest concerning the sick cow. The government vet had been out and carried out the testing on the whole herd. Now it was a matter of waiting for the results. Brock prayed that they'd be spared the difficulty of dealing with a positive test. The good news so far was that only one cow had exhibited symptoms, and according to Cayd, she appeared to be getting better.

The room was filled with conversation and laughter as family members caught up on each other's lives. The tinkling of glassware and the chime of cutlery on crockery only added to the din. Emma kept tossing curious glances in Brock's direction, her gaze resting meaningfully on Kelsey each time. Brock avoided the silent question in her eyes. He was falling hard for Kelsey, but that was nobody's business. At least, not yet. They had the little matter of the loan to deal with first.

Once that was done, no matter the outcome, he'd be free to pursue a relationship with Kelsey out in the open. Of course, there was the added complication that her home was on the other side of the world and her mother was waiting desperately upon her return, but he was confident that if they decided to move forward together, they'd be able to work through those challenges.

Taking advantage of having Raine seated across from him, Brock asked about their business.

"Everything's fine," Raine replied. "I've managed to hold down the fort. I owe you a few days, anyway. Take all the time off you want."

Brock chuckled. "More than a few days. I seem to recall when you were courting Isabella, you went missing in action for weeks at a time. Clocking up frequent-flier points like they were going out of fashion," he teased.

"Hey!" Raine protested. "It wasn't my fault the love of my life lived in Sydney!"

Beside him, Isabella turned and pressed a quick kiss against her husband's cheek. "Aren't you lucky it was only Sydney. Imagine if I'd lived overseas."

Brock groaned. "Exactly! Look at Kelsey!"

The words were out of his mouth before he realized. As all eyes turned toward him, heat exploded across his face.

Great. I was trying to keep a tight lid on whatever this is between Kelsey and I... Now I've blown it...

He hazarded a glance at Kelsey, but apart from an adorable pink blush staining her cheeks, she appeared mostly pleased.

Before anyone at the table could respond, Kelsey spoke. "Raine. Isabella. I meant to congratulate you on your pregnancy. Such exciting news!"

Her words fell into a sudden silence. Brock choked on the food in his mouth.

Shit. I meant to say something to her. Tell her it was a secret... Now it's too late. Shit.

He found the courage to glance at Raine and Isabella. Isabella's eyes were wide with surprise. Raine's expression had turned dark. As if sensing the sudden tension, Kelsey looked from one to the other and then to the faces around the table. Everyone stared at her with various degrees of curiosity, surprise and delight. She ducked her head, embarrassed at the realization she'd unknowingly let the cat out of the bag.

"You're having a baby?" Emma exclaimed, looking from Raine to Isabella, her eyes shining with excitement.

Isabella nodded. "Yes. We are."

"That's wonderful news," Brock's mother said, clapping her hands.

"Congratulations," Bob murmured, his gaze reflecting his pleasure in the announcement.

"I-I'm sorry," Kelsey stammered, her gaze briefly scanning those present. "I didn't realize you hadn't been told."

"It's my fault," Brock said. "I told Kelsey when she was back in Brisbane."

Isabella frowned. "Why would you do that? We wanted to wait until the danger period had passed before we told anyone."

"It's a long story. Kelsey was meant to meet with Raine and me about the loan. Raine was called out at the last minute to attend your ultrasound appointment. I had to offer Kelsey some kind of explanation for Raine's absence."

"So you opted for the truth," Isabella finished. "Fair enough."

Brock swallowed a sigh of relief, pleased Isabella appeared to be taking this so well. He glanced at his brother and was relieved that Raine's earlier irritation also seemed to have passed.

"When are you due?" their mother asked.

"The end of November," Isabella replied.

Ellen clapped her hands together. "A spring baby! How lovely! The weather will be perfect that time of year."

"What's the weather got to do with giving birth?" Raine asked drolly.

"Not the birthing part, silly," his mother replied. "It's the getting up in the middle of the night. November's still pleasant. Not too hot or cold. Perfect weather to be nursing a baby."

"Okay. Sorry I asked," Raine mumbled, color staining his cheeks.

Everyone around the table laughed and once again, the conversation resumed. Brock squeezed Kelsey's hand under the table.

"Sorry," he murmured. "I meant to tell you to keep that news to yourself. The truth is, I forgot all about the baby until now."

"That's all right," Kelsey said. "I understand. You've been kind of...distracted since we arrived."

He grinned, relieved that she wasn't going to hold it against him. "Too right."

Their gazes caught and held, and Brock's pulse skyrocketed. In an instant, he was back on the mountain, surrounded by the glory of nature, making love to Kelsey with his mouth. The memories had his cock straining against the zipper of his jeans. He bit back a groan and shifted uncomfortably, glad that nobody could see.

To his relief, his father tapped on his glass with a fork, distracting Brock from his predicament.

"I'd like to propose a toast to the first Fairfax grandchild," Bob said. "To Raine and Isabella. Let the family dynasty continue."

Everyone touched their glasses together amid another round of good cheer and murmured congratulations. Brock touched his glass to Kelsey's. The look in her eyes sent a rush of pleasure through him, giving him hope for the future, a future he was suddenly eager to explore. She'd said she wanted to get married and have children. He wanted that too. Had he finally found his soul mate, the woman he could make a life with? He couldn't wait to find out.

After dinner, Kelsey excused herself from the table and wandered out onto the front veranda. Though it was wonderful to be surrounded by so much family and in a room filled with so much love, it was a little overwhelming. She'd never had that. Growing up, her family had been comprised of her parents, her grandparents, and her. No aunts and uncles, no cousins. Now she'd lost one set of grandparents, a grandfather, and her father. Her family grew smaller by the day.

She loved the idea of being part of a large family Sharing adventures and the joy of being together. And so much love. She was disappointed her time at the station was coming to an end. Tomorrow, she'd return to Brisbane and resume her life. She suddenly wished Brock was coming with her, that he was already part of her life. She was falling in love with him. Hell, maybe she was already there.

It was too bad her life was so complicated. Not only because of the loan situation—that would be resolved one way or the other very soon. But she lived in the US and her mother grew sicker by the day. There was no way Kelsey could move permanently to Australia, and she couldn't expect Brock to give up his business and move to the States. And even if he was willing to give up everything that was important to him now, what if later he came to resent her for all that he'd given up for her?

She sighed, full of confusion and uncertainty. Up on the mountain, lying in Brock's arms, the world had felt right, like nothing and no one could come between them. Now she wasn't so sure. And there was the little matter of her deliberate omission of a significant truth for which she was terrified Brock might never forgive her.

"Do you mind if I join you?"

She looked up from where she sat on an old wooden rocker as Raine stepped out from the front doorway. She shook her head and indicated the chair beside her. "Of course not."

As Raine settled himself into the empty chair, Kelsey apologized once again for spilling the beans about the pregnancy.

He waved away her apology. "Hey, forget about it. It's fine. You weren't to know. If anyone's to blame, it's that dolt of a brother of mine. Besides, Isabella's more than fourteen weeks now. We're over the danger period."

"Thank you for being so gracious," Kelsey replied. "I bet neither of you were expecting your news to be shared that way."

Raine chuckled. "You're right. That's not exactly how we planned to tell the family."

Kelsey squirmed in her seat, but there was no anger in his tone.

"So, what do you think of Marlowe Downs?"

She drew in a deep breath and eased it out. "I've never been to a place quite like it. The vastness, the beauty of it, the sheer scope of what you're doing here. Brock explained how you had to cull most of your stock, but this is still an impressive enterprise. I can see why you all love it so much."

Raine nodded. "Yes, the place gets in your blood. Although I was never cut out to be a cattleman, I keep getting drawn back, and while I've chosen a career off the station, I'd hate to see it go under. It would devastate Mum and Dad."

Kelsey pursed her lips and remained silent.

As if suddenly aware of what he'd said, Raine grimaced. "I didn't mean that the way it sounded. Please don't think I'm pressuring you to approve that loan. I understand how business works. Banks are no different to any other business. We all need to make money."

She sighed with relief. "Thank you. I've already had this discussion with Brock. He also understands my decision is nothing personal."

Raine sent her sideways glance. "How are you and Brock getting along?"

Kelsey flushed, grateful for the darkness that concealed her discomfort. She cast around for the right words and then merely shrugged. "Okay, I guess."

"He likes you. A lot. I can tell."

Kelsey's discomfort deepened, but she was also overcome with happiness. "Do you think so?"

"Oh, yeah," Raine replied with certainty. "He's head over heels. The only thing I want to know is, do you feel the same way about him?"

She wasn't used to being put on the spot about her feelings and certainly not about feelings of love, but she liked and respected Raine. She wanted to give him an honest answer.

"I like him a lot too. Actually, more than a lot. I'm falling in love with him."

Raine grinned in the darkness. "Good. That's great. Because I'd hate to see him get his heart broken again."

Feigning ignorance, she asked, "Has he had his heart broken in the past?"

"Kind of. At least, he believed so at the time. To tell you the truth, I don't think he loved Cecelia as much as he thought he did. But she did a number on him and messed with his head. She lied to him about a lot of things, important things. He had some real trust issues for a while. Not that I blame him. Still, I'm glad to see he's gotten over her."

Her heart stuttered. "He has?"

Raine's expression remained somber. "Yes. I believe he has. And it's about time too."

A cautious warmth spread through her at Raine's words. Things were looking promising. She was in love with a potential husband who, if Raine was to be believed, was also in love with her. And she'd managed to find him well before her thirtieth birthday. She was so desperately close to securing the promised bounty that might very well save her mother's life. All she had to do was get him to the altar within the next six months.

"Just don't go breaking his heart," Raine warned, cutting through her thoughts.

"I won't. I promise," she managed, crossing her fingers which lay hidden in her lap in the dark.

"And always be upfront with him. No lies. No mind games. Don't fuck with him. That's all I ask."

Kelsey tried to smile, but it came out more like a grimace. The guilt over her deceit rose to the surface, dimming her burgeoning happiness. She forced the feelings aside. When the time was right, she'd tell him.

When she was sure of his feelings for her, sure that he wouldn't misconstrue her motivation, she'd reveal all. She'd have no other choice. Her grandmother would make sure of that. No doubt she'd demand proof of Kelsey's marriage and might even want to meet him before she agreed to hand over the money and when she did, there was no way the woman wouldn't crow from the rooftops her success over the deal.

No, there was nothing for it but to tell Brock the truth. She just had to find the right time to do it.

Chapter Fourteen

♥

As Brock's ute bounced across the rutted dirt track that led out to the highway, he tried not to think about where they were headed. Kelsey's time on the station had come to an end, and she was on her way to catch a plane back to Brisbane. His gut churned with disappointment and dread. He hated the thought of them being apart, even for a few days, but there were things that needed to be done on the station, particularly if any of the tuberculosis tests came back positive.

It appeared Kelsey was also in a somber mood. She'd been quiet ever since they'd left, staring blindly at the passing scenery, answering in little more than monosyllables each time he posed a question. The sound of her phone cutting through the silence was almost a relief. Before she could pull the device out of her handbag, it was picked up by the Bluetooth in Brock's ute.

"Hello? Are you there, Kelsey?"

Brock guessed from the thick American accent that the caller was Kelsey's mother. A moment later, she confirmed it.

"Mama! It's great to hear from you. How are you?"

"I'm doing fine, honey, I had a good day today. How about you? How's that good-looking cowboy doing? Have you snagged yourself a husband yet?"

Brock stared at Kelsey in surprise. Her face turned crimson. Frantically, she tapped on the screen of her phone, obviously trying to get it off speaker.

"Oh, Mama! You're so funny. Always telling jokes. By the way, I'm with Brock right now and you're on sp—"

"Jokes? Isn't that why you went down there?" her mother spoke over her. "I wouldn't be disappointed if you came back with a ring on your finger, but that has nothing to do with your grandmother's million dollars. You know how I feel about that."

Brock frowned in confusion. Kelsey continued to look painfully embarrassed. With a final, sharp stab at her phone, she finally managed to get it off speaker mode, and Brock was left with only her short and stilted end of the conversation.

What the hell's going on? Snagged herself a husband? A million dollars? What's that all about?

No sooner had Kelsey ended the call with her mother than Brock pounced.

"I thought you said your mother had cancer. You didn't tell me she was also suffering from dementia."

Kelsey frowned. "She isn't suffering from dementia."

"Then what was that all about?"

A fresh wave of heat washed over Kelsey's face. She couldn't believe what had just happened. Her phone must have automatically connected to Bluetooth, recognizing her device from the time she'd traveled with Brock from the airport.

The conversation he'd just overheard... How utterly embarrassing. How am I going to explain it? If only he'd just let the whole thing lie...

She should have known better. She couldn't blame the keen interest and burning curiosity tinged with confusion that now filled his bright green eyes. If their positions were reversed, she would have felt the same.

She tried for a laugh. It came out more like a croak. "Oh, you know how it is. Mothers, right? I'm an only child. My mother's desperate for me to get married and give her grandchildren. That's all that was."

The look Brock gave her made her doubt that he'd accepted her explanation, but to her relief, he dropped the subject. All the way to Roma airport, he talked of this and that. He shared interesting facts about the landmarks they passed, including how once when he was eight, he'd become separated from his family and had ended up lost in the National Park. And for all the time she let him talk, she felt guilty for not telling him the truth.

By the time they reached the airport, it appeared Brock had finally run out of things to say. There was a somberness about him that made her realize she hadn't been much of a traveling companion, limiting her answers, and likely raising his suspicions again. She wanted to ask him when he'd be returning to Brisbane, but something held her back.

Their relationship was still so new, the ground before them rocky and uncertain. The loan business still had to be resolved. Then there was the matter of whether they were going to see each other again. She hoped the answer was a resounding yes, but she was suddenly unsure. As Brock hoisted her suitcase off the back of his truck, she quietly murmured her thanks.

"What time's your plane leave?" he asked.

"Ten fifteen."

"You still have more than an hour to wait, then."

"Yes. I'd rather get here early and wait than miss it."

He gave a lopsided grin. "That eager to see the last of me?"

Her gaze bore into his. "Of course not. I've loved spending time out on the station with you."

He nodded. "I'm glad. I've loved having you there."

He awkwardly glanced away. She looked down at her feet. She wasn't sure what had changed between them, but something surely had.

Was it the phone call? Is that what's playing on his mind? Is he wondering what my mother meant when she talked about husbands and million-dollar windfalls?

Kelsey suspected that he was. Too bad. There was nothing she could do about that now short of telling him the truth, and the way things stood between them now, that probably wasn't a good idea. If he knew that she'd actively sought him out as a potential husband and that there was substantial sum of money up for grabs, he'd get the wrong impression, and she wasn't about to take that risk.

"Well, I guess this is it, then," he muttered, and kicked at the dirt with his boot.

She nodded. "I guess so."

Without warning, he leaned in for a kiss. The briefest touch of his lips that only left her yearning for more. She thought of the passionate kisses they'd shared over the past couple of days and swallowed a sigh.

"I'd better get going. Cayd needs me back at home."

"Sure. Let me know when you have the results from those tests."

He nodded. "Of course. Have a good flight," he added.

She lifted her hand and gave him a wave. "Thanks. See you around."

With that, he turned away from her, climbed into his truck, and drove away.

Her shoulders slumped. She wasn't sure what she'd expected, but she'd definitely hoped for more than that. He could have been seeing off anyone. They both knew there was something between them, but it appeared that at this stage, Brock wasn't prepared to act on it.

Would our parting have been different if my mother hadn't called?

She bit down hard on a surge of disappointment and irritably brushed away sudden tears. She'd fallen in love with him, and she had only herself to blame. She wished she knew how he felt. Raine seemed certain Brock had developed strong feelings for her, but what if Raine was wrong?

How did I manage to complicate my life so badly? I should have told him upfront, made joke of it.

What she should have done was kept him at a distance. Treated the visit as only a business trip, nothing more. Too bad she hadn't been able to do that, hadn't *wanted* to do that. Now she was stuck with this awful empty feeling of disappointment and a yearning for so much more.

The one thing she was glad about was that he hadn't asked her about the loan. She couldn't see herself approving it, no matter how much she wanted to. She'd loved everything about Marlowe Downs and had great admiration for the people who lived and worked there,

but as she'd told Brock from the outset, the numbers just didn't add u
p.

Brock returned to the station in a daze. The sun was no longer as bright. The sky no longer as blue. It was as if a light had been dimmed and it was all because Kelsey was no longer around. It irritated him that she'd come to mean so much to him so quickly. That she now had the power to affect his enjoyment of the day. It seemed ridiculous. They'd known each other less than three weeks and for most of that time, they'd barely had contact. Crazy stuff, and yet, he couldn't deny the strength of his feelings for her.

As he turned off the highway and hit the dirt road that would take him back to the homestead, he made the decision to return to Brisbane as soon as possible. He needed to get back to his life. Raine had been holding everything together, but it was time for Brock to pick up the slack. He had clients he needed to call, investments to assess, and about a thousand phone calls and emails to deal with.

During his few days with Kelsey, he'd steadfastly ignored everything to do with work, but now she was gone, it was time to throw himself back into the melee once again. Besides, what better way was there to fill the void left by Kelsey's departure?

But first, he needed to lend his support to Cayd and the rest of his family, who might very well be facing the loss of what was left of their herd. He didn't hold out much hope of the loan being approved. Surely Kelsey would have said something if she'd been angling in that direction. Now there was the possibility that they had an outbreak of tuberculosis, things looked even grimmer. He'd have to let the bank know if the test turned out to be positive. There was no way they'd get the money then. Even worse, they'd have to destroy any animal with the disease.

As he parked the ute near the shed, he spied Isabella leaning over the sliprail watching a newborn foal. Brock climbed out of the vehicle and strode over to where she stood.

"He's a little beauty, isn't he?" Brock commented.

She turned shining eyes upon him. "I was here when he was born only an hour ago. Look, he's still covered in afterbirth."

Brock looked across the railing. What she said was true. The foal's mother stood nearby, protectively watching her offspring as he negotiated his first few shaky steps.

"I can't believe I got to witness that," Isabella continued. "The miracle of birth. Never could I have imagined being privileged enough to be part of it."

Isabella had been born and raised in the city of Sydney. She'd never spent any time in the bush. Brock understood her enthrallment with watching an animal give birth. Over the years, he'd witnessed the birth of many animals, mostly calves, but each one had been completely magical just the same. He understood exactly how Isabella felt. His only regret was that Kelsey had missed the experience.

His sister-in-law's head was tilted to one side as she stared with delight at the beautiful interaction between the mother and her foal. Brock noticed Isabella's hand had crept to her stomach and now cupped the barely visible bump. Brock was thrilled for her and his brother that they were on the way to being parents. At the same time, he felt a sudden yearning so deep, it snatched his breath away.

That's what I want... A loving wife... A family...

At that moment, Isabella turned and looked at him. She smiled. "What's the matter? Why the sad face? Don't tell me it has nothing to do with Kelsey leaving. I saw the way you two looked at each other. I won't believe you if you say there's nothing going on between you."

He didn't bother to deny it. "You're right."

Isabella regarded him curiously. "You're single and available. What's holding you back?"

"The loan, for one," Brock replied, playing it safe. "For a while, I thought we were in with a chance, but now that looks doomed."

"What loan?"

Brock frowned. Raine and Isabella appeared to be as close as any couple could be. Brock just assumed his brother had told her about the station's precarious financial predicament. But perhaps that wasn't the case...

Backpedaling now, he tried to come up with an answer. "Um... Did I say loan? What I meant was...um..."

Shit. Damn you, Raine. You could have given me some warning...

Isabella glared at him with narrowed eyes. "What loan?" she asked again, her tone now deadly serious.

He looked around in panic, praying for Raine to appear. It shouldn't be up to him to bring Raine's wife up to speed. Obviously, Raine had been trying to spare Isabella the worry about the farm, but he could have filled Brock in on his plan to keep his wife in the dark.

Isabella set her hands on her hips. Her eyes flashed with determination. "I'm not moving until you tell me what's going on. What loan are you talking about?"

"He's talking about a loan we applied for on behalf of Marlowe Downs. The station's drowning in debt. We need help."

Brock sighed with relief at the sight of his brother. He looked at Isabella and nodded. "Yes. What he said."

Isabella rounded on her husband. "The station's in financial trouble? Why didn't you tell me?"

Raine scowled. "I didn't want to worry you, especially with you being pregnant. We both know the first trimester can be tricky, and we've been waiting so long for a baby." His expression grew earnest. "You've been going through IVF. Six attempts before we had success. That time was so tough on you. Hormones all over the place. Emotions awry. You had it hard enough dealing with the ups and downs of it all, let alone worrying about anything else. When you did fall pregnant, I didn't want to jeopardize anything by adding to your stress."

Isabella's mouth thinned in a stubborn line. She crossed her arms over her chest and continued to eyeball her husband.

"You should have told me, Raine. I'm your wife. I deserve to know something like that."

Raine's shoulders slumped. "I agree. And I'm sorry. I would have told you at some point. Just...not then. I couldn't take the risk that something might happen to you or our baby."

Isabella's expression softened. She stepped closer to Raine and placed a hand flat against his chest. "That's okay. I understand. You were only thinking of me." She cupped a hand over her bump. "And our baby. That's really sweet. Just don't keep things like that from me again."

She framed his face with her hands. The look that she bestowed on Raine was so filled with love, a lump of emotion lodged in Brock's throat, and he had to look away for a moment.

"We're in this together," Isabella continued, her gaze still fixed on her husband. "We're a team. Your worries are my worries, okay?"

Raine nodded and smiled. "Okay." He took his wife in his arms and kissed her soundly.

Brock averted his gaze again. He was beset by another surge of yearning so strong, it was almost painful. There was so much love and respect between his brother and his wife. They had each other's backs. He wondered what that would be like. Having a partner who loved him unconditionally and would support him no matter what.

Images of Kelsey flooded his mind, but he resolutely pushed them away. He couldn't think about her like that. Not yet. They had something special going on, but it was also very fragile. It had come to life on the vast plains of the outback. There was no guarantee those feelings would transfer to the hustle and bustle of the city when she was back behind her desk making or breaking other people's dreams with the stroke of a pen, and he was back in his boardroom, closing deals.

"So, tell me again about this loan, Brock," Isabella said with a grin, disengaging herself from her husband and walking over to him.

He shrugged. "There's not much to tell. Kelsey already turned the loan down once. I managed to persuade her to come out here and see for herself what we did. I hoped it might help to change her mind, but I don't think it did. When I dropped her off at the airport, she didn't say anything about it."

"What will happen to Marlowe Downs if you don't get the money?" Isabella asked.

Brock grimaced. "It could be the end of Fairfax beef. Our Plan B is to try to liquidate some of Fairfax Investments assets and cover the shortfall that way, but that's going to take time."

Isabella's mouth dropped open in shock. "The end of Fairfax beef? You have to be kidding! Your family has been farming cattle for generations! We can't let that happen."

Brock offered her a humorless grin. "You're right. It's not ideal."

A look of determination filled his sister-in-law's face. "I want to help. How much do you need?"

"Isabella—" Raine protested.

"I don't think—" Brock said before she cut him off.

"How much?"

He glanced at Raine, who shrugged in defeat. Brock eyed Isabella again. "Five million."

"Done," she said with a grin.

Brock frowned. "*What?*"

Isabella shrugged. "I inherited ten million dollars from my father. It's just sitting in investment accounts."

Brock shook his head in confusion. "You can't do that! You can't just give us five million dollars."

Isabella chuckled. "Of course, I can. I just did. It's yours." She turned to her husband, "Unless you'd rather not."

"It's your money," Raine said.

Isabella rolled her eyes on a groan. "No, it's *our* money. We're married. What's mine is yours and vice versa, right?"

"Of course," Raine replied.

"We'll pay you back," said Brock.

"Of course, you will, with interest." Isabella smiled.

Brock chuckled, hardly daring to believe their money problems might have just been solved. He stepped forward and spontaneously hugged her. Then he whooped and slapped his brother on the back, and while he was relieved their financial woes had come to an end, he was even more relieved that the loan business no longer stood between him and Kelsey. He was free to call her, to see her anytime he wanted. He just had to scrape up the courage.

Chapter Fifteen

♥

Kelsey stared up at the ceiling and started counting sheep. It was past two in the morning, and she had a big day ahead of her at the office. But try as she might, the walls of her Brisbane apartment seemed to be closing in on her, and there was nothing she could do about it.

Ever since she'd returned, her mind had been stuck on Brock. She was lonely without him. She missed him. She missed the wide-open spaces and the silence of the bush. Here, it seemed like every twenty minutes there was a siren wailing outside her window, to say nothing of the rumble of the passing cars on the street below.

The city was never quiet, not like the outback. Even the frogs and crickets eventually went to sleep. She'd been tossing and turning for hours. It felt like she'd been tossing and turning ever since her return. Her problem was, she couldn't stop thinking about Brock. The sweet moments they'd spent together, the laughter, the fun. The sultry kisses. Something as simple as the touch of his hand. There wasn't anything about him that she didn't want to experience again.

It had been three days since she'd returned to the city. Three days since she'd last spoken to him. She didn't know when he planned to return, or whether he'd look her up when he did, and that not knowing was driving her crazy. Of course, she'd have to call him soon about the loan application.

She'd kept herself occupied at work by running the figures again for Marlowe Downs, but no matter which way she looked at them, she couldn't approve the loan. She knew how much they needed the money and she wished there was something else she could do, but her hands were tied.

All she could hope for was that when she gave Brock the bad news, it wouldn't be the end of things between them. He'd given her every indication that he understood she'd make the only decision she could, but that didn't mean when it came down to it that he'd take the news well, or that he'd want anything further to do with her.

Brock dropped into the old rocker that had stood on the front veranda of the Marlowe Downs homestead for as long as he could remember. Cayd handed him a mug of coffee and sat in the chair opposite, his own mug of steaming, black brew in his hand. No sooner had Cayd taken his first sip than his phone rang. He checked the screen and cursed.

"It's the Biosecurity guy."

Brock's gut clenched. They'd been waiting three days for the tests to come back. It seemed the waiting was over. Brock prayed hard the results would be the ones they wanted. Cayd answered the call. The longer Brock listened, the larger the knot of dread in his gut grew.

At last, Cayd ended the call and looked at Brock. His expression was bleak.

"Half the herd has tested positive."

Brock sat up in surprise. "Half the herd? *Fuck.*"

"Yes, fuck is right. We're going to have to kill them all, and no doubt there'll be some kind of quarantine period. Isabella's money won't do any good. We won't be able to restock. That's it. We're done."

Brock hated the defeat in his brother's voice. He'd never seen Cayd like that. It killed him that something they could have prevented had they not cut back on costs would ultimately bring about their demise. Then a thought struck him. He frowned.

"How the hell can *half* the herd have tested positive? There was only one cow who displayed symptoms. Only a single cow who'd separated herself from the herd. You saw them. You were there. Even when we were doing the testing, it was only one cow, and since then she's improved."

Cayd sat forward. "You're right. Something's off."

"The tests must be wrong. That's all there is to it."

Cayd shook his head. "But how? The government vet oversaw everything. He was there every step of the way."

"Yes, but how many people were there that day helping out? The place was swarming with them. All those people from Biosecurity. Neighbors. Employees. I even saw that asshole, Todd Whittaker, poking around, pretending to help. The prick. I bet he's just loving this." Brock frowned as another thought occurred to him. "Do you think Whittaker could have had something to do with this?"

"What do you mean?"

"He could have swapped the samples."

Cayd looked at him with a healthy dose of skepticism. "Why would he do that?"

Brock ran a hand through his hair in frustration. "You know how much the Whittakers want this place! Only the other day, he goaded me again about selling to them. What better way to force our hand than to discover a TB outbreak?"

Cayd continued to look doubtful. "I'm not sure even Whittaker would stoop that low. Besides, how could he pull it off?"

"I don't know, but something's not adding up. We both checked over all those cows. So did Justin, Lachlan, and Aiden. Hell, even Dad cast his eyes over the herd. The only cow we could find who looked anywhere near sick was the one I'd already identified, and by the time she was tested, she seemed to be recovering. It doesn't make sense that half the herd's tested positive. Something's up."

Cayd stared off in the distance and remained silent. Finally, he said, "How are we going to prove it?"

"We can't prove it. All we can do is ask for the herd to be tested again."

"The vet's not going to agree to that. He spent all day out here as it is."

"Then we need to convince him. We can't sit by and do nothing. We can't sit by and watch the people from Biosecurity come in and slaughter our breeding stock. I won't let it happen."

Cayd regarded him steadily. "Look, I don't want to lose the herd either, but I just can't see you convincing the vet to do another round of testing."

"Be that as it may, I'm not giving up," Brock replied. "He must know there were no other cows exhibiting symptoms. Surely he also thinks the results are odd. I'm going to put it to him anyway.

Make him think about it for more than a second. Tell him about the ongoing animosity between us and the Whittakers. Maybe he'll draw the same conclusion as us."

"It's worth a shot."

"Damn right it is."

"Are you going to call him, or will I?"

"Leave it with me."

All of a sudden, he wished that Kelsey was still there. He wanted to tell her about the shit results. He wanted her understanding, her empathy. He wanted to kiss her and hold her close. She'd asked him to tell her when he got the results. Now they were in. They weren't what they'd wanted to hear, but at least they gave him an excuse to call her—in case he was looking for one. Which he wasn't. Not really. Maybe a little bit.

He reached for his phone.

Kelsey mindlessly tapped numbers into her calculator and then made entries on the forms in front of her. She was supposed to be preparing for a big presentation to the bank's board of directors, but she'd been acting on autopilot ever since her return from Marlowe Downs, and keeping her mind sharp and focused on her job had been proving difficult.

The trouble was Brock. She'd fallen in love with him, and she wasn't sure he felt the same way. Then there was the business about the loan. Her stomach still churned with nerves at the thought of giving him that bad news. His family desperately needed that money and now she'd gotten to know and care for them, her decision was especially hard.

Still, there was nothing for it. She was the boss. Sometimes that meant having to make difficult decisions. There was no point putting it off any longer. She reached for her phone.

Before she could dial Brock's number, the phone rang in her hand. Her heart skipped a beat when she saw who it was.

Brock. Of course, it is...

Drawing in a deep breath, she squared her shoulders and plastered a smile on her face before answering.

"Brock. It's great to hear from you again."

"You, too. The farm's not the same without you here."

His deep tones shivered over her skin like a sensual caress. Almost instantly, she was back in his arms, kissing him for all she was worth. With an effort, she pushed the memories aside and forced herself to speak.

"I've been meaning to call you. I—"

"We got the test results back. They're positive for tuberculosis. Not just one. Half the herd."

She gasped. "Oh, no! Half the herd! That's terrible."

"Yeah. It was a shock. And it doesn't fit with the evidence. We're hoping the department will agree to rerun the tests."

"What if they won't?"

"Well, if Biosecurity have anything to do with it, we'll have to slaughter them."

Her heart clenched. "Oh, Brock. I'm so sorry. That's shocking."

"It gets worse. If the department refuses to test again, and we're stuck with the positive results, we're going to have to go into quarantine. I'm not sure for how long, but it could be a number of years."

"*Years?*" she exclaimed. "That will ruin you!"

"Yeah."

He sounded so defeated, so full of angst and pain. And why wouldn't he? His family had farmed there for generations, and it was about to all be destroyed.

"How are you holding up?" she asked quietly.

"Not good. Everyone's in shock. We never expected these kinds of results. We're all walking around in a daze."

"Well, if there's anything I can do..."

"I'm coming back to Brisbane. I'd like to see you again."

Her heart stuttered. "I'd like that too."

"Great."

She heard the relief in his voice and was pleased she wasn't the only one feeling a little uncertain.

There was an awkward pause. "Anyway," she said. "I'm at work right now and I'm preparing for a meeting with the board."

"I'd better let you go, then."

"Yes."

"I'll call you."

"Please do."

"Soon."

"Great." With that, she ended the call.

With a sigh that was both filled with relief and excitement, she leaned against her chair and pumped her fist in the air.

Yes! He's coming back to Brisbane! He wants to see me again!

Though she was sad about the positive TB test and what that meant for Brock's family, she couldn't help the thrill of excitement and anticipation that flooded through her. Brock was returning to Brisbane. She only hoped he wasn't coming back to renew his case for the loan. He had to know that the positive tests had shot that hope to hell. At least she wouldn't have to justify her decision to turn them down. That was something.

Despite all the terrible things happening on the farm, Brock was looking forward to seeing Kelsey again. In fact, he welcomed the distraction. His call to the government vet had proved frustrating. The man refused to entertain the thought that someone of Todd Whittaker's stature in the community would stoop so low as to swap the samples. No matter what Brock said about the inconsistencies in the results, the vet wouldn't be swayed. In the end, Brock lost his patience and had handed the whole sorry mess over to Cayd. Maybe he would have more luck.

In the meantime, he couldn't deny the uptick in his pulse rate the closer he drew to Brisbane. His plane had been delayed taking off from Roma. It was already late in the afternoon. The most sensible thing to do would be to go home, shower, unpack and go to bed and make plans to see Kelsey in the morning. Only, she'd be at work then, and he didn't want to wait that long. He wanted to see her *now*.

The days he'd spent apart from her had been agony. He'd thought about her all the time. Even with all the drama going on at the farm, she'd never been far from his thoughts. He couldn't believe how quickly he'd gotten over his trust issues. Then again, she was nothing like Cecelia. Kelsey's honesty was one of the things he loved about her.

Calling her the moment he arrived back in Brisbane would show her how eager he was to see her, but he didn't care. He was ready to put his heart on the line and declare his love for her and hope she felt the same.

Unlocking the door of his townhouse, he took the steps two at a time to the upstairs bedroom. He tossed his overnight bag on the floor and then pulled out his phone and stared at the screen for a few moments.

This is it. Potentially the beginning of the rest of my life... All I have to do is dial her number and hope for the best...

He had a good feeling about them. There was no way they could have shared such passionate kisses without her feeling something for him. She'd told him she wanted to get married and have a family one day, so he knew she wasn't shy of commitment. Although he wasn't yet ready to get down on one knee, he sure as hell needed to be with her. Starting now.

Tapping her contact details, he waited as the call dialed.

"Brock! Hi."

She sounded breathless, which was good. That meant she was excited to hear from him, didn't it? He cleared his throat of a sudden rush of nerves and spoke.

"Hi, Kelsey. I'm home."

"You're back in Brisbane?"

"Yes. Are you doing anything this evening? I'd really like to catch up."

He heard her sharp intake of breath and then she was laughing. "Yes! Of course, I'd like to catch up! I've missed you!"

Relief poured through him, and he found himself laughing with her. "I've missed you too. God, you can't imagine how much. You're all I've been able to think about."

"Me too," she admitted quietly.

In short order, they agreed to meet at a swanky restaurant in the city in an hour's time. Brock ended the call, grinning like an idiot.

"Yes!" he whooped, punching the air triumphantly.

Shucking off his clothes, he strode into the shower. There wasn't a moment to waste.

Kelsey had changed her outfit four times before she finally decided on the ankle-length, one-shouldered Rhea Costa gown she'd bought more than three months ago and had never worn. Even then, she wasn't entirely satisfied. Though the cerise-colored, formfitting dress clung to her curves and emphasized all the best bits of her figure, this was the first time Brock had seen her in evening attire, and she wanted to blow his mind.

She teamed the outfit up with large gold hoop earrings and a matching gold bracelet given to her by her grandmother on her twenty-first birthday. It was a reminder that her grandmother could be extremely generous when she chose. After slipping on a pair of three-inch black stilettos, she turned this way and that in front of the mirror, assessing the ensemble with a critical eye.

A glance at her phone and she realized she was almost out of time. Satisfied or not with her appearance, it was time to leave. She liked to be punctual. She hoped Brock was someone who also appreciated that quality. Tardiness was a pet peeve of hers, whether it was being late for a business meeting or a date.

A date. I'm going on a date with Brock Fairfax...

Only just a few short weeks ago, she could never have imagined such a thing. *Brock Fairfax.* One of the city's most eligible bachelors. And her. Plain old Kelsey Garland from Tampa, Florida. Stepping out with not only a good man, but one who could have graced the covers of many a glossy magazine.

How did I get so lucky? I hope it holds.

The best thing was, he wasn't a commitment-phobe. They'd talked about marriage and babies in the general sense. He wanted both. With a bit of luck, she'd walk down the aisle with the man of her dreams before she turned thirty and get to pay for her mother's treatment.

In her bathroom, she sprayed perfume on her wrists and behind her ears, then she touched up her lipstick and fluffed up her loose hair. Her briefcase sat on her bed. She regarded it a moment or two and on impulse, picked it up. On the off chance she went back with Brock to his place and spent the night, she wouldn't have to return to her apartment before leaving for work the next morning. She had a number of early meetings. This way, she could spend every available minute with him until she was forced to leave for work.

It was fortunate she'd also begun leaving a change of clothes in her office, mostly for the times when she needed to go straight to the office from the airport after a long-haul flight. The thought that she might spend the night with Brock filled her with a mixture of nerves and excitement. Taking one last look at her reflection, she left.

Chapter Sixteen

♥

Brock had never been to the restaurant he'd suggested, and he was slightly apprehensive that it might not live up to his—or more importantly, Kelsey's—expectations. But the minute he stepped foot inside Alchemy, his misgivings drifted away. First of all, there were the spectacular views. Perched alongside the Brisbane River, the restaurant looked out on the Story Bridge. At this time of night, the bridge was well lit with golden light and only added to the ambience of the place.

He spied Kelsey perched on a barstool, looking breathtaking in a full-length, hot-pink sheath dress that hung off one shoulder and was draped around her body in such a way that it emphasized every curve. She looked cool and sophisticated and as elegant as their surroundings. As if sensing his gaze, she swiveled on the stool and faced him. Her eyes lit up with delight. His gut clenched.

How did I get so lucky?

He strode over to where she sat and kissed her lightly on the cheek. "You look beautiful," he said.

She grinned. "And you're right on time."

He gave a half shrug. "I like to be punctual."

Her smile widened. "Good. So do I."

She gave him a slow once-over. Her eyes gleamed with approval and something more. His pulse kicked into overdrive. Desire surged through him. He'd taken more time than usual with his appearance, which was a little odd given she'd already seen him in business attire, along with his farm clothes. But this was their first date, and he'd wanted to make a special effort.

The Tom Ford suit was one of his favorites. After discarding pale-blue, lemon, and bright red business shirts, he'd finally settled on plain white. Which tie to wear with it had been the next excruciating decision. On a normal day while dressing for the office, he chose whichever tie was closest to hand. But this was a date with Kelsey. A *first* date. More time on the decision-making process was required. A lot more time.

He'd narrowed it down to three: a navy-and-silver striped tie, a textured black tie, or a more flamboyant emerald-green with navy stripes. After much back-and-forth, he'd gone with the green. It kind of matched his eyes. He hoped she noticed that.

"Like what you see?" he asked, his voice husky with need.

"I do," she murmured, her gaze intent on his. "I particularly like your tie. It matches your eyes."

Heat rushed through him again. "Thank you." He perched on the barstool closest to her. "Can I get you a drink?"

"Yes, please. I'll have a glass of red. Merlot if they have it."

"I think I'll join you in that."

Brock signaled the bartender and placed their order. He was pleased for the distraction. His suit pants were already uncomfortably tight, and they hadn't even been shown to their table. He wasn't sure how he was going to endure the sweet torture of being so close to Kelsey and not being able to tear her sexy dress off. He sucked in a deep breath and tortured himself with the question as to whether she wore underwear.

"This place is lovely," Kelsey said, oblivious to his thoughts. "The view is spectacular."

He dragged his gaze back to her. "Yes. The Story Bridge is so close, it looks like we could reach out and touch it."

"It looks so magical, all lit up, and I love how the lights reflect on the water."

He followed her gaze and looked out through the open bifold doors and across the river. "You're right. It's beautiful."

His gaze tangled with hers. The air between them grew charged. His chest went tight. He couldn't look away from her if he tried.

"Mr Fairfax, we have your table ready."

It took a moment for the maître d's words to penetrate the fog of desire that enveloped him. Kelsey touched his arm and he almost gasped. He blinked and cleared his throat and then focused on the waiter.

"Thank you. We're just waiting for our drinks."

Right on cue, the bartender appeared with two wineglasses. Brock took the drinks and, after waiting for Kelsey to precede him, followed her and the waiter to their table. He was pleased to see it had a perfect view of the river.

"Thank you," Kelsey murmured as the waiter pulled out her seat and handed her a menu. He left a second menu for Brock.

"I'll give you some time to look over the menu," the waiter said, and then quietly walked away.

Brock set the drinks on the table and took the seat opposite. He looked around them, suddenly nervous. He cast around for something to say.

"This is nice." He almost groaned as the lame words fell out of his mouth.

Kelsey merely smiled. "It's lovely. Have you been here before?"

"No, but I've heard good things. Have you?"

"Have I been here before?"

"Yes."

She shook her head. "No."

They were spared any further awkward conversation when the waiter reappeared. "Are you ready to order?"

Brock flushed. "I'm sorry, can you give us a few more minutes?"

The waiter gave a brief smile. "Of course."

Brock glanced after the departing waiter and then grinned at Kelsey. "Anyone would think he was in a hurry to go somewhere."

"Maybe he has a hot date." She giggled.

Brock bit back another groan at the image her words conjured. Her giggle had a straight line to his cock. In an effort to distract himself, he opened the menu and scanned what was on offer. Kelsey did the same.

"I think I'll have the antipasto for starters and the gamba d'anatra for my main."

He cocked an eyebrow. "You like duck?"

"I do. Especially when it's accompanied by peppers, capers, eggplant, olives, chorizo, and red wine jus," she said, reading off the menu. She looked across at him, her eyes wide. "What's not to like about that?"

He laughed. "You're right. That sounds good. But I think I'll go with the grain-fed eye fillet."

She rolled her eyes. "But your family runs a cattle station. You can have steak anytime you want. Don't you want to try something else?"

He chuckled and shook his head. "What can I say? I like beef."

"Well, at least have the tortina alia cipolla for starters."

"The tortina alia cipolla?" he said, repeating the words as best as he could. "I'm afraid my Italian's not as good as yours."

"That's all right. It's a tart with roasted onion, pickled mushrooms, and whipped marinated feta. Does that sound good to you?"

"I don't know. I'm more of a meat-and-potatoes man, if you know what I mean."

She smiled. "There's nothing wrong with that, but how about you live on the wild side tonight?"

The hum of innuendo, along with the invitation that shone in her eyes, sent his pulse into overdrive. He wouldn't have cared what she suggested he eat. At that moment, he was willing to agree to anything.

"Sounds like a plan," he murmured.

Her eyes flared with delight, and his gut clenched in response. He wanted nothing more than to grab her hand and get the hell out of there and find somewhere they could get horizontal together. But that would be rude and way too presumptuous. Besides, this was their first date. He wanted to wine and dine her and entertain her with witty conversation. Well, the being witty part might be a stretch, but he wanted to create memories with her. And he also really wanted to get her naked, and that thought was currently overtaking everything else. In desperation, he reached for his wineglass and drained it.

When he set the empty glass back down and looked at her, she was regarding him with bemusement.

"Thirsty?"

He flushed and averted his gaze. "Something like that."

To his relief, the waiter reappeared, and they spent the next few moments giving him their order. He went with the tart for starters and the steak for main. Kelsey gave the waiter her order, the Italian words sliding easily off her tongue.

"Where did you learn to speak Italian?" he asked after the waiter had gone.

"My mother's parents were Italian. They've both passed now, but I have fond memories of sitting in Nonna's kitchen watching while she cooked. She made the best gnocchi!"

As the conversation flowed, along with the wine, Brock's earlier nervousness eased. By the time their mains were served, he was thoroughly enjoying Kelsey's company, although his erection hadn't eased. A casual brush of their fingers as one or the other reached for condiments was all it took for him to maintain a raging hard-on. If Kelsey noticed his continual surreptitious attempts to adjust himself under the table, she didn't say anything, but he could tell from the glittering desire in her eyes that she was as turned on as he.

When the waiter stopped by to ask if they wanted to order dessert, Brock was relieved when Kelsey shook her head. "Thank you, but I couldn't eat another bite."

With undue haste, Brock paid the bill and then ushered her out of the restaurant. They had barely cleared the entryway when she grabbed the lapels of his suit jacket and tugged him toward her.

She tilted her head backward and then leaned forward and pressed a lingering kiss against his lips.

"I've been wanting to do that all night," she murmured.

Needing no further encouragement, Brock groaned and pulled her close. His lips ravaged hers like a starving man, and she kissed him back with just as much passion. Oblivious to the people coming and going around them, they remained locked in each other's arms until at last, breathless and with hearts pounding, they were forced to come up for air. When they finally pulled apart, they stood there grinning at each other like idiots.

"God, I missed you," he rasped.

Her eyes flared in response. "I missed you too." She waited a beat and then asked, "Your place, or mine?"

Kelsey's heart raced like she'd just finished a marathon as the taxi weaved its way through the traffic to Brock's townhouse. He told her he lived on the north side of town, away from the water, but with a fabulous view of the city. It was farther out from her one-bedroom apartment in the heart of Brisbane, but she was dying to know everything there was about him, and spending the night in his home was a great way to start.

As the driver pulled up outside a small block of sleek and stylish townhouses, nerves and excitement rushed through her. She'd been tingling with anticipation from the moment she'd spied Brock walking toward her in the restaurant. He'd looked sophisticated and sexy in a custom-tailored Tom Ford suit. The navy-blue fabric was complemented by his tie. The emerald-green color was the exact shade as his eyes. She could tell he was pleased when she commented on that.

Though she was sure the food was superb, she hadn't tasted a bite. Her stomach had churned with nerves and excitement, and it had been all she could do to swallow anything. Why she'd ordered a starter *and* a main was beyond her. Thank goodness for the red wine. That at least had taken the edge off her nerves and had at least allowed her to maintain her end of the conversation.

Brock held open the door as she climbed out of the taxi and then took her hand and led her up a neat, paved path that was bordered by a low hedge that ran all the way to the front door. When he'd first issued the dinner invitation, she'd hoped to end the night in his bed. Now that they were outside his townhouse, a fresh wave of nerves assailed her.

She tightened her grip on his hand. He shot her a reassuring look. She drew in a deep breath.

"We don't have to go inside," he said. "I could give you a good-night kiss right here and send you off in the taxi. As much as I want to get naked with you, this is your call."

His tone was gentle, insistent. He wasn't going to pressure her into doing anything she wasn't ready for. His words and tone helped to allay her nerves. She wanted this. Wanted *him*. Had wanted him from the first moment she'd set eyes on him in person. The pictures of him she'd found on the Internet hadn't done him justice, and though she'd caressed the hard planes of his body through his clothing, she yearned to touch his skin.

Dragging in a shaky breath, she forced her gaze up to his. "I want to get naked with you too. That's all I've been able to think about."

A smile of relief split his face. "Me too."

She grinned slowly, her nerves dissipating. "Then what are we waiting for?"

With that, they half ran, half stumbled toward Brock's front door. He fumbled with the key. Kelsey took it from him and inserted it into the lock and turned the knob. Brock pushed the door open with his hand, found the light switch, disarmed the alarm, and waited for her to enter.

Her eyes were immediately drawn upward to the high ceilings. Cathedral-like, they soared above her head, as high as the top of the staircase that stood off to her left. The floor was polished marble. The stairs were carpeted. An enormous chandelier hung in the huge cavity, casting soft beams of yellow light around the room.

The area in front of her was comprised of a generous open-plan kitchen and combined living and dining room which extended out through large sliding glass doors to what looked like an impressive deck and entertainment area. Stone benchtops were complemented by modern stainless-steel appliances. The whole area was as neat as a pin, with not a single thing out of place.

"You have a lovely home," she commented, stepping forward and dropping her briefcase on an expensive-looking white leather couch.

He shrugged. "It's nice enough." He tugged her by the hand toward the staircase. "Come on. There are much more interesting things to see and do up here."

The sexy wink that accompanied his grin set her pulse racing. Kicking off her stilettos and hitching up her dress, she ran up the stairs behind him and followed him down a wide, carpeted hallway. They passed a bedroom and a bathroom and a second bedroom that a quick glance showed was decorated as an office. Brock came to a halt at the end of the hallway and waited for her to catch up. Grabbing her around the waist, he planted a kiss on her mouth.

"What took you so long? You can explore all you like tomorrow. Tonight, your time is mine."

He kissed her again. She wound her arms around his neck and clung to him, kissing him back. He walked backward into his bedroom, taking her with him. Their lips remained fused together until they were forced to come up for air. Kelsey took a moment to look around her.

High ceilings were also a feature upstairs, along with another generously proportioned room. Brock's king-sized bed fit comfortably, along with matching bedside tables. In stark contrast to the impeccable neatness of the downstairs area, Brock's bed and floor were strewn with clothes. She blinked in surprise and looked at him with eyebrows raised in silent question.

He blushed adorably. "Sorry about the mess. I...ah...I couldn't decide what to wear, and then I ran out of time to put it all away again. I'd actually forgotten I'd left it like this."

Her gaze scanned the collection of suit pants, jeans, casual slacks, business shirts, and ties that were scattered all over the place and her heart melted.

She grinned. "I'm glad I wasn't the only one."

He chuckled, still looking a little embarrassed. "What can I say? I wanted to impress you."

She closed the distance between them and took hold of his lapels, pulling him forward until their bodies touched. She caught his swift intake of breath.

"You don't need clothes to impress me," she murmured against his lips.

Just like that, the fire simmering between them reignited. Flames swept through her core. Their lips met and melded. Their fingers got busy with their clothes. Kelsey loosened Brock's tie and then went to work on the buttons on his shirt. Shrugging out of his suit jacket, he reached around her and unerringly found her zipper. He slid it down at the same time she pushed the shirt off his shoulders and tossed it to one side.

Fully clothed, he was a fine specimen of a man. Half-naked, he was magnificent, with broad shoulders and a muscular, well-toned chest, the faintest scattering of blondish-brown hair across his pectorals, and bulging biceps that spoke of hours in the gym. He might have spent most of his time behind his desk, but he had the body of a man who did much more physical work than that.

She splayed her hands against the warmth of his chest. "You're beautiful," she breathed.

Instead of responding, he pushed her dress off her shoulders and then slid it all the way down her hips. It pooled at her feet. She stepped out of it and stood before him, clad only in her strapless bra and panties.

Brock stared at her in awe. "*You're* the one who's beautiful."

In a rush to get naked as quickly as possible, they each removed their remaining clothes. Impatiently, Brock undid his belt and shucked off his pants and underwear. Kelsey reached behind her and undid the clasp of her bra. Her panties went the way of her dress. And at last, they were naked. Pressed together, skin to skin, they sighed simultaneously.

"You feel so good," Brock rasped.

Kelsey merely moaned as her fingers explored the musculature of his chest. She bowed her head and pressed kisses against his skin and flicked at his nipples with her tongue. Without warning, he bent and picked her up and took the few steps to his bed. He lowered her gently to the mattress and followed her down.

Chapter Seventeen

♥

Brock was on fire. Every nerve ending zinged. He was taut with need and desire, but this was their first time together. He had to make it last. He'd wanted to spend time planning this seduction. Have champagne on ice. Scatter the room with rose petals. But there had been no time. His desire had hijacked his plans. He hoped Kelsey wouldn't be disappointed.

With every vestige of self-control he could muster, he slowed his racing heartbeat. Kelsey lay on her back, staring up at him. Slowly, deliberately he kissed her, this time taking his time. He nipped at the edges of her lips, pressed kisses against her eyelids, the soft skin of her cheeks. Then he moved lower.

He nuzzled at her ears, kissed his way down her neck. He sucked on the skin where her neck met her shoulder until she moaned and shifted restlessly beneath him. Then he kissed his way to her breasts. Full and round, they overflowed his hands. He bent his head and took one hard nipple into his mouth. She gasped and arched against him.

"You like that?" he murmured against her skin.

"Yes!"

He shifted his attention to her other breast, laving her nipple until it also stood in a hard peak. Then he made his way lower, kissing his way across her flat stomach, pausing to delve his tongue into her belly button and then burying his face in her womanhood.

As his tongue stole out and began to lick her soft folds, her hips came off the mattress on a gasp. "Brock!"

He raised his head. "You don't like?"

"I like it too much. Please, don't stop."

He returned to the task with renewed enthusiasm. She tasted sweet and musky, her whimpers of need only fueling his desire. He was rock-hard and desperate to plunge into her moist heat, but he wanted to make this as good for her as it was for him.

He continued to love her with his mouth. She buried her fingers in his hair. Her breathing got faster and shallower. He kept up the rhythmic pressure of his tongue and caressed her with his fingers before slipping two of them inside her and mimicking the action of his tongue.

Suddenly, she was there, crying out in relief, pulsing against his hand. As she quieted, he drew back up beside her and took her in his arms. Their lips met in another crushing kiss, her passion no less forceful despite her recent orgasm. If anything, the fire inside her seemed to burn hotter. She pushed him to his back and kissed and caressed him over and over, her hand moving from his chest to his stomach and lower.

When her fingers closed around his cock and started stroking, he shuddered.

"Do you like that?" she asked with a cheeky grin.

He growled, "I like it a lot, but if you keep doing it, I'm not going to last."

Her eyes glinted with challenge. She tightened her hold and then flicked her tongue over the sensitive tip. Then her mouth opened, and she took him all the way in. He bit back a groan, closed his eyes, and gave himself up to the sensual onslaught. She had a wicked way with her mouth and tongue that was slowly driving him crazy. When he didn't think he could stand it a moment longer, he pushed her back and again reversed their positions.

She stared up at him, her eyes wild with desire. He leaned over and grabbed a condom from his bedside drawer and quickly sheathed himself before positioning himself between her thighs. Her legs fell open in silent invitation. His cock prodded at her entrance, and then, in one swift thrust, he was in. Surrounded by her tight, wet warmth, he was in heaven. Slowly, at first, his hips moved in rhythm as he plunged in and out. With each thrust, the sweet yearning inside him swelled.

Kelsey's eyes were closed, her face taut with concentration. She clung to him, moving with him, meeting his thrusts, matching his passion. Her little whimpers of need escalated into moans. He could tell she was once again teetering on the edge of an orgasm. And then she was there, crying out, her inner muscles convulsing around him. His movements grew faster, more frantic, until he was at the precipice. With a shout of triumph and relief, he free-fell over the other side.

He collapsed against her, savoring the musky scent of her hair. Breathing fast, he did his best to regain control of his pulse rate. Her arms came around him and held him close. She pressed a tender kiss against the side of his face. His heart swelled with love. He thought he'd been in love with Cecelia, but that had felt nothing like this. Like he was safe. Like he was secure. Like he was home.

Kelsey shifted under Brock, silently urging him to move off her. While she'd welcomed his weight only moments earlier, now that their passion had receded, she was uncomfortable. Mumbling an apology, he shifted to the other side of the bed. His arm snagged around her waist, dragging her with him.

She loved that even though the sex was over, he still wanted that kind of closeness. It told her that this was more than just a casual encounter. It was definitely more than that for her. She wondered if she had the courage to tell him how she felt.

I'm nearly thirty... If I can't say what I feel now, then when?

The pep talk did the trick. She needed to rip off the Band-Aid, know right upfront if he had serious feelings for her. She'd never needed to have serious feelings to have sex in the past, but the stakes were higher now. She was in love with him, and he had the power to hurt her. She probably should have ascertained his feelings before she'd slept with him, but logic hadn't been in the driver's seat.

But now that the passion had cooled, she wanted to put it all out there. She wasn't in the business of playing games, and quite frankly, she didn't have the time. If she had any hope of securing the money, she needed to act fast.

"I hope this doesn't come as a shock, but I'm falling in love with you, Brock."

There, she'd said it. There were a few seconds of silence. She glanced at him from under her lashes, her heart beating hard. His eyes were wide with surprise and jubilation. Some of the tension inside her eased.

Brock stared at Kelsey with incredulity, still unable to believe what he'd heard. "You're falling in love with me?"

She laughed a little uncertainly and nodded. "Yes. In fact, I'm already there."

He grinned and hugged her hard. "That's fantastic! Because I'm in love with you too."

"Really? I... I can't believe it!"

He hugged her again and kissed her full on the mouth. "I never expected for it to happen, and definitely not so fast. It wasn't that long ago that I didn't think I'd ever be able to trust a woman with my heart again. I can't believe how wrong I was and I'm so grateful to Raine for insisting it was time for me to set that hurt aside and try again."

Her expression filled with surprise. "Raine told you that?"

"Yes. He and Isabella are so loved up, he urged me to give it a go. He knew what had happened with my last girlfriend, but he also knew I wanted to get married and have a family of my own one day. Apparently, that could only happen if I gave love another go. And here I am."

The smile Kelsey gave him was luminous. His heart flooded with love. Nothing had ever felt so good, so right. So perfect. He felt like pinching himself to make sure this wasn't a dream.

Then his smile faded at all the challenges they were facing. The problems with the station aside, she lived on the other side of the world. Her mother was sick. Very sick. As soon as Kelsey had the money together for her mother's treatment, she'd be returning home.

When she noticed his change in demeanor, Kelsey frowned. "Brock? What is it? What are you thinking about?"

"Us." He sighed quietly. "Things are so complicated. Being together is great, but what about your mother? She lives in the US. And she's unwell. You're going to return there just as soon as you can. And what about afterward? Are you going to be willing to leave her and return to Australia once the treatment's finished? What if it isn't a success?"

The longer he spoke, the deeper Kelsey's frown lines became. Her hand slipped from his chest, and she eased back, putting some distance between them. From the way she bit her lip, he could tell she didn't have any answers. He understood that. It was far easier to revel in the feelings of love and euphoria and all the good things that came with that, than to spend time worrying about all the difficulties they faced moving forward.

"You're right," she finally responded. "There's a lot I haven't wanted to think about, but my mother's desperately ill and nothing's going to change that. She'll begin treatment in the US as soon as I can make it happen. How long I'll be there, I can't say."

He looked at her closely. "Is there a chance you won't return?"

Once again, she took a long moment to respond. Then she nodded. "Yes, unfortunately there's definitely a chance I won't return. Depending how the everything goes, my mother might not be well enough to travel. Or she might need me. I'm her only family. I won't abandon her permanently."

"Of course not. And I wouldn't expect you to. My family's just as important to me. I'd never judge you for putting your family first."

She sighed. "Then where does that leave us?"

He compressed his lips, hating the grim prospect before them. "I don't know."

To his relief, Kelsey reached for his hand and squeezed it. "We don't need to get too bogged down with all this right now. I don't have the money yet."

Brock eyed her steadily. "But I do."

She sat back in surprise. "I couldn't ask you to give me the money! We're talking about thousands of dollars!"

"You didn't ask," he replied pointedly, "I offered. There's a big difference."

"That's semantics. I couldn't take your money. It wouldn't be right."

He frowned, genuinely confused. "Why not?"

She shrugged hopelessly. "Because you don't have any money. You came to me for a loan, remember?"

"That was for five million. There's a big difference between that and what you're talking about. I could spot that much at least."

"But... I hardly know you! Who offers an almost-stranger thousands of dollars?"

He looked away in an effort to hide his sudden hurt. "Ouch! I'm sorry, I thought we meant more to each other than that. Who tells a stranger they're in love with them?"

Remorse immediately flooded her face. She leaned forward and framed his face with her hands.

"Oh, Brock! I'm sorry! I didn't mean that the way it sounded Of course, you're not a stranger. My goodness, we just made love! I'm in love with you! I know we haven't known each other long, but I want to spend the rest of my life with you."

Her passionate plea and the genuine contriteness in her expression softened his hurt, along with her declaration of a future with him. Though the way forward was hazy right now, the knowledge that she felt the same way was enough. Yes, they had a lot of logistics to work through, but he was quietly confident things would sort themselves out. If they loved each other enough, things would be all right. Wouldn't they?

Kelsey woke the next morning to find Brock asleep beside her. After spending a few minutes gazing at his handsome profile and marveling that such a man could be in love with her, her need to use the bathroom finally drove her from the bed. Afterward, she pulled on Brock's bathrobe hanging from the door. One last glance in his direction and she slipped out of the bedroom and down the stairs.

Her briefcase was where she'd left it on the couch. Digging around inside it, she pulled out her phone and checked her messages. She was relieved to discover her first meeting of the morning had been pushed back half an hour. That wasn't much, but it would give her just enough time to stop by her place first and change. She was relieved she wouldn't have to sneak into her office in her evening clothes.

After sending off a few quick replies to her more urgent emails, she checked the time. It was just after six. That would be about eight the evening before in Tampa. She hadn't spoken to her mother since her return from Marlowe Downs. After everything that had happened, she couldn't wait to give her the news. She dialed the number and waited for the call to connect.

"Kelsey? Is that you?"

"Hi, Mama. How are you doing?"

"Not too bad. It was a lovely day here today. Beautiful spring weather. What's been happening with you?"

Kelsey drew in a deep breath and eased it out over a smile. "You wouldn't believe what's happened!"

"Oooh, I can tell it's good news. Now I'm excited. Tell me, please."

"Well, you remember how I told you about Brock Fairfax and how I went out to his station in the outback?"

"Of course. I spoke to you briefly on your way back to the airport, remember?"

"Oh, yes. How could I forget?"

"So, your news has something to do with the handsome cowboy, does it?"

Kelsey grinned.

Brock came awake to the distant sound of laughter. Looking across the empty bed, he guessed it could have only been coming from Kelsey. Tossing off the covers, he pulled on his boxers and made his way toward her voice. He was halfway down the stairs when he heard her mention his name. Peeking around the banister, he saw she was on the phone.

"They don't call them cowboys in Australia, remember, Mama? But yes, my news most definitely has everything to do with Brock."

There was a moment of silence when presumably her mother responded. Brock felt a little guilty about eavesdropping, but he was curious as to what she'd say to her mother about them.

"I've fallen in love with him, and he says he loves me too! How amazing is that?"

Once again, there was a pause while Kelsey listened to her mother's response.

"I understand, Mama. It's all happened incredibly fast, but it feels so right. He's an incredible man."

A warm glow filled Brock's chest. It was nice to be described like that, especially when she had no idea he was listening in.

"You're right. We have some things to work through. The distance thing is a real concern. And with you being in Florida and the cancer treatment and everything..."

Kelsey broke off while she listened again to her mother's reply.

"Yes, Mama. I understand. I won't get grandma's money until after the wedding, and that's only if we marry before I turn thirty. I'm hoping to convince Brock to go for a short engagement."

Brock frowned, trying to make sense of Kelsey's words. Then she spoke again.

"I know. But there might be another solution. Brock's offered to pay for the surgery."

Another pause. And then, "Absolutely! I'm shocked too. But that's the kind of man he is. So wonderful, so generous. I can't wait for you to meet him."

Kelsey listened to her mother's response and then laughed. "He hasn't even proposed yet, but I think that's only a matter of time. His feelings seem to be as strong as mine. And he's nearly thirty too..

He's mentioned in a theoretical sense of wanting to get married one day. I hope that's how he feels about me."

Brock's frown deepened. Something was awry. He couldn't put his finger on it, but there was disquiet stirring in his gut. He was still trying to make sense of what Kelsey had said when he realized her conversation was winding up.

"You too, Mama. I love you. Talk soon."

With his heart thumping, Brock spun on his heel and bolted back up the stairs as quietly as possible.

Chapter Eighteen

♥

With a sigh of contentment, Kelsey dropped her phone back into her briefcase and stood. It was always good to talk to her mother and even better when her mother sounded so well. Almost her old self. Of course, that might have had more to do with Kelsey's good news.

Her mother was thrilled that Kelsey had found love, although she'd cautioned her to take things slowly. The speed at which things had happened worried her, but Kelsey was fine with it. Her mother didn't know Brock. Didn't know how wonderful he was. Or that he wanted to marry and settle down as much as she did. And knowing she might also collect a cool million dollars as a wedding gift was icing on the cake.

As she ran up the stairs, she couldn't keep the smile off her face. Entering Brock's bedroom, she hoped he was still asleep. She'd wake him with sweet kisses all over his sexy body.

Disappointed to hear the shower running, she paused for a moment until an idea formed. It was bold and a little bit naughty, but she was almost certain he'd like it. Dropping the bathrobe to the floor, she opened the door to the bathroom and stepped into the shower. Brock's eyes were closed as he lathered his hair with shampoo. She slipped in behind him and clasped her arms around his slippery chest.

He tensed momentarily and half opened his eyes. For an instant, she thought he was upset, but then a slow smile curled up his lips. He rinsed the shampoo from his hair and then crowded her until her ass was pressed against the shower wall. With the water sluicing off them, they indulged in a passionate kiss.

His cock was already thick and hard against her stomach. Heat burned through her core. Clinging to his shoulders, she arched her back, grazing her nipples against his chest. He reached down and grasped the back of her thigh, lifting her, opening her. He positioned himself until his cock nudged at her entrance.

She loved the hard feel of him against her, the insistence of his cock as he unerringly pushed inside, filling her, stretching her wide. Then he angled his hips and thrust up hard. She gasped. In the back of her mind, she registered they weren't using a condom, but she was on birth control, and they were both too far gone to stop.

Brock pounded into her, his hold on her hips almost painful. The night before, he'd been all patience and tenderness. Today, he was wild and passionate and furious. She loved both sides of him. As her desire began to build, her nails raked his back. He lifted her off the floor, pinning her to the wall, as she tightened her legs around his hips. She leaned into him. Wrapping her arms around his neck, she was overcome with a need to be as close as she could get.

As the rhythmic pounding continued and the warm water poured down her back, Kelsey's excitement overwhelmed her. She cried out as her inner muscles contracted around his cock. At the same time,

Brock shouted his relief and thrust faster and faster, finally finding his release.

She slid off his cock and down his body and did her best to catch her breath. The water had turned lukewarm, but was pleasant on her overheated skin. She looked up at him and grinned.

"Good morning."

He smiled. "Good morning to you too."

While Kelsey finished dressing, Brock went downstairs to start the coffee. Now that the fog of sex had cleared, he pondered Kelsey's conversation with her mother. He was of two minds about whether to confront her. He'd have to admit to eavesdropping, but at least he might get to the bottom of what was going on. He hoped he'd completely misunderstood what she'd seemed to be saying.

The reference to collecting money upon her marriage was similar to the comment her mother had made on their way to the airport. Kelsey had brushed it off at the time, but having heard it again, and in connection with him, his suspicions were roused. But he owed it to her to give her a chance to explain before he went off half-assed, dreaming up scenarios that might not be true. His gut clenched with anxiety.

On his way past the couch, he noticed a sheaf of papers half hanging out of Kelsey's briefcase. The name "Fairfax" typed in large bold letters across the top page snagged his attention. Curious, he walked over to take a closer look.

Tugging the folder out of the briefcase, he flicked through the first few pages. There were photos of his family and then larger photos of him and his brothers. There were detailed bios on each of them. He was surprised to discover his bio was twice the length of his younger brothers'.

A prickle of alarm raised the hair on his arms. *Strange.*

"What are you doing?"

He jumped. A guilty flush spread across his cheeks. He hadn't even heard her approach.

"Um...nothing." He tapped the dossier against his thigh. "What's this?"

He held it up toward her. Her eyes went wide for a fraction of a second and then her expression cleared. She shrugged.

"It's a file on your family."

"I can see that," he replied in a neutral tone.

"It's no big deal. I research all my clients, especially the ones asking for millions of dollars. I like to know as much about a client as possible. The figures on the loan application don't always tell the whole story. Why do you think I agreed to go to Marlowe Downs? I wanted to get the full picture before I made a final decision."

"And have you?"

The sound of her phone ringing interrupted them. She pulled it out of her briefcase, checked the screen, and frowned.

"I'm sorry, but I need to take this."

She turned away and took a few steps toward the entryway. Giving her privacy, Brock went into the kitchen and started the coffee machine. Her explanation sounded reasonable enough, and why else would she have the dossier? He thought again of her mother's comment about snagging a husband and Kelsey's earlier reference to getting money on her wedding day, but then dismissed them. As far as he knew, she'd never been anything but upfront and honest with him before. There was no reason to suspect anything was awry now. Maybe he was just a bit sensitive about the whole deception thing. Or maybe not. He needed to think about it.

By the time she'd finished her phone call, he had her coffee waiting for her. She gave him a lopsided smile.

"Oh, you're so sweet. That smells so good. But I'm going to have to take a rain check. I'm needed at the office."

He looked at her in surprise. "You don't have time for coffee?"

"No. I have to go. I've meetings this morning, and I have to stop by my house to change." She looked down at her evening dress with a rueful smile. "I'm a little overdressed." She kissed him briefly on the lips and then strode across the living room. Collecting her briefcase, she waggled her fingers in his direction and smiled. "I'll call you."

And with that, she let herself out.

Kelsey stood on the footpath outside Brock's townhouse and waited for her Uber. She was still a little shaken that he'd found her dossier on his family. Though what she'd said about researching all her clients was true, she'd paid particular attention to the Fairfax men. And why wouldn't she? She'd been on the hunt for a husband, and their family had just happened to include several eligible bachelors.

She was embarrassed Brock had seen the dossier. She'd forgotten it was still in her briefcase. Declarations of love aside, she didn't want him to know that she'd actively sought to engage his personal interest. She was concerned that he might misconstrue her attraction to him, that he might think she'd systematically set out to woo him in order to secure a husband, which she had in the beginning, but her feelings for him were very real.

The Uber pulled up beside the curb. Blowing out her breath on a heavy sigh, she opened the car door, greeted the driver, and climbed in the back. Right now, she didn't have time to focus on Brock and what he might be thinking. She had a day full of important meetings which needed her utmost attention. Before that, she had to stop by her place and change. The knowing smirk on the driver's face when he'd seen her dress had underscored that need.

Brock spent the first part of the morning attending to emails and phone messages that had come in during his absence. Raine had done his best to respond to the more urgent matters, but there was still plenty of correspondence to work through. The problem was that his concentration kept being interrupted by thoughts of Kelsey.

He was high on the feelings coursing through him, and yet he was worried at the niggling doubt. Somewhere between leaving his townhouse and arriving at work, he'd decided he needed Kelsey to clarify the conversation he'd overheard. There was no doubt it had been about him. He needed to know what she'd meant—money upon her marriage, convincing him on a short engagement, referring to his offer to pay. In his mind, it was beginning to sound like he was a pawn in some elaborate plan. He needed to call her and seek an explanation.

With that thought in mind, he reached for his phone. To his surprise, it rang in his hand. He checked the screen and answered it.

"Cayd. What's up?"

"I finally got the guy from Biosecurity to take another look at those positive tests."

"Well done. What did he find?"

"It's as you suspected. Todd Whittaker switched the samples."

"Fuck. How did he do it?"

"You remember that day the team from Biosecurity came to do the testing, it was pandemonium here. We had five hundred head of cattle to test. The department was short staffed, and they'd asked for help. Our neighbors were good enough to respond to the call, but that meant there were people everywhere. Turns out Todd helped a little more than most," Cayd said dryly.

"Where did he come up with the positive samples?"

"That's the best part," Cayd replied. "Turns out his own herd is infected. The tests all came from his cattle."

"How did the Biosecurity people discover that?"

"Once I went back to the vet and convinced him there was no way we could have half our herd infected, especially without them displaying any symptoms, he started investigating other possibilities. We both knew Todd had been on our farm the day of testing and he already knew there wasn't a lot of love lost between us and the Whittakers. The vet went over to Wyambee Station and found a large number of sick cows. Todd had no choice but to confess."

"Where did they get TB from? It's been eradicated in Queensland."

"Yeah. Apparently, he imported a stud bull from Africa a couple of months ago. It must have been carrying the disease."

"Bastard. How the hell did he think he was going to get away with this?"

"Well, he almost did. If we hadn't insisted there was something awry, we'd be finished. It goes to show how desperate he is to own Marlowe Downs. Stupid thing is, though, he wouldn't have been able to use the station for a number of years anyway, until it was cleared of the disease."

"Are they going to prosecute him?" Brock asked.

"Who knows? Probably not. He's about to have a large number of his herd slaughtered. Some would think that's punishment enough. No doubt there'll also be a period of quarantine. It's been so long since the government had to deal with tuberculosis, they probably don't even have a plan."

Brock grimaced. "Typical. Still, at least we're in the clear."

"Yeah. I wanted you to know as soon as I found out. I'll let everyone else know right after this."

"What about the sick cow?"

"She's fully recovered. It was just a cold."

"Fantastic. Thanks for your call. It's great news. I bet everyone at home will be thrilled."

"Yeah, and relieved."

Brock ended the call, then leaned back in his chair feeling lighter than he had for a while. A battle where they'd come out on top. Good on Cayd for pursuing Brock's suspicions. The station still had a future. Which reminded him. He still needed to tell Kelsey the family no longer needed the loan.

Kelsey was on her way back from a quick bathroom stop between meetings when her phone rang. She looked down at the screen and her heart skipped a beat while nerves jumped in her belly.

Brock.

Drawing in a deep breath, she smiled as she answered the call. "Hello. How are you?"

"Great. How's your day going?"

"Not too bad. Busy. It's good to hear from you."

"I just had a call from Cayd. The positive TB results were false. They came from another farm."

She frowned. "I won't pretend I have the faintest idea how cattle testing for tuberculosis is done, but how could that happen?"

"It shouldn't have. It was our trusty neighbor, Todd Whittaker. It's his herd that's infected. He switched the samples so it looked like it was ours."

"Wow," she breathed, genuinely shocked.

"Yeah."

"At least that's one less thing for you to worry about. That's great news."

"Yes. The best news I've heard all day." He paused and then added, "What are you doing tonight? How about we go out and celebrate?"

Her heart stalled and then started beating overtime. He didn't seem to be miffed about the dossier. She was pleased he hadn't turned it into a big deal and that they appeared to be back on sound footing.

"That would be great. Do you like seafood?"

"I love seafood," Brock replied.

They agreed to meet in the city at Kelsey's favorite seafood restaurant.

"I'll see you there at seven," he said.

"Sounds great. Should I pack an overnight bag?"

It was rather forward of her, but she hoped Brock responded in kind.

"For sure. Or maybe I could pack one? I'm curious about where such a hot bank manager lives."

His cheeky comment made her smile and she responded in kind. "By all means. I'd be happy to show you my pad."

The day dragged on. Brock lost track of how many times he glanced at his watch. His niggling sliver of doubt about Kelsey's motivation for being with him was far outweighed by his desire to be with her again. Raine was due back in the office that afternoon, so Brock was hopeful he could get away early. He needed to go home, shower, and look over his wardrobe. It had taken him four changes of clothes the last time. Hopefully, he'd be more decisive this time around when he was confident of the end result.

He settled on a simple white polo shirt and a pair of navy-blue slacks. No tie. No jacket. Casual, but smart. Perfect for the restaurant Kelsey had chosen and for the unseasonably warm autumn weather. Not that Brisbane got particularly cold, unlike the southern Australian states, where it often snowed in late autumn.

He arrived early and took a moment to appreciate the water views as he sipped a beer. His position at the bar also gave him an opportunity to watch Kelsey as she climbed the stairs to the restaurant door right on time. He thought she'd been stunning the night before in the hot-pink number. Tonight, she blew him away in a royal-blue sheath that fell midthigh and hugged every sweet inch of her. The color brought out the brilliance of her blue eyes and complemented the warm tones of her skin.

His gaze took in her generous cleavage and then dipped lower. She turned slightly sideways through the entry door, giving him a view of her profile. The rounded globes of her ass were perfectly outlined beneath the stretchy fabric of her dress. His hands ached to palm them.

Blood rushed to his groin, and he cursed. They hadn't even said hello and his cock was already rock-hard. He wondered if it would be rude to skip dinner and go straight to bed and return to eat later. Would she be shocked if he suggested that?

Yeah, probably.

Their relationship was still so new. They had so much to work through, to discuss, to discover. She'd surprised him with sex in the shower, and he was all for doing more of that as often as they could. But emotionally, he felt like he was on a rollercoaster, not quite in control. He needed to slow things down. If this thing between them had what it took to last forever, there was no need to rush. He just needed to convince Kelsey.

Chapter Nineteen

♥

Kelsey stepped into the entryway and smiled at the maître d
who greeted her.

"May I help you?" he asked with a smile, an appreciative glint in
his eye.

"Yes, thank you. I have a table booked for seven. Kelsey Garland."

The man consulted his iPad. "Oh, yes. Kelsey. Your dinner guest
has already arrived. He's waiting by the bar. Let me know when
you're ready to be shown to your table."

"Thank you."

The man showed her the way to the bar. She spotted Brock almost
immediately. Tall and broad-shouldered and impossibly handsome,
he stuck out from the other men like a prized bull surrounded by
steers. Her heart did a quick somersault as nerves mingled with a
clench of desire. He had his back to the bar, sitting nonchalantly on
a stool, legs spread wide and watching her walk toward him.

I can't believe he's mine...

The thought brought a whimsical smile to her lips and an added
sway to her hips as she approached him.

"Hey, you," she whispered in a sultry tone.

"Hello, gorgeous." He looked her over through heavy-lidded eyes, making it clear he appreciated what he saw. "How about you come a little closer and give me a kiss."

She wanted to crawl into his lap, but managed to restrain herself and leaned closer, brushing her lips against his in a teasing taste.

"A little closer," he murmured.

She moved in between his legs and upped the ante, sliding her hand up the side of his face before plunging her fingers into his hair. She fused her lips to his, putting everything she felt for him into the kiss. When they finally broke apart, they were both out of breath.

She smiled. "Hey, you," she said again.

"It's good to see you again. It's been so long."

"I know. I didn't think the day was ever going to end."

"Me, either," he admitted with a smile.

"Kelsey! Fancy seeing you here."

Surprised to hear her name, Kelsey turned and came face-to-face with one of her staff. She bit back a groan. Rochelle Williams had been passive-aggressive toward her ever since Kelsey had refused to hand over the Fairfax account. Kelsey was almost certain the woman had wanted the account to gain access to the eligible Fairfax men. Not that Kelsey could blame her. After all, she'd had the same idea.

Kelsey forced a smile. She hadn't seen Rochelle since her return from Marlowe Downs. "Rochelle. How're you doing?"

The other woman's gaze rested pointedly on Brock before sliding back to Kelsey.

"I'm doing fine, but not as well as you. It looks like you got what you wanted." Once again, the woman looked at Brock and then back at Kelsey.

"I'm not sure what you mean," Kelsey replied tightly, hoping her colleague hadn't witnessed their recent passionate display.

"Oh, come on. No need to be coy. I saw the two of you kissing. Surely you're not going to pretend this is a business dinner?"

Kelsey noticed a frown now marred the smooth skin of Brock's forehead. He stood abruptly, towering over the petite Rochelle.

"I'm Brock Fairfax," he said, holding out his hand toward Kelsey's loan officer.

"Rochelle Williams. I work with Kelsey. Did she tell you how she fought off all of us for your account?" Rochelle shot Kelsey a narrow-eyed look before bestowing a brittle smile on Brock. "Yes, she's a smart one, is our Kelsey. She knew exactly what she wanted and how to get it. Or should I say, *him*. And look at how well things worked out for her. She snagged herself one of Brisbane's most eligible bachelors. Clever girl."

Kelsey's face burned with embarrassment and humiliation. The malicious glint in Rochelle's eyes worried her. Deciding to go on the offensive to minimize the damage and shut the woman down, she laughed.

"Oh, come on, Rochelle. Our high-powered clients are always managed by the bank manager, you know that. I was just ensuring service of the Fairfax account was undertaken at the appropriate level. Now, if you'll excuse us, we have an evening to enjoy."

Turning abruptly, she hooked her arm through Brock's and steered him in the direction of the maître d, who'd thankfully caught her eye. She snuck a glance at Brock, and her stomach sank. Confusion and a hint of anger clouded his gaze. But he continued to walk with her, allowing her to take the lead. As the maître d' showed them to their table, she tamped down hard on her burgeoning panic. She needed to stay in control of the situation. So much was at stake.

Brock took his seat, still looking far from amused. He stared at Kelsey across the table. "What the hell was that all about?"

Brock's head spun, and it wasn't from the beer. First the mother mentioned snagging a husband, now the work colleague intimated as much. Try as he might to keep his doubts about Kelsey in check, they came at him in a rush. Her work colleague seemed to think that Kelsey had deliberately set out to meet him with a view to starting a relationship. He hated how calculated that appeared. Suspicion stirred in his gut.

No, I won't jump to conclusions. I'll give her a chance to explain...

He couldn't deny the guilty look on her face. Her cheeks were rosy, and she had trouble meeting his gaze. Icy tentacles of dread began to unfurl in his gut. Beneath the table, his fists clenched as he braced himself for the worst.

Kelsey's chest expanded on a deep breath. Her shoulders slumped on a sigh. "I'm sorry about that. Rochelle's one of my senior loan officers. When your application came in, she was keen to take on your account. Given the substantial sum of money you were after and the complexity of your assets, it was appropriate that it stayed with me. She wasn't happy about my decision."

"Was that before or after you researched my family?" he shot back.

She bit her lip. Her gaze glanced off his. "After."

"So, you looked us up on the Internet and discovered we were a family of some worth and then you decided to take on our account to see if anything other than a loan came of it." His gaze turned piercing. "Is it true? Were you on the hunt for a husband?"

The color in her cheeks flared brighter, but she finally looked at him. "You're right. The reason Rochelle's so mad is because she wanted the opportunity for herself to meet such an eligible bachelor. I took that opportunity from her and used it for myself."

Anger lit through him. All this time, she'd not only orchestrated their meeting, she'd done it solely for the purposes of meeting him in the hope they might strike it off. He recalled her mother's mention of a million dollars, and his anger increased. He was deeply suspicious that not only did she set out to snag a husband, but she was also being paid to do it.

He glared at her. "What about the million dollars your mum mentioned?"

Kelsey's heart raced. She bit her lip against a rush of emotion that tightened her throat and threatened to undo her. Everything was unraveling. Everything had come out wrong. Why she'd thought she'd be able to keep it from Brock, only heaven knew.

Even if Rochelle hadn't done so, her mother had already more or less let the cat out of the bag. And her grandmother would have eventually done so too, if they'd gotten that far. Oh God, he'd made it sound so cold and calculating, when it was anything but. Were they finished before they'd really begun?

From the way he scowled at her, the signs weren't encouraging. He was obviously angry and hurt and likely jumping to all the wrong conclusions. Not that she could blame him. She'd not been as upfront and honest as he seemed to think she was. For a moment, she was ashamed of her subterfuge. He deserved better. She needed to find the right words and quickly to convince him, or otherwise all would be lost, and she was terrified her heart might never recover.

What if he doesn't believe me?

No. She refused to think like that. She needed to pull on her big-girl panties and tell the truth and hope he loved her enough to understand and forgive her. Before she could speak, Brock glared at her and pushed back his chair in a move to leave.

"There's something I haven't told you," she blurted.

His eyes narrowed, but he remained seated. She drew in a shaky breath and plunged in.

"I'm twenty-nine years old," she said in a rush. "My biological clock's ticking. I want to get married, have a family. Unfortunately, my body won't wait forever. I was vaguely aware of your family. When your application came across my desk, I did some research. I discovered that Raine was married, but that the pair of you had several single brothers of marriageable age. I leaped at the opportunity to meet all of you, or at least some of you. You, in particular, caught my eye. Even more so after that first meeting."

The longer she spoke, the darker Brock's expression became. "So, Rochelle was right," he cut in. "You orchestrated a meeting knowing full well we weren't viable to get a loan, just so you could try and snag yourself a rich husband."

She flushed, but bravely held his gaze. "I'm not so sure about the rich part. You were seeking a substantial loan, remember?"

Brock cursed softly. "Don't give me that bullshit. You did your research. You would have known that Fairfax Investments is one of the most profitable businesses in Australia. We turned over ten billion dollars last year." His expression turned cruel. "You're nothing more than a gold digger."

"No!" she exclaimed, mortified that he would think that of her. "No, that's not it at all. You don't understand."

Brock shook his head, his eyes full of disgust. "To the contrary, I understand all too well." Once again, he made as if to stand. She reached across and managed to grab his arm before he could do so. "Please, Brock. Let me explain. Remember what I told you about my mother?"

"That she has cancer. I mean, is that even true?"

"Of course, it's true! How could you think I'd lie about something like that?"

He merely shrugged and removed her hand from his arm. His eyes turned cold. Desperation clawed at her insides. She had to make him see.

"My grandmother offered to give me a million dollars if I married before I turned thirty."

Brock's expletive filled the air. "You have to be kidding! So, that's what this has all been about. It's nothing to do with your sick mother. It's all about a payday. A million dollars. I can see how appealing that would be. No wonder you were on the hunt for a husband. I was just the poor sucker who happened your way. Did you even love me at all?"

"Of course, I did! I do! I'm madly in love with you. Okay, I wanted to find a husband. But that's not why I accepted my grandmother's challenge. That money might very well save my mother's life. I told you we can't afford the treatment she so desperately needs. And my grandmother wouldn't hand it over any other way. So I set about finding someone. I went on countless dates. I did everything I could to increase the odds. That meant going out with lots of men. And I did, way too many to count. But none of them rocked my world. None of them were my soul mate.

"When the opportunity to meet you came across my desk, I was naturally interested. You were good-looking, sexy, ambitious. On paper, at least, you appeared to have great husband potential. I discovered your older brother had recently married and by all accounts was happy. I hoped he might have inspired you to try it out.

"Of course, you could have been a total asshole or unsuitable in some other way. If that had been the case, I would have kept looking. If I didn't find the right man, I was prepared to make a business marriage with someone suitable in order to secure the money. I wasn't prepared to let my mother die because of my belief that marriage is for life. I wasn't letting what I wanted jeopardize her access to treatment that very well might save her life. And then I found you."

Brock continued to glare at her. "How do I know you're telling the truth? That this isn't a load of bullshit?"

She blew out her breath on a noisy sigh. "You don't. All you have is my word. Have I ever lied to you before?"

He shook his head. "I don't think so, but how do I know? I wasn't expecting this deception."

She didn't respond to that. Instead, she tried again to make him understand her dilemma. "What would you have had me do? Announce as I walked into your boardroom that I was a single woman in need of a husband and that you'd caught my eye? You would have run a mile, and I wouldn't have blamed you. No one says upfront that they're on the hunt for a mate. It's just kind of assumed, isn't it?

It's not like I had to force you to be interested. I could tell from the outset there was a spark between us. Are you going to deny that?"

He held her gaze a moment longer and then lowered his to the table. "No, I'm not."

"There was an immediate and incredible chemistry between us that gave me hope. I wasn't sure if that spark would develop into something more or fizzle out, but I was willing to give it a try. That's why I accepted your invitation to Marlowe Downs. I tried not to give you false hope over the loan. I was upfront about its chances. But I wanted to spend more time with you and see if whatever it was between us could lead to something more."

She stared at him now, refusing to let him get away so lightly. "And it did. And you were just as invested in us as I was. So what if I wasn't totally upfront about the way we met? I took advantage of an opportunity. So shoot me. But I meant it when I said that if you'd turned out to be an asshole, I would have met with you, talked about your application, and left as quickly as I could, and you would never have heard from me again. There's no way I would have accepted your invitation to Marlowe Downs."

His expression remained implacable, but she sensed the slightest softening around his mouth. Feeling encouraged, she continued. "Until I got to know you, I wasn't sure if you were what I was looking for. Good looks and wealth are great, but if that's all there was, I wouldn't have been interested. Looks fade, and money can come and go.

"The reason I fell in love with you is because you're a wonderful man. I'd love you regardless of your looks or financial status, and I'd marry you in a heartbeat, regardless of my grandmother's million dollars."

She dragged in a ragged breath. "I can't make you believe me. That's up to you. I might have taken steps to ensure our paths crossed, but that's as far as it went. What happened after that was completely real."

A lump of emotion lodged in her throat, making it difficult to speak, but she forged on. "I fell in love with you, and that scares me because I realize I'm probably going to have to relocate to Australia permanently and leave my friends and family behind. That's terrifying, because what if things don't work out? And what about my mother? It's a huge decision, but I'm willing to take the risk because I love you. But if you want out, as much as that will hurt, I'll understand and respect your decision. But if you leave here believing the worst of me, I'm not sure I'll ever recover."

Brock's mind reeled. He wanted to believe Kelsey, but what if he were wrong? What if it was Cecelia all over again? A woman lying to get close to him, to claim him for her own. His anger reignited.

He leaned across the table and glared at her. "How can I believe you when you've been deceiving me all this time with your ulterior motives? I feel like the joke's on me!"

Her expression grew desperate. "Please, Brock. Think about the way we made love. Do you think I could have faked those responses?"

A surge of impatience burned through him. He scrubbed his hands through his hair. "How can I believe you? How do I know what's real and what's fake? You've admitted to deliberately seeking me out with the aim of luring me into a relationship. That's so...pre-meditated."

Her expression morphed into defiance. Anger flickered in her eyes. "So? Why is that such a crime? I liked what I saw and read about you. I had the fortunate opportunity to meet you. So I did."

He groaned aloud. A part of him wondered why he was being such an asshole. What did it matter that she'd set out to meet him with the possibility that he might be husband material front and center in her mind? It shouldn't have mattered. But it did. It was like Cecelia all over again. He pushed back from the table again, and this time, he stood.

"I'm sorry, I need to get some air. Enjoy your dinner." With that, he started to turn away. At the last minute, he swung back to face her. "By the way, don't worry about that loan. We've secured money elsewhere."

Her jaw was set at a stubborn angle. "Good, because I was going to deny it anyway. As I've already told you, your family's too big a risk for the bank, with or without the positive tuberculosis results. Don't take it personally. Business is business. I'm only doing my job."

He laughed humorlessly. "Right. Of course. No doubt it was all part of your scheme to get me to fall in love with you. You led me to believe you were on our side, that you were fighting for us to get that loan approved. All you were doing was fighting for yourself, doing everything you could to snag the husband you've been angling for all this time. Thank God I discovered your deceit before it was too late."

She looked up at him bleakly and said quietly, "I'm not Cecelia, Brock."

He started in surprise. Before he could respond, her phone began to ring. She looked at her screen and frowned. "It's my mother's neighbor," she muttered and answered the call.

Brock looked around him. Some of the other diners were casting curious glances in their direction, but most were absorbed in their own conversations. He wanted to leave, but to his great irritation, he was also concerned about Kelsey. His gibe about her lying about her mother's cancer had been said to hurt her. He didn't really believe she'd made that up. After all, he'd overheard them talking about it.

As Kelsey ended the phone call, she looked up at him with eyes that were wide with shock and fear.

"My mother's been taken by ambulance to hospital with a bad infection. She's in serious condition. My neighbor's not sure if she's going to pull through."

Brock stared at her, dread filling his gut. "Oh, Kelsey. I'm sorry. I—"

"I need to go." She pushed back her chair and stood.

"Where are you going?" he asked.

"To the airport."

With that, she slung her handbag over her shoulder and rushed out the door.

Chapter Twenty

♥

Kelsey's heart pounded with fear and concern for her mother, along with the fear of losing Brock. The hurt she'd seen on his face pained her, and that he thought she'd deceived him, just like his ex-girlfriend, was devastating.

She hadn't meant to hurt him by not telling him the full story upfront, but she stood by her argument that it would have been nonsensical to announce at the beginning that she was on the hunt for a mate. Still, Brock's hurt and confusion were real, and she hated that she was responsible for that. However, there was no point worrying herself sick over what had been said and done. Right now, her priority had to be her mother.

While she waited for an Uber, she opened a search engine and began to look for flights. It didn't take long for her to realize she couldn't get a direct flight to Tampa. Her best option was to fly to Dallas and then get a connection. Though there were several flights available, the only flight departing that night had already left. The earliest she could leave was first thing in the morning.

Though she chafed at the delay, there was nothing she could do. That was part of the downside of living so far away from home. On her way back to her apartment, she looked up the number for Tampa General Hospital. When the receptionist answered, she asked to speak with her mother.

"Let me see if I can find her," the woman said.

Kelsey heard the sound of keys being tapped on a keyboard. A moment later, the woman said, "Oh, she's still in the emergency room. She hasn't been admitted yet."

"Can I speak with her?"

"No, there aren't any phones by the beds in emergency, but I can put you through to the nurses' station. Someone should be able to tell you what's going on."

"Thank you."

While Kelsey waited to be connected, she drew in a couple of deep breaths. Her heart still beat frantically. She needed to stay calm. After what seemed like an interminable amount of time, the phone was answered by a man.

"Emergency. Can I help you?"

Kelsey explained who she was and why she was calling.

"Right. She's been seen by the doctor, and IV antibiotics have already been started. It appears she's been battling the infection for several days. It's lucky she called the ambulance when she did."

"She's going to be all right, though, isn't she?"

"Hopefully. We'll have to see how quickly she responds to the antibiotics. I assume you're aware of her cancer diagnosis?"

"Yes, of course."

"Yes, well, that's an added complication, but we're doing the best we can."

Kelsey's stomach clenched with dread. The nurse was far from reassuring. It was clear Kelsey's mother was in serious condition. She pushed down on a fresh surge of panic.

I have to get over there as soon as possible...

The timing couldn't be worse for her to be leaving, but she had no choice. She just hoped there was still something left of her and Brock's relationship to fight for when she returned.

Brock took a cab back to his townhouse, his head still full of Kelsey and her revelations. Through the whole twenty-minute trip, he kept circling through their argument. The truth was, he didn't know what to think, didn't know how he was supposed to feel. Hurt, angry, confused. But he was still in love with her. He wanted to accept that her actions were no big deal, but he felt taken advantage of. She'd taken steps to meet him and get to know him. And all along, she'd been assessing him as potential husband material.

Was that so wrong? She didn't seem to think so. But he was too close to the whole situation to know. As he let himself into his house, disarmed the security system, and flicked on the downstairs lights, he was no closer to understanding her arguments.

I need to talk to someone... Someone with more experience with women than me...Raine.

Digging out his phone from his back pocket, he dialed his brother's number. He was grateful when Raine answered almost immediately.

"Brock. What's up?"

"Oh, hell. Where do I start?"

"Does this have anything to do with Kelsey?"

Brock sighed. "How did you know?"

"An educated guess," Raine said dryly. "Plus, you forget I've been in the throes of new love. I know how it plays with your head. Is there anything in particular that's got you all worked up?"

Raine's calm tones helped Brock settle his thoughts. Throwing himself down on the couch, he sighed heavily. Giving Raine the shorthand version of what had happened, he sat back and waited for his brother's reply.

"So, you're feeling put out that she took one look at you on the Internet and decided you might be someone she wanted to meet."

Brock grimaced. The way Raine put it, it didn't seem like such a big deal. "She deliberately sought me out for the sole purpose of checking me out as a potential husband," he corrected.

"I'm sorry, there's something I'm missing here. What's so strange about a single woman of a certain age actively looking for a mate? Besides, hadn't you already decided it was time to settle down? Didn't we have that very conversation the day you were due to meet? You'd as much as admitted you were ready to dip your toe in the dating pool again. If Kelsey hadn't come along, no doubt you would have thrown yourself into the scene in an effort to make that happen. What's the difference between that and what Kelsey did?"

"Because a date's a date. This was a business meeting!" Brock exclaimed. "It just feels so *sneaky*!"

"Oh, Brock! Get over yourself! Think for a moment if the shoe was on the other foot. If you'd stumbled across Kelsey online and then an opportunity arose for you to meet. Wouldn't you have gone there with the thought in mind that she could be a potential girlfriend?"

Brock grumbled under his breath, but he had to admit Raine had a point. If he'd been in Kelsey's position, he definitely would have been interested in making her acquaintance to see if there was a spark.

"Are you in love with her?" Raine asked quietly.

"Of course, I am! That's why I'm so cut up about her deception! When she told me what she'd done, I was right back there with Cecelia! I'd been deceived all over again!"

"Oh, Brock! Please! Don't be so dramatic. You can't tell me what Kelsey did comes anywhere close to the level of deception Cecelia engaged in."

Brock blew his breath out on another weary sigh. Raine was right. What Cecelia had done was systematic deception that had started from their very first date and continued for the entire three months of their relationship. She'd lied about everything, from what she did for a career to what she drove and where she lived and had taken active steps and had engaged others to reinforce her deception. Kelsey's failure to tell him that she'd had an ulterior motive for their meeting didn't come anywhere near that level of deceit.

The truth was, he was in love with her. He wanted to be with her, regardless. Despite everything going on with her mother, she'd said she was prepared to move permanently to Australia, give up her family and friends, and commit to him. Was he prepared to do that for her? What about his business? *His* family and friends?

He realized nothing was more important to him than Kelsey. He'd do anything for her. He loved her.

I need to apologize... I need to tell her how I feel... I need to book a ticket to Tampa...

The thoughts tumbled one after the other, filling him with a nervous kind of energy and panic. He thanked his brother with a muttered "I've gotta go find Kelsey" and abruptly ended the call. He jumped up from the couch and started pacing. At the same time, he scrolled through his contacts for Kelsey's number. He wasn't sure if she'd take his call, but he had to try. With his heart in his throat, he dialed.

The call rang out and eventually went through to voicemail. He bit down on his disappointment and ended the call. What he had to say needed to be done in person. He just hoped he hadn't left it too late. If need be, he'd fly all the way to Tampa to apologize.

With renewed determination, he took the stairs two at a time and strode into his bedroom. Ignoring the barrage of memories that bombarded him as he entered the room, he set about filling a suitcase. He'd heard the weather was balmy in Florida most of the year round, so he threw in mostly shorts and T-shirts. A couple pair of jeans. A jacket. Underwear and socks. Shoes. Toiletries, cologne, and a hairbrush, and he was done. He zipped up the suitcase and once again reached for his phone.

A quick search of the airlines told him the only available flight was leaving first thing in the morning. Booking a one-way ticket, he sent up a silent prayer that Kelsey would also be on that flight. With a bit of luck, he'd have at least nineteen hours on the plane to convince her that he was sorry and that his feelings for her were real. He hoped that was enough time.

Kelsey checked her luggage through and joined the queue to go through security. She dropped her phone, house keys, and jacket into the plastic container and set it down on the conveyor belt to be scanned. Brock had called her the night before, while she'd been on the phone to the hospital. He hadn't left a message, and she hadn't been in the mood to return the call.

Now she wondered if she should have made the effort. She was about to get on a plane for nineteen hours. Way too much time to spend with her thoughts, not knowing what Brock had been planning to say.

Dammit... I should have just called him back...

She bit back a sigh and walked through the security scanner. To her chagrin, she set off an alarm.

"Excuse me, miss. You need to take off your shoes and then walk back through the scanner," the security guard said.

Holding on to her patience, she did as he asked. Thankfully, this time, all was well, and she was allowed to leave. She recovered her personal items from the conveyor belt and started to pull on her shoes.

"It's amazing who you meet at the airport."

The familiar, deep voice went right through her, leaving her tingling in surprise. She turned and saw Brock standing less than five yards away. The sight of him had her wanting to throw herself in his arms and yelp for joy, and maybe cry a little, and then thump him for putting her through the worst night of her life, but the saner part of her urged caution.

"What are you doing here?"

"Catching a plane. Isn't that what people do at airports?"

The teasing glint in his eyes went a little way to easing her tension. When they'd parted the night before, he'd been an angry, disillusioned man. She wondered what had brought about the change.

She hardly dared to ask where he was going.

"I'm off to Tampa, in case you're wondering."

She stared at him, her eyes wide, hardly daring to believe what he'd said. "You're going to Tampa?"

He smiled. "Yes. Isn't that where you're going?"

Her heart skipped a beat, and she could feel her stupid tears starting to well. "Yes. But why are you going?"

He took a few steps closer, then reached out and framed her face with his hands. "I'm going wherever you're going. To be honest, I don't care where that is." His expression turned serious. "I'm sorry for being angry with you. I was hurt and upset and... I don't know. It was stupid. If our situations had been reversed, I would have done everything I could to meet you. I can't blame you for wanting to do the same thing. In fact," he added with a lopsided grin, "I'm flattered."

A rush of joy exploded in her heart. To her chagrin, she burst into tears and threw herself into his arms and planted kisses on every available inch of skin. While he wrapped her in his arms, she was momentarily beyond words as she tried to reel in her emotions.

"I'm so glad!" she sniffled, leaning back to look up into his beautiful green eyes. "I hated being at odds with you. I wanted to return your call from last night, but I was scared you were going to call things off permanently. I didn't want to deal with that along with everything going on with my mother..."

Brock's expression sobered. Tenderly, he brushed the tears from her cheeks. "How is she?"

"I'm not sure. She was receiving treatment when I spoke to the hospital last night. It's a wait-and-see situation. Depending on how well she responds to the antibiotics...or not..." Her voice hitched. She couldn't bear the thought that her mother might not pull through.

Brock folded her in his arms once again and pressed a comforting kiss against her hair. "She's going to be all right, you need to believe that. And when we get there, I'm going to ask her for your hand in marriage."

For the second time, Kelsey was overwhelmed with emotion. She blinked back another rush of tears.

"You don't have to rush into a proposal, Brock. We still have so much to learn about each other. My grandmother's bribe has no bearing on any of this."

Brock frowned and held up his hand. "Whoa. Okay, I think it's time for you to explain more fully to me about this offer of money. You referenced it last night, but quite frankly, in my outrage at having been taken advantage of by my bank manager, I didn't take it in."

With a sigh, she took him by the hand and led him away from the crowds of people heading toward their gates. They found a quiet spot where they could talk with a modicum of privacy.

"Okay. I'll try to explain it more fully." She drew in a breath. "My grandmother offered to pay me a million dollars if I marry before I turn thirty. Apparently, she's desperate to see me hitched."

Brock's eyes widened. "That's one hell of an incentive."

"Yes, and in the interest of being completely upfront and honest, if it means giving my mother a chance to live, I'll get married in a heartbeat. I know how that sounds—awful, right? But I love her with everything that I am. She gave me life. She loves me unconditionally. If I had the chance to save her and didn't do it and she died, I'd never forgive myself.

"But my feelings for you are real. Falling in love with you was unexpected, but I'll count it as one of the most wonderful blessings I've ever received. I can't make you believe that what I feel for you is genuine and has nothing to do with the money, but I hope and pray you do. That's all I can say."

The tears were back, but there was nothing she could do to stop them. Brock draped an arm over her shoulders and pulled her close.

"Now I understand better what's at stake, I don't know how you stopped yourself from marrying the first man who came along. I mean, your mother's life depends on this treatment."

Kelsey's heart clenched at the reminder. She swallowed against a lump that lodged in her throat and swiped at her tears. "Yes. I was lucky she never once pressured me into marrying for the sake of the money, despite the fact she knew as well as I did what was at stake. In fact, she wanted me to promise her I wouldn't marry for anything but love."

"She sounds like a remarkable woman."

Kelsey hiccupped. "She is."

Brock planted a tender kiss on her lips. "I'm looking forward to meeting her."

Kelsey smiled through her tears and hoped the look she gave him conveyed all the love she felt for him.

"By the way," he added, "my offer still stands."

"What offer?"

"To pay for your mother's treatment."

"I appreciate that. But those costs could run into the hundreds of thousands of dollars."

"So I'll sell some stock. Cash in some investments. Don't worry, I'll find the money."

"We've already been over this."

"And I'm still at a loss as to why it's such a big deal for you. I want to do this for you and your mother."

She gave him a hopeful look. "If we marry before I turn thirty, we'll get the money from my grandmother. Then you wouldn't need to sell anything."

Brock shrugged and pulled her in close for another hug. "I'm keen to make you my wife as soon as possible, but if that doesn't happen in time, that's fine too. Your Mum's going to get that treatment one way or the other. I promise you."

Kelsey was so choked up with emotion, she could barely speak. "I love you so much, Brock Fairfax. You have no idea how much."

"If it's even half as much as I love you, I'm a very lucky man."

He bent his head and sealed their declarations with the sweetest, most tender kiss.

Epilogue

The back garden of Kelsey's grandmother's palatial Florida home had been transformed into an elegant wedding venue. The lush greenery that surrounded the perimeter stood in stark contrast to the huge bouquets of magnolias tied in strategic places, their pungent perfume heavy on the clean summer air. An ornamental lake, complete with flowering lily pads and snow-white geese, provided a beautiful backdrop for the ceremony.

Kelsey smoothed her hands over the soft fabric of her wedding dress. The gown was the perfect combination of classic and modern. From the moment she'd laid eyes on it in the bridal boutique in Tampa, she'd known it was the one.

Layered organza was carried through to the straps of the subtly sheer bodice. The deep V-neckline mirrored the open V-back and created a look that was soft, yet sexy. The lace-covered bodice extended into a princess-inspired silhouette, with lace appliqués gently falling over the circular-cut tulle skirt. The full, frothy hemline extended into a long train. It was exactly the kind of gown she'd always dreamed of.

As the time drew nearer for the ceremony, she was nervous with excitement. She glanced at her mother's reflection in the mirror as she put the final touches to Kelsey's hair. A rush of love overwhelmed her, knowing how blessed she was to have her mother with her.

Thanks to Brock's generosity, her mother had undergone the experimental treatment. It was now more than eight weeks since she'd finished the course, and so far, she appeared to be doing well. It was still early days, but so far, her blood work was good and her doctors were pleased with her progress. Kelsey would be forever grateful for her husband-to-be who'd made it possible.

Now the day had come when they were going to make their love official, and she couldn't wait.

"You look beautiful," her mother whispered. "I just wish your dad were still here. He would have loved to walk you down the aisle."

Kelsey swallowed against the lump that had lodged in her throat and blinked back a rush of tears. "He *is* here, Mama. Right by my side. Where he belongs."

Her mother nodded and sniffed and turned away to dab at her eyes. "He would have loved Brock," she murmured.

Kelsey smiled. "Yes, he would have. He's the best husband a woman could wish for."

And it was true. Since their emergency dash to the US three months earlier, Brock hadn't left her side. He'd put his business interests on hold and had focused everything on her and what needed to be done.

He'd been there while her mother had battled the infection, and later, when the doctor walked Kelsey through the whole process of what would happen during the experimental treatment. There were risks involved, and there was no guarantee of success, and it was important both she and her mother were made aware of that. And though she'd been scared, having Brock there by her side made it less stressful and difficult than it otherwise might have been.

I love him so much... My hero.

"I think it's time. Are you ready?" Her mother's gentle question broke through her thoughts.

She nodded. "I'm ready."

Pushing back the chair, she carefully stood and held up her long skirts. Her mother lifted the train and carried it gently over her arm. Together, they walked down the wide staircase of her grandmother's mansion and across the beautifully decorated patio to the garden where the ceremony was about to begin.

Matching white wooden chairs had been set out in neat rows on either side of a white carpeted aisle, most of which were now filled with guests. Kelsey recognized many of her childhood and university friends, along with a huge contingent of Fairfaxes. She was blown away that so many of them had made the effort to come all that way. Raine and Isabella, who was now more than six months through her pregnancy, turned to smile at her as she approached. She offered them a nervous grin.

As the string quartet began to play the beautiful strains of Pachelbel's *Canon in D*, Kelsey slowly proceeded down the aisle on her mother's arm. She fixed her gaze on the man who stood at the other end, watching her walk toward him.

Brock.

The tenderness and love in his eyes stole her breath. Her heart stuttered and her eyes filled with happy tears. He'd been a mountain of strength through her mother's ordeal, while Kelsey anxiously watched out for some of the many side effects, hoping against hope that the treatment would work. Brock never wavered in his support for her and her mother in whatever capacity he was needed.

As she reached his side, she caught a glimpse of her grandmother out of the corner of her eye. The old woman beamed with approval. Kelsey gave her a cheeky grin as her mother moved into position beside her. The two women smiled at each other. Another miracle.

Kelsey was glad that her mother and grandmother had finally called a truce. After so many years, her grandmother had at last set aside her animosity for her only son's wife and embraced her daughter-in-law as she should have done right from the beginning. Better late than never.

Kelsey had cried when her grandmother had asked her mother to move in with her, telling her that there were far too many rooms in her house for just one person and she could think of no one better to share it with. Knowing the two most important women in her life now had each other to rely on filled Kelsey with happiness and relief.

The wedding dance was over, the cake had been cut, and the reception was winding down, along with the guests. Brock surveyed the happy crowd of well-wishers and couldn't contain his joy. He and Kelsey were now husband and wife, and he couldn't be happier. After the past few hectic months of hospital and outpatient visits and supporting both Kelsey and her mother through a very difficult and concerning time, it was nice to be able to take a breath and relax. They wouldn't know for some time whether the treatment had worked for Maria, but so far, the signs were looking good.

He spied Kelsey talking to his sisters and headed over to steal her away. He was about done with the celebrations. It was time to take her back to the sumptuous hotel room he'd booked and make love to her for the rest of the night.

Drawing her away from his family, he led her to a spot in the garden that overlooked the glassy lake. The moon rose high, casting a yellow path over its silvery surface, burnishing everything in gold. Taking her in his arms, he kissed her thoroughly.

"I've been wanting to do that all night," he murmured against the silkiness of her neck.

She chuckled. "Then what's been holding you back? We're married now. No one's going to stop us."

She tilted her head back, and their lips met in another heated kiss. By the time they drew apart, they were breathless.

"I think it's time to head to the honeymoon suite." He winked.

"Sounds good to me."

Hand in hand, they strolled back to where the wedding guests were gathered and bid everyone a farewell. Having opened the door to the five-star hotel room he'd arranged to have decorated with candles and rose petals, Brock lifted Kelsey into his arms and carried her over the threshold. She gasped in delight at the romantic scene that greeted her. Even he was impressed.

More than a dozen candles cast their golden glow over the darkened room. Thousands of fragrant rose petals covered the king-sized bed. A bottle of champagne was cooling in an ice bucket on the bedside table, along with two crystal champagne glasses. Still in his arms, Kelsey kissed him lingeringly on the lips.

"This is so beautiful. You went to so much trouble. I love it."

He slid her body slowly down his until her feet reached the carpet, pressing her against his rock-hard cock.

"Can you feel how much I want you, Mrs Fairfax?"

She grinned. "I want you just as much. But first, my grandmother gave me this." She handed him an envelope. It had Kelsey's name written on the front of it.

"It's addressed to you."

She rolled her eyes. "We're married now. What's mine is yours, and vice versa. Please, I want you to open it."

Slowly, he did as she asked. He pulled out a check made out to her for a cool million dollars.

"Looks like grandma came through for us." She chuckled.

"So it does," he said, tossing the check over his shoulder and then burying his face in her breasts.

"There's just one more thing," she gasped as he pulled the low neckline to one side and began to suck on her nipple.

"Can't it wait until later?" he grumbled. "I'm busy making love to my wife."

"Grandma said there's another million in it if we give her a great-grandchild within the first year."

Brock lifted his head and cocked an eyebrow, a speculative gleam in his eye. "Another million? That's a lot of money."

She nodded sagely. "It is."

Brock grinned. "I've always loved a challenge. Especially one that will be as pleasurable as this one. Let's get cracking, then, shall we?"

With that, he swung her off her feet and lowered her into the middle of the bed, scattering rose petals everywhere. Watching her laugh at his antics, he basked in the joy on her face. This brave, beautiful, inspirational woman was his. Whether they stayed in the US or made a life back in Australia remained to be seen. Where they lived no longer mattered. As long as they were together.

The End

Get a free book when you sign up for Chris Taylor's newsletter at: http://www.christaylorauthor.com.au

If you enjoyed Brock and Kelsey's story don't forget to leave a review at your favorite digital retailer. Every review is really appreciated and helps with visibility so that other readers can find and enjoy my books.

A Cattleman's Quest is the next book in the Fairfax Family Series. Keep reading for a sneak peek at *A Cattleman's Quest*.

CHAPTER ONE

Cayd Fairfax brushed his hair back off his forehead and made a conscious effort not to pace, but it was difficult. The nerves had been swarming inside his gut ever since he'd woken that morning to the knowledge that today was the day three gorgeous, single women would descend upon his family's cattle station in outback central Queensland with high hopes of winning his heart. They were due to arrive at any moment.

It was right about now that he questioned the wisdom of agreeing to participate in the TV show, "Outback Bride," but it was too late to back out now. The TV producer, Lily Calimeris, stood a short distance away, her expression filled with expectation as she stared across the miles of grassed paddocks, seeking confirmation that the women weren't far away.

Cayd had met the women at a ritzy function organized by the TV station at a property on the outskirts of Sydney. He'd chosen to meet in person ten out of the hundreds of women who'd applied. From those ten, he'd narrowed it down to the three who he now waited for with equal parts nerves and excitement.

There was Marissa. A tall, leggy blond. Confident in her good looks. There was no doubt she was stunning, but he wasn't completely sure about the gray matter. Then there was Olivia. A cute, petite redhead. He wasn't sure how she'd do on the farm with her long, painted fingernails and immaculately blow-dried hair, but her cheeky smile had intrigued him, and she'd been as keen as any of the ladies to experience life on the farm. Last, there was Chelsea, with her short, curly brown hair and friendly smile. She was attractive without being head turning. Her "can-do" attitude was appealing, and she had experience working on a farm, but he wasn't sure if she was already in the friend zone. Still, he was prepared to give her a go and see how things developed.

"How are you feeling?"

The TV producer's question startled him from his thoughts. He blinked and turned to Lily with a smile.

"You know. Nervous, excited. I can't figure out which. All this has suddenly become real. I'm starting to wonder what the hell I was thinking when I signed on for this."

She nodded. "Don't stress. You're not the first farmer to have second thoughts. In fact, this is my tenth season and I don't think

I've ever had a farmer who was entirely comfortable with his decision. You're out of your comfort zone. That's okay. Think of it as a challenge. You want to find a wife, right?"

Cayd shrugged. "I guess."

"And we're going to do our best to find you one. This show isn't called "Outback Bride" for nothing." She grinned.

His gut clenched. Even with only a smattering of makeup, there was no denying the woman was striking. Then again, she was in the TV industry. Weren't they all beautiful? With her long black hair and warm brown eyes framed by impossibly thick long lashes, it was all he could do not to return her grin. She might have been petite—barely coming up to his chest—but everything was in proportion, except for her breasts. They were at least a size or two larger than her slight frame might otherwise have dictated.

Not that he minded. He'd always been a boobs guy and she had a very nice rack indeed. Too bad she wore an engagement ring. While he was always in the mood to appreciate a beautiful woman, he drew the line at dating another man's fiancée.

And then he mentally shook his head.

Why am I even thinking like that? I have three gorgeous ladies about to arrive any minute. Ladies handpicked by me. Surely one of them will prove to be my match... If things go to plan, I could be engaged myself before the month's out.

The possibility blew his mind. While his primary motivation for taking part in the TV show was to garner publicity for his farm stay venture, the thought of hanging out with three beautiful women for a couple of weeks all vying for his attention had sounded fun. The idea that one of them might even be his future wife was hard to imagine, but as Lily had said, it was a challenge and one he was definitely up for.

"Just so you know, this show has a good track record for success," the stunning producer added, drawing closer. "Out of the fifty couples over the ten seasons so far, more than half of them are still together and they have a total of forty-five children between them." She grinned. "Not bad, hey?"

He nodded. "That's a reasonable success rate, for sure."

She rolled her eyes at his understatement. "Now, don't forget what we talked about. You can't show any lady preferential treatment. It's important to keep the viewers guessing about who your final pick will be. There'll be a farewell dinner this Sunday night. That's when you'll choose one lady to send home. The final two will stay on the farm until the next farewell dinner at the end of the second week. It's important you don't give too much away. We don't want to know which lady you're planning to choose until the very last moment, okay? Our audience love the suspense."

He chuckled to hide another wave of nerves. "Okay. I hope when the time comes that *I* know which one I'm going to choose."

"Don't worry. You'll get plenty of time with all of them, along with some one-on-one time. Again, make sure you share your time with the ladies equally. Although, if you're drawn to one over another, then that's okay. Sometimes the ladies can get a little put out if that happens, but a bit of drama is always good for the show and even better for the ratings."

He hid a grimace. He wasn't sure what Lily meant by "drama", but he was pretty sure it was the kind of thing he'd rather steer clear of. He'd never been any good at playing games, especially where relationships were concerned.

At twenty-seven, he'd had a few serious relationships, but none that had lasted longer than twelve months. The closest he'd come to falling in love was with Emily Dwyer back in high school. They'd dated their senior year and had given up their virginity to each other. He'd been desperately in love with her back then and couldn't have imagined a future without her in it.

Unfortunately, she'd had other plans and had broken things off with him a month after their high school graduation. She'd gone off to university in Brisbane and he'd returned to the station. At the time, he'd been heartbroken and had convinced himself there'd never be another girl for him, despite his mother's gentle insistence that he'd get over her. Over the ensuing years, there had been other women in and out of his life and truth be told, he could barely remember what Emily looked like.

So much for being broken hearted... Looks like Mum was right...

Witnessing the joy in his older brothers as they found the love of their lives had filled Cayd with a sense of yearning to have what they did. Now Raine's wife, Isabella, was due to give birth to their first baby in two weeks, and from what Brock had said to him only yesterday when they'd spoken on the phone, he and his new wife, Kelsey, were also trying hard to add to their family.

Being one of ten children, Cayd had always been surrounded by family. They centered him, gave him security, made him whole. He'd gotten to an age where having a family of his own had become important. If he could find a potential wife by taking part in a TV show and give his farm stay project a boost along the way, then why not? As long as the drama Lily hinted at didn't get out of control. He shuddered at the thought of being caught up in a catfight.

"Looks like they're nearly here," Lily murmured.

Cayd stared in the direction of the front drive and noticed a cloud of red dust billowing up into the air. "Yep. I'd say they're about three minutes away."

A fresh wave of nerves swarmed his belly, and he drew in a deep breath.

This is it... The moment I've been waiting for...

Beside him, Lily chuckled softly. "Relax, Cayd. They're your ladies. The ones you chose. They're not going to eat you up."

Easy for you to say...

He shot her a tight-lipped look and then forced himself to relax. "You're right. It's not like I haven't met them already. I'm sure we'll all be fine."

Lily Calimeris glanced sideways at her latest farmer. He was the epitome of a tall, strapping cowboy. Tanned from years out in the sun, the denim-colored chambray shirt brought out the piercing blue of his eyes. The Levis emphasized his narrow hips and hugged his muscular thighs. His feet were shod in battered, dusty boots that were definitely not for show. To top it off, he wore a black Akubra that was accompanied by a wide, white sexy smile.

There was no doubt he was a handsome devil. That would play well for the cameras and was most definitely good for ratings. But there was also an authenticity about him that was equally attractive. He wasn't playing at cattle farming. He was the real deal. So different from her fiancé, Alexander Vasco.

An accountant for a small, family run accountancy firm in the Sydney suburbs, Alex drove a hybrid car, owned an electric scooter and wore a suit and tie every day. He barely saw the sun. The only time he tanned was during the summer when she'd force him out on weekends to the beach. Still, he might not be a red-hot cattleman, but he was hers. And she loved him. That's all that mattered.

The cloud of red dust drew closer. Any moment, and the ladies would be there. She turned and walked over to the camera crew who'd been lounging against the homestead fence in the shade.

"We ready to roll?" she asked.

Nigel, the cameraman who usually accompanied her on these trips, saluted her. "Ready when you are, boss."

"Good. Let's get some footage of the vehicle arriving and then keep filming while the girls step out of the car. I want their initial reactions, including when they greet Cayd. Got it?"

Nigel and his offsider nodded. "Got it," they mumbled.

Lily turned away, confident in their ability to do as she'd asked. Most of the crew had been together for a long time. With ten seasons under their belt, they had this down to a fine art. In anticipation of the imminent arrival, she returned to Cayd's side. She shot him a sideways look and noticed the tension around his mouth. No doubt the nerves were about to kick in tenfold. She'd witnessed many a nervous farmer at this point in the game and she knew just how to get them to relax.

She squeezed his bare forearm just below his elbow, where his shirt sleeve had been rolled up. In a distant part of her brain, she registered the warmth of his skin and the strength of his muscle beneath her fingers. Ignoring the pleasant sensations that tingled up her arm, she gave him a reassuring smile.

"Relax, Cayd. Smile. Ignore the cameras. Pretend they're not even there. In fact, the best thing to do is not to pay any attention to whether they're rolling or not. Think of them as a tree, or a fence post. Present, but unobtrusive." She pulled a face. Her eyes twinkled with good humor. "Well, as unobtrusive as two cameramen recording your every move can be."

The sound of the 4WD drew closer as the vehicle appeared out of the dust. Lily gave Cayd's forearm another friendly squeeze.

"Right. Here they are. Let's see you looking beyond excited to meet your ladies. Big smiles, Cayd."

Cayd's heart thumped. He wasn't sure if it was from the hot little producer's casual touch or the fact that his women were about to arrive. A late model white Toyota Landcruiser swung into the driveway and came to a halt in front of them. No doubt the vehicle had been clean and shiny when it had left Sydney. Now it was covered in red dust. The station had been in flood less than a year ago, but there was no evidence of that now. It had been more than two months since it had rained and the grass was drying off.

No doubt the show's producers had chosen the 4WD on purpose. This was their tenth season. They had previous experience driving on outback roads. Lily had told him the show had been sponsored by Toyota. In Brock's opinion, the 4WD Land Cruisers were the only vehicles tough enough to withstand the harsh conditions. The dirt roads out there left a lot to be desired.

Cayd glanced sideways at Lily. She held a clipboard and a pen in her hands. The camera crew had shifted into place. They'd already filmed a segment of him talking about how excited he was to welcome three beautiful ladies to his farm. He'd been pleased to be able to speak the truth. His initial motivation for signing up for the show might have been to breathe life into the farm stay project he hoped to get off the ground in the near future, but he was almost as keen to spend time with the women. Finding an outback bride wouldn't be the worse thing that could happen.

Marissa was seated in the front, next to the driver. No surprises there. At twenty-eight, she was the oldest of the three ladies he'd chosen. She was also the most confident. In fact, she'd surprised him by challenging him to an arm wrestle the first day they'd met. He'd let her win and she'd crowed about it the rest of the day. It had been fun to hang out with her and he looked forward to spending the next two weeks getting to know her better.

Surreptitiously, he wiped his now-sweaty palms on the side of his jeans. The cameras kept rolling. Lily kept issuing instructions.

"We need a close up of the vehicle with the dust coming off it," she said. "That gives it the authentic country look."

Cayd wanted to roll his eyes but stopped himself just in time. This is what the producers wanted. An authentic outback experience to be shown to their city viewers who apparently found all things country romantic. Even the dust.

Marissa was the first to climb out. Dressed in designer jeans and boots that looked so shiny they must be new, she looked the epitome of an urban cowgirl. The designer plaid blouse with the top three buttons undone gave him ample view of her impressive cleavage and completed her sophisticated look.

Not waiting for any instructions from Lily or the camera crew, she came straight up to him and greeted him with a kiss on the lips. The look in her eyes left him in no doubt she was attracted to him, and he was fine with that. It was one of the reasons he'd chosen her. She was as tall as he was. They'd fit together well. He was curious to see what might develop between them.

"I'm sorry, Marissa. We didn't get any of that. Can you greet Cayd again?" Lily turned to the cameramen. "And get a close up of both of them," Lily instructed. "I want shots of their faces."

Marissa winked at him. "How about a hug?"

He grinned. "Sounds good to me."

He stepped forward and drew her in his arms. "Welcome to Marlowe Downs."

"Can we get a smile, Cayd?" Lily asked.

He smiled at Marissa. She smiled back. He winked. She grinned. He could think of worse things than to be flirting with a beautiful woman.

"Okay, cut. I think we have enough," Lily said. She smiled distractedly at both Cayd and Marissa. "Thanks, guys. That was great."

The rear doors opened and Lily turned her attention to the other two girls. "Okay, Olivia. Chelsea. Who's next?"

Olivia climbed out of the 4WD and stepped forward a little hesitantly. She'd told him she was twenty-six, but her lack of confidence and open, innocent face made her appear younger. Cayd met her halfway. Lily called "action" and the cameras started rolling again.

It had been a week since he'd first met the women at a function center organized by the television station on the outskirts of Sydney. It was obvious both Olivia and Chelsea were feeling as awkward and nervous as he was.

Olivia approached him with a shy smile. "Hi. It's good to see you again."

"You, too."

She was even shorter than the producer, but she had a tidy figure and a cute button nose and a pleasant smile that put him at ease. He pecked her on the cheek and hugged her briefly. "Welcome to Marlowe Downs."

When Cayd dropped his arms and went to step out of the hug, Lily shook her head.

"Sorry, Cayd. Just give us a few more moments. We need a bit more footage of that hug."

Cayd swallowed a groan and complied. Greeting Olivia in such an orchestrated way felt unnatural, but he understood this was what was required. They were filming for a TV show, after all. He drew the woman into his arms and held her close. The difference in their height made things a bit awkward, but short of lifting her off her feet, there wasn't much he could do. Unperturbed, Olivia sent him a flirty grin.

"You're taller than I remembered," she teased.

He chuckled and then looked at Lily for a signal that he could now release his hold. She nodded.

"And...cut. Thanks, Cayd. Thanks, Olivia." She turned to where Chelsea stood waiting near the vehicle. "Last, but not least, Chelsea. I'll tell you when we're ready."

Cady pushed down a surge of impatience. This was only the opening scene of the girls' arrival on the station and it had already taken up far too much of his time. He understood that filming took time, and they didn't always get the shot they wanted the first time, but this was a working station. He had jobs that needed to be done.

As if sensing his irritation, Lily sidled up close and pulled him to one side.

"It's okay, Cayd. I understand. This is all so new, and you're not used to having every minute of your life put under the microscope. But you signed up to be part of a TV show. This is how it works."

He managed a tight smile. "I understand. I guess I wasn't expecting everything to take so long. I mean, I haven't even taken them to their lodgings, or showed them around."

Lily's brown eyes filled with understanding. "Hey, I get it. You're not the first farmer I've dealt with on this show. It takes a little getting used to, having me and a camera crew following your every move, but like I said, try and forget we're here. Be as natural as possible. We'll do our best to remain invisible."

With that, she shifted away and went to speak with Chelsea. A few moments later, Lily called "action" and Chelsea stepped forward and smiled at him.

"Hi, Cayd. It's so nice to see you again. Thank you for inviting me to your farm."

Cayd smiled and pecked her on the cheek. He followed that with a hug, keeping one eye on Lily who nodded to let him know when it was fine to step back. At twenty-three, Chelsea was the youngest of his ladies. His gaze scanned over her from top to toe. Faded blue jeans and a no-nonsense plaid shirt. Her well-worn work boots were testament to the fact this wasn't the first time she'd been in the bush. She'd told him during their first meeting that though she'd been born and bred in the city, she'd grown up spending weekends on her grandparents' hobby farm a couple of hours south of Sydney. Though their fifty-five acres was only large enough to run a couple of cows, three sheep, a goat, some chickens, and a pet pig, she'd always loved spending time there and she was sure she'd love his cattle station just as much.

Cayd had a few doubts. There was a big difference between a hobby farm that ran a menagerie of livestock that were mostly regarded as pets, and a working cattle station that spanned more than two hundred thousand acres and supported Cayd's parents, brothers and sisters and a handful of employees. Still, he'd invited her there and he was eager to see where things went. She wasn't as drop-dead gorgeous as Marissa, or as pretty as Olivia, but she had her own appeal and he was prepared to keep an open mind, like Lily had urged him to do.

Speaking of Lily....

Chapter Two

♥

Cayd looked around and found Lily in conversation with one of the cameramen a short distance away. Talking shop, technical terms he barely understood. Like his guests, she wore a pair of Levis and a blouse that was tucked in at the waist. Her leather belt emphasized the smallness of her waist. Her boots, while obviously not new, weren't quite as battered as Chelsea's. No doubt Lily had been on many a farm before. This was her tenth season as a producer on "Outback Bride" after all.

She laughed at something one of the cameramen said and Cayd's gut clenched involuntarily at the throaty sound of it. His initial attraction to her hadn't diminished. It was only the presence of a weighty engagement ring on her finger that kept it in check. She was off limits. But that message was still making its way to his cock.

Her hair had been pulled back into a ponytail, making her appear as young as the women he'd invited back to the station. He had no idea how old she was, but he guessed she was close to thirty.

As if becoming aware of his scrutiny, she turned her head in his direction. Their gazes locked. For half a beat, he was mesmerized.

She gave him a friendly wink and then turned away, once again focused on her conversation with the cameraman.

Cayd felt the impact of it all the way through him. He pressed a hand against his chest and dragged in a breath.

This is crazy... She's taken... Get a grip.

He'd invited three beautiful ladies back to his farm, one of which he hoped might become his wife. After all, that was the idea of the show. It wasn't called "Outback Bride" for nothing. He was expected to find love.

Yeah, with one of my ladies... Not with the sexy producer who's already engaged to someone else... Hell...

He didn't realize he'd groaned aloud until he caught sight of the frown that marred Marissa's smooth features.

"Cayd? Is everything all right?"

"Yeah. Sorry. I'm fine. I was thinking about the cattle I should be mustering. This is taking a lot more time than I anticipated."

She nodded with understanding and grinned. "But it's more fun than mustering, right?"

He shrugged. "Yeah, I guess."

She pouted. "That doesn't sound very convincing! We've come a long way to spend time with you. We drove for miles. You need to sound happier about us being here than that."

He flushed with embarrassment. "You're right. I didn't mean that the way it sounded. Of course, I'm thrilled to have all of you here. I can't wait to show you around."

She ambled closer and lowered her eyes and licked her lips and then ran a painted fingernail down his chest. Her voice dropped to a husky drawl. "That's more like it."

His gut tightened. Blood rushed to his groin. Though he was a little surprised by her forwardness, he wasn't repulsed by it. Confident women who were prepared to go after what they wanted were incredibly attractive.

As if sensing one of her rivals was moving in on the prize, Chelsea linked her arm with his and turned him away from Marissa.

"I can't wait to see the cattle. How many do you run?"

"In a good season, we run about twenty thousand. During the drought and then the flood, we were forced to destock. We got down to five hundred of our prime breeding stock. That's all we could afford to feed. Fortunately, the seasons have been more favorable in recent times. We're in the process of restocking now. We're currently running about five thousand head. A long way to go before we get back to our earlier stocking rates, but it's a good start."

Olivia had come up behind them. Her eyes were wide with disbelief. "Did you say twenty thousand cattle? Where do you put them all?"

From the corner of his eye, Cayd caught Lily's chuckle. He smiled at Olivia. "This station covers two hundred thousand acres. That's a fair bit of land. Plenty enough to run that many cattle. Don't worry, they all have somewhere to sleep."

At that, Lily snorted. Once again, their gazes clashed before sliding away. Once again, Cayd experienced a visceral reaction to the beautiful producer.

This is madness... I have three beautiful women to choose from and she's not one of them... Best remember that.

With that thought firmly in his mind, he spread his arms wide to encompass Chelsea, Olivia and Marissa and drew them away from Lily and her camera crew and toward the homestead. From behind him, he heard Lily instruct the crew to film them as they walked across the wide expanse of green lawn and neatly tended flower beds that bordered the wide front steps.

"I'll show you to your lodgings later," he told the women. "Right now, let's go and have some coffee and cake."

Lily watched after Cayd and his ladies while they walked up to the homestead. Marlowe Downs was nestled in a valley and was surrounded by mountains on three sides. Only an hour's drive from the beautiful Carnarvon Ranges, the reds and golds and khaki greens of that landscape were reflected all around them. As far as farms went, it was one of the most spectacular Lily had seen.

Of course, Cayd had told her they were in the middle of a good season and that accounted for the lush greenery, the flourishing gardens, the thick ground cover that now grew in paddocks that not so long ago had been bare. The clear blue sky was dotted with fluffy white clouds and the fresh country air carried a hint of honeysuckle, no doubt wafting across from the flower-laden Murraya tree that stood in one corner of the front yard. All of it contributed to the welcoming feel of the place.

And then there was Farmer Cayd. Tall, broad shouldered, and sexy has hell. She could see what the women had gone for. It was no surprise that Cayd had received more applications from wannabe wives than any farmer in the history of the show. Given that this was their tenth season, that was saying something.

Lily had been with the show for the past five years and had seen her fair share of cute farmers, but there was something about Farmer

Cayd that drew her. That wasn't good. He'd chosen three lovely ladies to spend the next two weeks with. At the end of the first week, he'd send one of the three home. By the end of the second week, it was hoped he'd fall in love with one of them, or at least be interested enough to invite them to stay on.

A twinge of jealousy surprised her. She was engaged to a lovely man who thought the world of her. She had no cause to be wishing for anything more. That wasn't fair to Alex. He'd loved her since they were children. Besides, the name of the show was "Outback Bride." It was her job to see that by the end of the series, a potential wedding was on the cards. That was her only priority. She wasn't getting paid to get distracted. She had a job to do. She needed to set aside any feelings she might have toward the sexy cattleman and focus solely on that.

Linking arms with Marissa and Olivia, Cayd strode toward the homestead. Chelsea followed a couple of steps behind. Though the TV executives had asked, for the sake of the show, that he pretend this was his station and he lived on it alone, it was very much a family-run operation and a family home. Both of his parents and most of his siblings still called the place home. His younger brothers, Justin, Aiden, and Lachlan all lived in the homestead and worked on the station. It was ludicrous to expect viewers to believe a two-hun-dred-thousand- acre cattle farm could be operated by just one person, but apparently that was what the TV executives were going w ith.

At Lily's request, his family had been kind enough to agree to stay out of sight of the cameras until such a time as the TV execs were ready to introduce them to their viewers. The show worked on the pretense that this was Cayd's home. The ladies were expected to help cook and clean and assist with other farm chores. The reality was quite different. His mother would be responsible for most of the cooking and cleaning, as she usually was, but apparently having Cayd and his ladies waited on by his mother didn't make for good TV. Nor was the fact that at twenty-seven, he still lived with his parents.

Cayd didn't give a toss about any of those things. He loved living with his family on the station. His younger sisters, Marnie, and Skyla, though both living in Brisbane, still called the farm home and though his older sister, Maggie managed the neighboring station, she still dropped in regularly for visits, as did his sister, Emma, who worked for the Royal Flying Doctors and was rarely in one place long enough to put down roots. She was also a regular visitor to Marlowe D owns.

They were a close-knit family and got on well most of the time. Cayd liked to bounce ideas off his father who'd lived on the station all his life, as had his parents before him. There was something about that history, handing a farm down through the years to later generations that appealed to Cayd. He hoped one day to raise his own family there.

But first, I need to find a wife...

The three girls he'd chosen were all very different. He'd never had a type. He'd dated blondes, brunettes and everything in between, though Chelsea was his first redhead. Each of the ladies he'd chosen had their own appeal: Marissa—stunningly attractive and confident in her appeal. Olivia—cute and disarming. Chelsea—sweet and pragmatic. He looked forward to spending time with them and getting to know them better. He wasn't sure yet if one of them was wife material, but he was prepared to give it his best shot. After all, getting publicity for his new venture wasn't the only reason he'd agreed to participate.

The smell of freshly baked apple and cinnamon cake wafted on the air as they entered the large and airy country-style kitchen. The room was his mother's domain, but in accordance with the contract he'd signed for the TV show, Ellen Fairfax had made herself scarce. But not before setting out a plate of delicious-smelling cake and a pot of fresh coffee. The women stood around the large island bench and *oohed* and *ahhed* over the spread.

"Someone's been busy in the kitchen," Marissa said and raised an eyebrow at him.

The sound of the front screen door slamming saved him from answering. Cayd looked up as Lily and the camera crew entered the room.

"Just keep on doing what you're doing," she instructed. "Ignore the cameras. We'll keep out of your way as much as possible."

Doing his best to carry out her instructions, Cayd poured the coffee and then offered milk and sugar. He and his ladies chatted amongst each other and Cayd did his best to act natural and ignore the cameras. Lily continued to give directions to each of them and the crew. The screen door slammed again and was followed by the heavy tread of boots on the polished floorboards that lined the hallway. A moment later, Lachlan appeared in the open doorway that led to the kitchen. He took one look at the crowd and cursed under his breath.

"Shit. Sorry. I forgot this was happening today," he mumbled and then beat a hasty retreat.

A part of Cayd wished he could join him. He wasn't used to being surrounded by young women all vying for his attention and though he'd willingly put himself in that position, he hadn't really thought it all the way through. His main goal had been to create publicity for the bed and breakfast project he hoped to get off the ground, and to have a little fun. But having his every movement, every conversation monitored and recorded was hard work and not exactly what he'd had in mind when he'd signed on. Still, it was too late for regrets now. The ladies were there and expecting big things. He'd best not let them down.

"Who wants a tour of the farm?" he asked.

He was met with a chorus of cheers. After finishing their coffee and rinsing the cups in the sink, he set his Akubra on his head and urged the ladies to follow him out the door.

Lily and her camera crew followed Cayd and his entourage out the front door and across to the machinery shed. Cayd disappeared inside the shed for a moment and then came out pushing a quad bike. Lily signaled to the cameramen to start shooting.

"Does anyone know how to ride one of these?" Cayd asked, looking at his ladies.

Both Marissa and Olivia shook their heads. Chelsea put up her hand. "I do. I've ridden a quad before on my grandparents' farm."

"Great." Cayd disappeared again and then returned with a second quad. He parked it beside the first one. "We can double up on them.

"I'll drive one. Chelsea, you can drive the other. Marissa and Olivia can ride behind."

Lily wasn't surprised when Marissa hastily volunteered to sit behind Cayd. She hid a smile as she watched Marissa tuck herself up nice and close behind the farmer. Her arms snaked out and caught him around the waist. She pressed her breasts against his chest. Irritation replaced Lily's amusement and she was forced to tamp down on another surge of jealousy. This wasn't good. She wasn't one of the ladies vying for his affections. She needed to remember that.

She twisted the engagement ring on her finger and conjured an image of Alex's smiling face. His Greek heritage was as obvious as hers in their dark hair, dark eyes and olive skin. Their families had been friends forever. She'd known Alex all her life. Three years older than her, it had long been understood by both their families that the two of them would one day marry. That day had now arrived.

Though they hadn't yet set a date, they'd been engaged for nine months already. Their families were growing impatient. She didn't know why she kept dragging her feet. She told her parents she was too busy to plan a wedding. And she was. But she knew that if it were Cayd Fairfax waiting for her to make things legal, she'd have walked down that aisle in a flash.

Stop this nonsense. We can't all marry men who look like movie stars. Alex is a perfectly lovely man. And he loves me to bits. He always has. And I love him.

She watched as Cayd handed out helmets and then waited until the women had put them on. Marissa predictably pretended to have trouble with her chinstrap and then smiled brilliantly up at Cayd when he offered to help. Lily only just managed to stop herself from rolling her eyes. She noticed that Olivia narrowed her eyes at Marissa.

Lily hid a grin, pleased that at least one of the girls was aware of the potential threat Marissa was to their chances of winning Cayd's heart. Lily made a mental note to have a quiet word with Chelsea, who so far appeared oblivious to Marissa's machinations. The viewers wanted drama. It was Lily's job to provide it. If that meant pitting the ladies against each other, then so be it. There was nothing like a catfight to send the ratings soaring. She might even get a raise. Now *that* would be something.

As the bikes roared to life and started forward, the camera crew filmed their departure. When they had the footage they needed, Lily and her crew climbed into their 4WD and followed along behind.

Cayd had offered to take the ladies for a quick tour around the station in the hope that the cameras would capture some of the station's natural beauty and perhaps encourage city viewers to take a road trip. Though it had been some time since the last fall of rain, the floods that had ravaged the land nearly a year ago had brought the place back to life. Thick pasture, overflowing dams, trees and shrubs that had been given a new lease on life. Then there were the multitude of birdlife that filled the clear blue skies. Surrounded by the red and gold and khaki landscape of the Carnarvon Ranges, it was a glorious sight and far removed from the steel-and-glass landscape of the city.

Marissa was pressed tightly against him, clinging to his waist. He enjoyed the feel of her breasts molded against his back. He glanced across at the other bike. Chelsea appeared more than capable of handling it, although Olivia looked a little scared. Cayd gave both girls a thumbs up. Chelsea grinned and returned the gesture. Olivia managed a brief smile.

They pulled up in a paddock that housed some of their cattle. No doubt the ladies had never been up close and personal to such huge beasts. As they climbed off the bikes and pulled off their helmets, he explained a bit about the breed.

"These are Droughtmasters cattle. It's an Australian breed of beef cattle. They were developed from around 1915. They crossed Zebuine, primarily Brahman cattle from the US, with British origin Beef Shorthorn and came up with the Droughtmaster. They were specially bred for the tough conditions experienced in North and Central Queensland and are resistant to ticks, heat, eye cancer, and drought."

"They're enormous!" Marissa exclaimed, clinging to Cayd's side.

He nodded. "Yes, although not as large as some of the other breeds."

"Do they come in different colors?" Olivia asked, inching closer.

"They're mainly red, like these ones, but there are variations from a golden honey color to a much darker red."

While Marissa and Olivia remained plastered to Cayd's side, he was interested to see that Chelsea felt confident enough to walk up to one of the beasts and attempt to pat it. The cow shifted slightly away, but was mostly unperturbed by the attention.

Marissa reached for his arm and clung to him. Olivia pressed close against his side. Amused, Cayd hurried to reassure them.

"It's all right, ladies. There's no need to be scared. They might be big, but these beasts are some of the most docile cows you can find. Go ahead, give them a pat. They won't bite."

Marissa shot him a doubtful look. "Will you come with me?"

Cayd chuckled. He wasn't sure if she was truly that frightened of the cattle, or if this was just another ploy to keep him close. Either way, he complied. Taking her hand, he led Marissa over to one of the beasts and stood next to her while she gingerly reached out to pat the sleek red side.

"She's so soft!" Marissa exclaimed. "I didn't expect that. And so clean. How come she's not covered in dust?"

"Oh, there's plenty of dust in her coat, don't worry. You can't live in this part of the world and not get covered in dust. It's just that it's red, like her. It blends in with her coat."

Marissa looked at him with wide eyes filled with wonder and batted her eyelashes at him. "You're so knowledgeable about your cows. That's such a big turn on."

Cayd's eyebrows rose at the frank interest in her eyes. He felt an answering stirring in his loins. The next couple of weeks with a woman like Marissa in the picture was going to keep things interesting. Very interesting indeed.

Chapter Three

♥

Lily was finding it increasingly difficult to remain unaffected by Marissa's constant touching of Cayd. It was obvious she wasn't going to waste any time staking a claim, but she barely knew him. How Cayd didn't get irritated with the woman's constant pawing, Lily didn't know, although when you looked like a real live Barbie doll, no doubt you got away with things ordinary women didn't. The other two girls better watch out or they'd be left behind in the dust.

It was up to Lily to even the playing field, or at least do what she could to ensure the other girls remained in the race. With that thought in mind, she drew Olivia aside.

"How about you ask Cayd if you can swap with Marissa and ride behind him to the next stop?"

Olivia's eyes widened with sudden comprehension. She gave Lily a grateful look and then walked back to where Cayd and Marissa were chatting quietly together. Lily signaled to the cameramen and instructed them to keep their focus on the two women. Her crew got into position and started rolling. She stood off to one side with her arms loosely folded over her chest and listened in while Olivia made her request.

"Of course," Cayd agreed affably. Olivia shot him a winning smile.

He threw an arm around her shoulder and gave her a friendly hug. He didn't appear to have a favorite among the girls yet, but time would tell. At the end of the week, he had to send one girl home. Right now, Lily wasn't sure which one of them that would be.

Marissa glared at Olivia and stomped off to climb on behind Chelsea. Lily stifled a giggle and silently congratulated Olivia for pulling off that move, no matter that it probably wouldn't have occurred to her if Lily hadn't put the thought in her head.

Lily refused to feel guilty. It was her job to create drama; to ensure each girl got a fair deal. It wouldn't do anyone any good if Cayd had an obvious favorite from the start. She'd warned him against giving any of the girls special treatment, but that didn't mean subconsciously he wasn't ordering the girls into a list of front runner to last. Besides, Marissa wouldn't have hesitated to do the same to the other girls if their positions had been reversed.

Cayd's gaze trailed after Marissa. It was obvious she was a bit put out, but there was nothing he could do about that. He'd been told to treat each of the girls fairly. Lily had been clear that it was important not to play favorites, at least in the early days. All three girls deserved equal amounts of his time to ensure he got to know all of them. According to Lily, their TV viewers always chose a lady to root for and it wasn't possible to know who'd gain their favor ahead of time. It would be months after filming finished that the show would go to air. Only then would they know who was popular among the viewers and who wasn't.

He admired Olivia for coming forward and asking to ride with him. Average height and average build, her bright red hair was now windblown and hung around her face in a tangled mess beneath her helmet, but her grin lit up her blue eyes with good humor and warmth. As he started the ignition, he glanced back at her.

"Put your arms around my waist. It's going to be a little rough where we're going."

She blushed, but her arms snuck out and loosely encircled his waist. She certainly wasn't as bold as Marissa, but that was okay. Confidence was appealing, but there was room for someone a little less forthright. That could be just as attractive.

Cayd waited while Lily and her crew returned to their vehicle and stacked their camera gear into the back. Putting his bike into gear, he indicated with his hand for them to follow him before he set off toward the billabong. The natural spring was fed from underground and was now full of sweet, clear water. Surrounded by tall reeds and shady gum trees, one side of it was bordered by a sandy shore.

As they drew up to it and switched off the bikes, the girls exclaimed in delight and surprise.

"Oh, this is amazing!" Marissa cried.

"An oasis in the middle of the desert. Who'd have thought?" Chelsea murmured.

"Is it safe to swim?" Olivia asked.

Cayd grinned. "Absolutely. Why do you think I brought you here?"

The November day was hot enough that a cool swim sounded sublime. The girls didn't need any more encouragement to kick off their shoes, roll up their jeans and paddle into the water. Cayd stood back with Lily while the cameramen captured the scene.

"I think you should join them," she said, shooting him a sideways glance. "Feel free to take your shirt off."

He looked at her in surprise and caught her teasing grin. His gut somersaulted. He looked back to his ladies. They were splashing and squealing and obviously having fun. It was hard not to want to be a part of it. Coming to a decision, he pulled off his boots and socks and set them to one side. Then he rolled up his Levis to his knees. He looked across at Lily who was staring at him. Slowly, he eased the buttons from his shirt and slipped it from his shoulders.

Her eyes slid boldly over him. When her gaze swept back to his, he was gratified to see a faint blush staining her cheeks. Once again, his gut clenched, and his pulse picked up its pace. He couldn't have said whether it was from the anticipation of joining his ladies, or from the avid interest in Lily's bright gaze.

Don't be ridiculous... She's not interested in me. I don't care what kind of look she's giving me. The rock on her finger tells a different story.

Deliberately turning his back on her, he strode toward the water. The ladies started cat calling. Chelsea let out a wolf whistle. Grinning widely, he stepped into the water. It was cool and refreshing on his heated skin. He continued walking until he was knee deep. Marissa instantly appeared by his side. She raked a fingernail across his bicep.

"Oh, boy. I thought you looked good in clothes. I had no idea you looked this delicious without."

Her voice was a throaty drawl. Cayd's body reacted instinctively to the raw need in her eyes. Blood rushed to his groin. He only hoped Lily wouldn't call them out of the water until he'd gotten his erection under control. Then Olivia sliced the water with her hand and sent a flood straight into his face. He sputtered in surprise, wiped the water out of his eyes, and then returned fire.

Before long, a full-blown water fight had erupted. Amid squeals of laughter, they all got roundly soaked. Beside him, both Marissa and Olivia's damp blouses now clung to their chests, doing very little to conceal their generous breasts. Once again, Cayd's cock thickened. Then Chelsea charged toward him and tackled him, following him down into the water, chasing all thoughts of erections and bountiful breasts away.

They both stood up, drenched. Cayd swiped at the water on his face. Chelsea laughed and flicked her short curls, obviously pleased with herself. Cayd frowned. Not only were his jeans soaked through, his phone had been in his back pocket and had also been submerged. He pulled it out and tapped the screen, relieved when it illuminated. Still, there was no telling if the dunking had caused serious damage. The biggest pain was that it was a five-hour trip to Rockhampton to replace it.

Something in his demeanor must have telegraphed to Chelsea that he wasn't exactly happy. She bumped her hip against his.

"Oh, I'm sorry, I didn't realize you had your phone. Now it's gone for a swim!" She appeared completely unrepentant.

"Yeah," he muttered, unimpressed.

"I left mine in my suitcase," Chelsea added. "No need for one out here, right? I mean, is there even phone service so far out here?"

"The service isn't great, that's true. But it works most of the time. Besides, this is a working farm. People need to be able to reach me.

This," he spread his arms wide, "is my office. Having fun with you and the others isn't how I usually spend my time."

Some of his anger must have finally penetrated. She flushed with embarrassment and averted her gaze. He cursed under his breath for coming down so hard on her. It had been an innocent bit of fun. She hadn't meant to submerge his phone. She hadn't even been aware it was in his pocket.

He made a deliberate effort to soften his tone. "Hey, I'm sorry." He tried on a reassuring grin. "Call me an asshole. Who cares about a stupid phone?"

Her relief was immediate. She smiled up at him and then punched him playfully in the arm. "You're a bit of a kidder, aren't you? For a moment there, I thought you were seriously upset about your phone."

With an effort, he suppressed another surge of irritation. The cameras were still rolling, adding to his discomfort. He glanced in Lily's direction and found her gaze on him. She was frowning. Embarrassment seared his cheeks. He was meant to be doing what he could to get to know his ladies, not antagonize them.

"Hey, Chelsea. How about you ride behind me on the way back," he suggested.

The woman's eyes lit up with excitement. At the same time, Marissa pouted. She pointed to herself and Olivia. "How are *we* supposed to get home?"

"I'm sure you or Olivia can work out how to steer the bike. We'll take it slowly, okay?"

He shot his ladies what he hoped was a winning grin in an effort to placate them. He was met with half-hearted smiles.

He sighed inwardly. When he'd signed up to be part of the show, he'd thought it might be fun. Keeping three women entertained and happy was harder than he'd imagined. And this was only day one. There was a whole two weeks of this left.

Hell. What have I let myself in for? How am I going to survive?

This time, he couldn't suppress his groan.

A Cattleman's Quest is available for preorder from your favorite digital retailer. It is due for release in October, 2023.

Also By Chris Taylor

The Munro Family Series (in order)
The Profiler
The Investigator
The Predator
The Betrayal
The Deception
The Negotiator
The Christmas Vigil (A novella)
The Ransom
The Defendant
The Shooting
The Maker

The Sydney Harbour Hospital Series (in order)
The Perfect Husband
The Body Thief
The Baby Snatchers

The Final Bullet
The Debt Collector
The Lab Test
The Stolen Identity
The Cliff-top Killer
The Likeable Fraudster

The Sydney Legal Series (in order)
An Accidental Murderer
At the Hand of her Father
A Woman Scorned
Lies and Deception
Ordinary Evil
The Ties That Bind
The Perfect Crime
A Toxic Inheritance
Malicious Love

The Craigdon Family Series (in order)
Callum
Joel
Isabella
Nicholas
Sophia
Flynn
Noah
Logan
Elizabeth

The Barrington Family Series (in order)
Broken Lives
Broken Promises
Broken Bonds
Broken Spirits
Broken Minds
Broken Vows
Broken Hearts
Broken Dreams
Broken Homes

The Fairfax Family Series (in order)
A Cattleman in Disguise
A Cattleman's Quest
A Cattleman's Daughter
A Cattleman's Secret Baby
To Catch a Cattleman
The Doctor and the Cattleman
To Rescue a Cattleman
A Cattleman's Heart
For the Love of a Cattleman

Bachelor and Brides Series (in order)
Matilda
Austin
Farrah
Benjamin
Verity
Denver

Ebony

Tyrone

Willow

Books by Chris Taylor writing as Bella Christian

This is Where it Ends series (in order)

Jessie's Story

Ryan's Story

Holly's Story

Sarah's Story

Veronica's Story

Acknowledgements

As usual, no book comes into being without a lot of help and support by my friends and family. A world of thanks must go to my editor, Linda Ingmanson. Thank you for turning my humble offerings into something truly amazing.

To my sister, Nicole Guihot, thank you for your excellent editorial comments and suggestions. Nic, I hope you like the final result.

To the fantastic writer organizations such as Romance Writers of Australia, Romance Writers of America and Romance Writers of New Zealand for all the help, support and encouragement they offer all authors, including me.

To my readers, thank you for your support and love for my stories. Your encouragement and enjoyment make this journey all worthwhile.

And lastly, to my friends and family, especially my husband and children. Thank you for putting up with late dinners and even later conversations as I've emerged day after day from the sometimes scary but always enthralling world I've created on my computer.

About the Author

Chris Taylor grew up on a farm in north-west New South Wales, Australia. She always had a thirst for stories and recalls writing her first book at the ripe old age of eight. Always a lover of romance and happily-ever-afters, a career in criminal law sparked her interest in intrigue and suspense. For Chris to be able to combine romance with suspense in her books is a dream come true.

Chris is married to Linden and is the mother of five children. If not behind her computer, you can find her doing the school run, taxiing children to swimming lessons, football, ballet and cricket. In her spare time, Chris loves to read her favorite authors who include Richard North Patterson, Sandra Brown, Kathleen E Woodiwiss, Colleen Hoover, Nora Roberts and Jude Devereaux.

You can find out more about Chris and **sign up for her newsletter** at her website:

http://www.christaylorauthor.com.au

Join Chris on Facebook at:

http://www.facebook.com/christaylorwriter